He poked the gun barrel even closer to Rollins' face. "I'm givin' ya ten minutes ta git a gun, mister. Do ya hear?"

Like all the rest, Zack stood at the bar waiting. He believed that his friend's remaining lifetime might well be measured in minutes, or even seconds, for Bret Rollins would not back down. The man simply knew no fear. Just as the allotted ten minutes expired, Rollins kicked the batwing doors open, and in one fluid motion, was inside the building. In his hands was a double-barreled shotgun, the barrels pointed directly at Hilly's midsection. "Now . . . now wait a minute. I didn't say nothin' about gittin a damm cannon." He took another step backward. "I . . . I tell ya what, he stammered. "Let's jist forget the whole thang. All right?" Rollins smiled, then nodded.

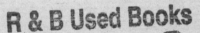 

**Other Books by Doug Bowman
from Tom Doherty Associates**

Gannon
Sam Curtain
The Three Lives of Littleton Blue
The H&R Cattle Company

THE
H & R CATTLE
COMPANY

DOUG BOWMAN

A TOM DOHERTY ASSOCIATES BOOK
NEW YORK

THE H & R CATTLE COMPANY

Cover art by Tim Newsom

A Forge Book
Published by Tom Doherty Associates, Inc.
175 Fifth Avenue
New York, NY 10010

Forge® is a registered trademark of Tom Doherty Associates, Inc.

ISBN: 0-812-56757-9

First edition: September 1997

Printed in the United States of America

0 9 8 7 6 5 4 3 2 1

1

"**N**o doubt in my mind that the horse is worth fifty dollars, Mister Davis," Zack Hunter was saying as he inspected the big bay. "But I just don't have that kind of money. Took everything I could scrape together just to give Ma a decent burial."

The man stood quietly for a while, tamping tobacco into his brierroot pipe. Though seemingly in good health, Lester Davis was well past the age of seventy. A successful farmer and horse trader, he was a man of means, and was said to have prospered during the Civil War by trading with both sides. He fired his pipe now and blew a cloud of smoke to the wind. "How 'boutcha uncle?" he asked. "Dalton's got money."

Hunter shrugged. "Sure, Uncle Dalton's got lots of money, but he damn sure ain't gonna give me any of it. You've been trading or trying to trade with him longer than I've been alive. I'm sure I don't have to tell you how tight he holds on to a dollar. He still owes me for building two bridges last summer, but I'll never get the money. He even refused to sell me a horse on credit."

The old man sucked his pipe stem again. "Credit ain't no good way o' doin' business, boy. Jist like myself, Dalton didn't git whur he is by keepin' a lotta money on th' books."

Hunter shook his head. "They taught us in school that the whole world runs on credit, Mister Davis, and I've been reading a lot of books. One country might owe another country a million dollars. Sometimes more. Then when they pay off the loan, everybody's happy 'cause both the borrower and the lender have made money."

Davis tapped out his pipe on the heel of his shoe, then began to scratch his beard. "Maybe so," he said thoughtfully.

"Whatcha gonna say next is that ya wanna buy th' horse on credit. Right?"

Hunter nodded. "It's the only way I could even hope to buy the animal." He ran his hand along the bay's muscular withers. "I'd want the saddle, too."

Lester Davis chuckled. "Th' saddle, too?" He took a seat on an upended nail keg, beginning to jerk hairs out of his nose with his thumb and forefinger. "I'll tell ya what, boy. Gimme thirty dollars down an' I'll sell ya th' horse an' th' saddle fer ninety dollars."

Hunter shook his head. "I couldn't do that, Mister Davis. I believe that's more than they're worth. Besides, I couldn't pay more than ten dollars down." He handed over the reins and turned to leave.

"Jist a minute, boy," the old man said loudly. "Don'tcha know nothin' a-tall 'bout horse tradin'?"

Hunter reversed the few steps he had taken. "I never was much for dickering, Mister Davis."

"Well, dammit, ya don't hafta dicker, but I wantcha ta listen. Whatcha gonna do with that milch cow over at th' cabin?"

"I already traded her for this Henry and two boxes of shells." He held up the rifle for Davis to see.

The old man inspected the rifle, then nodded. "Well, I know that they's a wagon over there, an' a turnin' plow an' a middle buster, too. An' I remember seein' a good porch swang. Gimme all them thangs, an' throw in that pocket watch I saw ya lookin' at a while ago. I'll give ya a bill o' sale fer th' horse an' saddle free an' clear."

Without a word, Hunter unhooked the chain from his belt. Then he laid his dead father's watch in the trader's hand. "I don't have any other choice, Mister Davis. I'll saddle the bay while you write the bill of sale."

A few minutes later, Hunter folded the document, shoved it in his pocket and climbed into the saddle. The old man stood at his stirrup, scratching his beard. "Dalton ain't gonna give me no shit when I go ta pick up them thangs, is he?"

Hunter looked the old man in the eye. "None of that stuff belongs to Uncle Dalton, and he's not likely to see you anyway. If he does, just tell him I traded with you."

The man nodded, and Hunter rode out of the yard at a gallop. He expected to be across the river and into Arkansas by sunup tomorrow, and he had no time to lose. The sheriff and a few others might already be looking for him, for yesterday afternoon twenty-four-year-old Zachary Hunter had killed a man.

The argument had started in a small grove of scrub oaks alongside Wolf Creek, where Zack Hunter and his best friend, Bret Rollins, had engaged two strangers in a four-handed game of draw poker. Betting recklessly, Rollins went broke quickly, as did the smaller of the strangers. Hunter and the larger man, who had introduced himself as Mose Mack, continued to play.

When it became obvious that the disagreement between the two players was about to come to blows, Bret Rollins decided to appoint himself referee of the fight. "Now, both of you listen to me," he said. "If a man goes down, the other must count to ten, giving the down man a chance to get up before hitting him again."

Even as Rollins was talking, Hunter kicked Mack in the groin, almost lifting the man off the ground. As Mack put both hands to his crotch, grimacing in agony, Hunter grabbed him by the hair, jerking his head downward. At the same time, Hunter brought his knee up full force into the man's face. Five times he did this, and each time the downward motion of Mack's face met the upward thrust of Hunter's knee, Rollins thought he heard something break. At last, Hunter released the man and let him fall to the ground. "One . . . two . . . three—"

"Hell, there ain't no use to count, Zack," Rollins said loudly. "You've probably killed the sonofabitch!" The big man lay in a motionless heap at Hunter's feet. Rollins, robbed of his chance to referee, began to walk around in circles, shaking his head. "You just couldn't wait, could you, Zack?"

"Nope. Didn't like all the rules you were laying down." Zack Hunter fought by only one set of rules: his own. His ability to bring a physical conflict to an abrupt halt was well known among much of the male population of Shelby County, and few men dared to trifle with him. He had been taught self-defense several years ago by his older cousin, Billy Olsen, who had later died in a hunting accident. Zack had spent one whole summer on the Olsen farm and had practiced Cousin Billy's lessons daily.

"There's no such thing as a dirty fight," Billy Olsen had said. "The only thing you need to be thinking about is how to get it over with as quick as possible. The idea is to put your man down any old way you can, and keep him there. What matters, and the only thing that matters, is that you win." Cousin Billy had then spent the rest of the summer teaching Zack the fine art of fistic persuasion. Zack had been fifteen that year, and he had not lost a fight since.

Now, still standing beside the fallen man, Zack touched him with the toe of his boot. He got no reaction. The big man had brought it all on himself, he was thinking. After all, the poker game had been the man's own idea, and it was not Zack's fault that the big bastard didn't know that a flush beats a straight. Hunter turned to Mack's partner, who had watched the entire exchange from his seat on a nearby log. "Do you know that a flush beats a straight?" he asked.

"Shore I do. I'll tell Mose when he comes around."

Hunter stamped his foot and exhaled loudly. "Why the hell didn't you tell him when the argument started?"

"Weren't none o' my affair," the man said, squirting a mouthful of tobacco juice. "Another reason I didn't say nothin' is 'cause I figgered Mose could whup both uv ya. I wuz watchin' th' cards. I saw yore han' an' I saw his'n. All 'at money there on th' blanket is fairly yore'n. I'd 'preciate it if ya'd jist take it an' leave."

"All right," Hunter said. He stuffed the money he had won in his pocket.

"No, no!" Rollins said loudly, his deep voice reverberating through the woods. He took a step toward the big man's partner. "It's not us that's gonna be leaving, fellow. It's you! Get your ass across that creek and over that hill. You'd better not even look back unless you want a dose of the same medicine your buddy got."

The man waded the shallow creek quickly and was soon out of sight. Rollins turned to Hunter. "Couldn't let that joker hang around here, Zack. He'd be hunting up the law ten minutes from now." He pointed to the lifeless heap on the ground. "That man's dead."

Hunter nodded. "I know."

After a short discussion, the men decided to move the body a few hundred yards downstream, hoping that if the exiled partner did return, he would think that Mack had regained consciousness and walked away under his own power. With one man at each end, they carried the corpse around the bend and covered it with brush. Then the friends went their separate ways, Rollins to his grandfather's house and Hunter to his own cabin, where he had been living alone since the death of his mother a few weeks earlier.

Zack spent a sleepless night but had risen this morning with a firm decision: he would head west as soon as he could get a good horse under him, and he had no intention of ever returning to Tennessee. Now he was pleased with the trade he had made with Lester Davis for the big bay saddler. He had never intended to use the plows or the wagon, and the pocket watch was a lousy timepiece. Nor had he expected to spend any time sitting in the porch swing. Old man Davis would no doubt reap more than the bay's worth when all his dealing was done, but right now Zack had what he needed most, and he was satisfied.

He turned the horse off the road and headed for his cabin, located in the middle of one of Uncle Dalton's cotton fields. Dalton Smith had given the cabin to his younger sister, who was Zack's mother. Zack expected the old man to ask him to vacate the building any day now. Smith had stood in the background with a vacant stare at his sister's funeral and had not even spoken to Zack. All because his nephew had recently informed him that he expected to be paid for his work.

Well, his uncle could have the cabin and everything in it, Zack was thinking as he tied the bay to the hitching post at the front door. He retrieved the saddle scabbard that had come in the trade for the rifle. Then he stripped two blankets from his bed, tying them securely behind his saddle. A few minutes later, he shoved the Henry in the boot and remounted.

He covered the three miles to his uncle's house in less than twenty minutes. He knew his uncle would be in the fields bossing his workers, so he rode straight to the barn. He helped himself to a good saddlebag from the tack room, then led his horse to the house. Once inside, he buckled his uncle's prized

Colt six-shooter around his waist and dumped a box of shells into his pocket. Then he took a pillowcase and headed for the meat cellar.

A few minutes later, he rode out of the yard, a smoked ham and half a slab of bacon tied to his saddle. By his own reckoning, he and his uncle were about even now.

An hour later, he was at the Rollins farm. Bret had seen him coming and stood waiting in the yard. "I see you finally got something decent to ride," he said, grabbing the horse's bridle. "How in the world did you manage to shake old man Davis loose from the bay?"

Zack dismounted. "Traded him everything I owned."

They walked a few steps and stood beneath the canopy of a large oak. Rollins tied the bay to a low-hanging limb. "I thought about you all night, Zack. Have you heard anything about what happened yesterday?"

"Only in my dreams. I'm gonna get the hell out of this part of the country before I do hear about it." He tightened the cinch another notch, then retied the knot in the pillowcase. "We've been talking about Texas for years, Bret. You still want to go?"

"Absolutely," Rollins said, his ever-present smile widening. "Can't leave today, though. As you well know, I lost my horse in a poker game last week." He pointed toward the small corral. "I'm not riding that damn mule out there anywhere." He removed his hat and began to scratch his head. "I'll tell you what let's do, Zack. You go on across the river and wait for me. I'll be there in two days.

"You can cross the river on the ferry at Rogers Point. Make your camp up there on the hillside in that big stand of timber. I'll meet you there the day after tomorrow. I've got to make a trip to Ellisville, then I'll have everything we need to travel in style."

Zack climbed into the saddle. "I believe that, Slick." It was a well-earned nickname that Hunter often used when referring to Rollins. "I'll be watching for you. Maybe I'll be able to see you when you get off the ferry."

Rollins nodded and headed for the corral to get the lazy mule. Hunter kicked the bay in the ribs and guided it toward the Mississippi River.

At a fishing camp near the water's edge, Zack bought a hundred feet of rope from a commercial fisherman, then caught the last ferry of the day. When he disembarked a few minutes later, he was in Arkansas, safely out of the Tennessee sheriff's jurisdiction.

He took to the woods immediately, riding halfway up the hill before halting at a small spring. He selected a camping site between two fallen trees, then picketed the bay on the long rope. He would move the horse to new grass occasionally, for he had no grain to feed the animal. After eating a pound of smoked ham and watering himself at the spring, he made a bed of leaves and added his blankets. Then he called it a day, for darkness was closing in fast.

He lay on his bed for a long time, thinking. He had no doubt that Rollins would be along later and that he would bring everything necessary to make their travel more comfortable. The man simply had a way of talking people out of things. He had a deep, musical voice that could not be ignored. When he talked, people listened, even though many of them knew that his morals and scruples were not of the highest order.

Rollins was exceedingly handsome, the best-looking man Zack had ever known: fair complexion, curly hair the color of corn silk, and big blue eyes that sometimes appeared to contain small particles of ice. His constant smile revealed rows of perfect teeth behind lips that the girls of Ellisville High had secretly voted most kissable. He was a good athlete, and had won about every organized footrace in the county. Zack supposed that Rollins had needed that speed more than once since his school days. Using one scheme or another, he had separated many people from their money, and a few times had narrowly escaped going to jail. It was after learning that Rollins had used his good looks and silver-tongued nature to get laid for free in a Memphis whorehouse that Hunter began to occasionally refer to him as "Slick."

Hunter and Rollins were identical in size, each standing six feet tall. They had weighed themselves at the cotton gin last week: Rollins, one-ninety-three; Hunter, two pounds more. Both men were twenty-four years old. There the similarity ended.

Hunter was dark, with green eyes and black hair, and although most women would have considered him handsome, they did not flirt, giggle and chase after him shamelessly as they sometimes did Bret.

Zack had known Bret most of his life, but would never have anything to do with him because he had pegged him as a sissy. Then came the day, when they were eighteen, that Bret fought Zack to a draw on the school playground. Though Zack used everything his Cousin Billy had taught him, Bret took everything he could dish out, and dished out just as much of his own. Zack realized early in the fight that he had misgauged his opponent. No, sir, Bret Rollins was no damn sissy. Not by a long shot. They fought till neither of them could stand without holding on to something, then called it a draw. They had been inseparable friends ever since.

Hunter held his position on the hillside for the next two days, moving about only when it became necessary to lead the bay to a new grazing area. He had just done this when he saw the ferry tie up on the west side of the river. He watched as a man leading two horses scrambled up the bank and stood looking in his direction. Still standing in the clearing, Zack began to wave his hat. The rider mounted and headed up the hill.

A few minutes later, Bret Rollins rode into the clearing. He was astride a beautiful roan that stood at least sixteen hands at the withers, followed by a heavily loaded packhorse. Smiling broadly, he dismounted beside Hunter.

"I see you made it," Hunter said.

Bret motioned toward the horses and the pack carried by the smaller of the two. "I got lucky, Zack. I believe I've got about everything we'll be needing."

Hunter answered with a broad smile of his own. He stood looking at the animals and the new packsaddle admiringly. When his eyes resettled on the roan, he chuckled, for he recognized the animal. Smiling again, he turned to Rollins. "I'm not gonna ask you what all you did for the good doctor's wife to get that roan, Slick. It's a well-known fact in Ellisville that she plays around, but I never heard it said that she pays a stud fee."

"Dammit, Zack, a man has to work with whatever tools he's got. She didn't need these animals anyway, they've got several more.'' Rollins began to pat his hip pocket. "She also decided that I needed a hundred dollars to buy things.''

Hunter walked around the animals again, chuckling and shaking his head. "I guess you've pulled it off, Bret. I just can't help wondering how she's gonna explain it to the good doctor. I mean, a man is bound to miss something as big as a damn horse.''

Rollins nodded. "I asked her that question. She assured me that she knew exactly how to handle the doctor.''

They unburdened the animals at the spring, then picketed them on good grass. The packhorse had been carrying more than a hundred pounds. Indeed, Rollins seemed to have everything they were likely to need: food, cooking utensils, blankets, a two-man tent and several changes of clothing. He had a Colt six-shooter in his saddlebag, and a double-barreled, ten-gauge shotgun in the saddle scabbard.

They spent the night at the spring. They did not set up the tent. The absence of rain clouds and the pleasing temperature of the June night made it unnecessary.

They talked till late. Though neither man had a particular destination in mind, each agreed that they would not slow down until they reached Texas. Then they would simply wander about till they found something that struck their fancy. Finding work was not an immediate concern, for they had both provisions and money, and plenty of green grass for their animals.

They headed southwest at daybreak, a route that would take them directly to northeast Texas. During the ride, Bret explained exactly how he had come by the horses and provisions. Aside from an occasional chuckle and a short comment, Hunter said little. He was not a long-winded talker, usually speaking only when he had something to say. Rollins, however, could talk all day about anything. Or nothing. He said that he did not believe Mose Mack's body had been found; otherwise, there would have been talk around Ellisville. Knowing that such news traveled like wildfire, Hunter was quick to agree.

Two hours before nightfall, they made camp a hundred feet off the road, beside a wide, shallow stream. A passerby informed them that the stream was known as Village Creek. As

Hunter kindled a fire, Rollins set up the tent, for he believed it would rain before morning.

It did not rain, however, and at daybreak there was not a cloud in the sky. Hunter dragged himself from his blankets at sunup to find Rollins sitting on a log in front of the tent. He had a fire going and the coffeepot steaming. Hunter poured himself a cupful, then noticed that Rollins was busy feeding bread crumbs to a stray dog.

"That's the ugliest dog I've ever seen, Bret," Zack said. "Probably got twenty different breeds in him."

"At least twenty," Bret said, then changed the subject. "If you want to wash up and shave, go ahead," he said, pointing to the creek. He handed Zack a razor and soap. "I'll fix something to eat while you're gone."

When Hunter returned from the creek, he found Rollins serving coffee to an old Negro man who had been walking on the road. With the dog still lying at his feet, its head resting on its forepaws, Bret had the man wound up in conversation.

"I live 'bout three miles down th' road," the man was saying. "Raise chickens. Don't make no differ'nce what I do, though. Th' weasels git 'bout half uv 'em 'fore they git big enough ta sell."

"Well, now," Rollins said. "That's a shame, and you can certainly put a stop to it." He began to pat the dog's head. "What you need is Ol' Rex here. Fact is, my partner and I are moving to the city, and that ain't no place for Ol' Rex. No, sir, he needs plenty of room to run and hunt." He rubbed the dog's head and ears. "Bad as I hate to, I've been thinking about selling him."

The man bent over the dog for a closer look. "I sho' ain't never seen nothin' looks like him," he said. "What kinda dog is he?"

"Bulgarian Weaselhound," Rollins said quickly. "Yes, sir, if you had him, there wouldn't be a weasel within a mile of your place after the first week. Five dollars and he's yours."

The man shook his head. "Couldn't pay no five dollars . . . might go three."

"Split the difference," Rollins said. "Four dollars."

"Nope. Won't pay but three."

Rollins dashed his coffee grounds into a bush. "Well, I'll

say this for you, Mister Chicken Man—you sure know how to drive a hard bargain." He hesitated for a moment, then added, "I'm gonna let you have the dog, but I guess you know that you're beating my socks off on the deal."

The old man took the tobacco sack that he used as a coin purse from his pocket. "Been knowed ta bargain a little, heh-heh." He counted out three dollars in nickels and dimes. Then he looped his belt around the dog's neck and led "Ol' Rex" down the road.

Hunter had stood beside the tent listening. He had just watched Rollins make more money off that mongrel than he himself had been paid for three days of digging ditches. The sale of the dog had come as no surprise to him, for he had seen Rollins operate before. Such things were second nature to him. Nor would it bother him that he might have taken the man's last three dollars. He would never give it another thought. He was an accomplished con man, and he did it more for pleasure than for money.

Hunter walked to the fire. "Bulgarian Weaselhound, huh? Is there even such a thing?"

"Hell, I don't know, Zack. It's like I said before. A man has to work with whatever tools are handy." He pushed the skillet onto the gray coals. "Let's have some breakfast, then head for Texas."

2

A hard day's travel through the lowlands brought them to White River, one hour ahead of a rainstorm. They picketed their animals and began to stretch the tarpaulin, tying it to saplings six feet above the ground. That done, they dragged the pack and their saddles underneath, then pitched the tent. Then they walked in opposite directions in search of dry firewood. A short time later, they had a fire going and coffee boiling.

Then the rain came. The men and their belongings stayed dry, however, for no wind accompanied the downpour. The water fell straight down and cascaded off the tarpaulin, one corner of which had deliberately been tied six inches lower.

Hunter placed a pot of water on the fire and added a few handfuls of dried beans. "You think anybody's found Mose Mack's body yet?"

"I would think so," Rollins said, refilling his cup. "If the smell didn't attract somebody, the buzzards probably did."

Zack nodded. He added salt, pepper and a few slices of bacon to the pot, then leaned back against his saddle. "I doubt that Mack's partner found him, Bret. I believe you scared him out of the county. And I don't intend to let the fact that Mack is not around anymore bother me. He insisted on a fight, and I did what I had to do."

Rollins broke a limb and laid the pieces on the fire. "Did you ever kick anybody in the nuts before?"

"Nope."

"Why'd you kick him?"

"Because I didn't want the big bastard hitting me. Maybe you didn't look him over real good, Bret. That joker's arms were as big as my legs."

"Sure I looked him over, Zack. But I've seen you fight big men before. You never kicked any of them."

Hunter stirred the pot. "I'm smarter now."

They talked till long after dark, then ate the beans by firelight. When the fire died on its own, they crawled into the tent. Neither man spoke during the night.

Hunter lay awake for a long time, thinking. He firmly believed that the thing with Mose Mack was over and done. The only witness who could identify Zack was Mack's traveling partner, and Hunter believed the man to be long gone. Maybe he was himself wanted by the law, for neither of the men had struck him as an upstanding citizen. Anyway, if the case ever came to trial, Bret Rollins would testify that Hunter had acted in self-defense. Zack believed that as a witness, Rollins could make a jury believe almost anything.

Bret was not only a smooth talker, he was proficient at a

host of other things. A highly skilled player of pocket billiards, he was sought after by members of Memphis pool tournaments, and dreaded by those who played for money. He could also make a pair of dice do unbelievable things. He was the happy-go-lucky type who would be well-off today and broke tomorrow. But he would never be broke for long. Not as long as somebody else had some money. More than once Zack had seen Slick talk one of his lady friends out of enough money for a stake, then head for Memphis. He would almost always return with a fat roll.

Several men had been fooled by Bret's pretty face in the past, and no doubt many would be again. He was an excellent scrapper, and few men could match his speed and fancy footwork. He could hit hard with either hand, and could deliver a punch quicker than any man Zack had ever known. And he did it with a cool head, never letting his temper get in the way of the business at hand. Zack remembered the time when Bret fought with a man over a pool game in Memphis. Bret had knocked him down three times before the man crawled to a barstool and pulled himself to his feet.

"Let me get my breath," he said, panting loudly. "Then I'm gonna try him again."

"I'd counsel against it," Zack had told the man. "Old Bret's been in a lot of ass-kicking contests, and a few times he's even had to furnish the ass. But, mister, I just don't believe you can climb that hill."

After thinking on it for a while, the man retrieved his hat from the floor and left the building. A short time later, Rollins was walking down the street counting his winnings, whistling an old Irish tune.

Bret had been raised by his grandfather since the age of three, after his parents perished in a hotel fire in Memphis. His grandmother died two years later, leaving the upbringing of young Bret to Grandpa Rollins and two of his female slaves. The women pampered him constantly, and the elder Rollins saw to his every whim, even buying the lad his own horse at the age of seven.

Young Bret lived a life of ease for most of his growing years, and was mostly left to his own devices. His grandfather owned a wide assortment of guns, and Bret tried them all, becoming especially proficient with the handgun and the long-range rifle.

Then came the Civil War. When the hellish conflict was over, the Rollins household had been reduced to near poverty. Not only were there no slaves, there were indeed fewer acres to plant. One tract of land at a time, Grandpa had been forced to sell off most of the farm, eagerly accepting offers that would have been scorned only a few years earlier. Young Bret had watched as his once-prosperous grandfather became a poor man, his vast holdings now reduced to a few acres for gardening and truck.

Tennessee had taken a beating during the war, and few people remained unscarred. Many wealthy men had been wiped out completely, with some reduced to standing in soup lines. The countryside had suffered immensely as well, for more battles were fought in Tennessee than in any other state. Even now, ten years later, visible signs of the devastation were everywhere.

As a schoolboy, Bret Rollins had always had money in his pocket. Zachary Hunter, however, had never had a dollar until he was old enough to earn it himself. Even then, paydays had been few and far between. The war and its aftermath had brought little change to the Hunters, for Zack and his mother had had nothing to lose. They had already been poor, depending largely on Uncle Dalton's shifting generosity for their livelihood.

Zack's father had died a year before the war began. He had been bitten by a poisonous snake while rabbit hunting, and died a few days later. Zack well remembered the day Will Hunter was laid to rest in the small cemetery at the end of the turnip patch as his wife and young son stood beside the grave, holding hands and crying. Despite the fact that he was disliked by Dalton Smith, Will Hunter had a host of friends throughout the county, and a large crowd of mourners stood on the hillside in the drizzling rain.

Uneducated, barely able to write his name, the elder Hunter had resigned himself to his designated fate of a lifetime of hard labor, but had sworn almost daily that his son would receive a decent education. And young Zachary had done so.

He studied hard and brought home good grades, and his father was proud.

Zack's mother had died recently of some mysterious illness. She had been sick for most of the year, but of late had been getting around more, her health seemingly on the mend. She had even hoed the garden on the last day she lived, saying it was a joy just to be alive and feeling well again. A few minutes after eating supper, she complained of a headache and went to bed early. She died sometime during the night. Two days later, Nellie Hunter was laid to rest beside her husband. Uncle Dalton had insisted that his sister be interred in the Smith graveyard, but relinquished the idea when informed by Zack that his parents would indeed rest side by side. Even then, the old man had refused to take part in the ceremony.

The loss of his mother was a crushing blow to Zack, and Rollins was quick to sense it. He moved into Zack's cabin and became a constant companion for more than a week, doing whatever it took to keep Zack thinking and talking about something else. Even though Hunter had good-naturedly run Rollins off after nine days, saying that he needed neither a cook nor a nurse, he would not soon forget Bret's concern.

It seemed that Zack had been asleep for only a few minutes when he smelled the coffee. Opening one eye, he saw that another day had arrived and that he was alone in the tent. He put on his boots, then crawled through the opening. After he poured himself a cup of coffee, he began to look around for Bret.

He found him fifty yards downriver, peeling the skin off a large catfish. "Caught him on a piece of cheese, Zack," he said, holding up his catch.

Hunter looked the fish over. "Where'd you get a damn fishhook?"

"Brought some from home. Weights and line, too."

Hunter chuckled. "Looks like it paid off." He watched Rollins throw the fish's head in the river, then walked back to the tent.

A few minutes later, they sat broiling fish over the campfire. "This won't take long," Rollins said. "Don't take much cooking for a fish. I think they're already about half done when you catch them.''

Hunter grunted, then began to eat.

They crossed the Red River a week later and camped on its west bank. Though three hours of daylight remained, they had decided on an early halt. They had been traveling since shortly after dawn, and both men and horses were weary. As they stood beside the campfire watching the boiling pot, which contained, among other things, a rabbit Hunter had shot two hours before, Rollins pointed to the river. ''Whoever named that river probably didn't have to think about it very long. The way the sunlight's hitting it right now, it's almost as red as blood.''

''Uh-huh. The man who named it saw the same thing you're looking at.''

Rollins thumped his forefinger against the crude map he held in his hand. ''According to this thing, we should cross the Sulphur tomorrow. Then we'll be in Texas.''

''That's the way I read it, Bret.''

''Well, I'll be damn glad to get there,'' Rollins said, pocketing the map. ''From what I hear, they don't have anywhere near as many laws and lawmen as Tennessee does. A man might actually be able to make a living without working.''

Hunter chuckled, then began to stoke the fire. He knew that Bret had long been conservative of his physical energy and was totally averse to any kind of toil that might bring a bead of sweat to the brow. ''I've read that Texas is a land of opportunity, Bret. Maybe you can find something that won't hurt your back too much.'' Hunter was laughing now.

''Go ahead and laugh,'' Rollins said. ''One of these days you'll know that I'm right. It's just like I've told you a hundred times: a working man is never gonna have a damn thing. He spends so much of his life working that he don't have any time left to make money.''

Zack stirred the stew. He had no argument against what he was being told. Of all the hard-working men he knew, none had anything more than food for the table. Those who were well-off, however, seemed to spend most of their time sitting on their asses, getting richer every day. ''There might be more than a little bit of truth in what you're saying, Bret.'' He dished up the stew and handed a bowlful to his friend.

"Hell, I know I'm right," Rollins said, blowing air into the steaming bowl. "And I intend to get mine any way I can."

When they had eaten, Hunter pulled up the pickets and moved the horses to new grass. Then he made a bed of leaves in the shade of the large oak and spread his blankets. They would not pitch the tent tonight; the skies were clear and they needed the cool breeze from the river. Rollins fashioned his own bed ten feet away, and the men stretched out, with both long and short guns close at hand. They were soon sleeping soundly, and neither man stirred until dawn.

Another week of travel brought them to the Trinity River, where they camped for the night. Just before sundown, Rollins asked directions from an old man who was passing by. "Ya ain't never gonna git ta Dallas if ya keep goin' west," the old man said. "Ya done missed it by more'n twenty mile." He pointed north. "Ain't no use ta cross th' river, jist foller it an' it'll take ya right inta town. Take ya 'bout a full day ta git there, 'cause th' travelin' ain't none too easy."

"Thank you, sir," Rollins said. "We appreciate the information."

"Name's Jenkins," the old man said, "an' I don't reckin it cost me nothin' ta tell ya." He took a wad of chewing tobacco from his pocket and poked it into his mouth, wallowing it around several times. "Shore would like to borry a dollar from ya till I see ya ag'in, though. This here's my last chew."

Rollins gave him a quarter, and the old man guided his mule north, toward Dallas.

Then the men began to look around for firewood. It had been a long day, and they were tired and hungry. Half an hour later, they had a fire going, with beans and onions in the pot. Rollins lay beside the fire on his elbow, waiting for the coffeepot to come to a boil. "You know, Zack, I can't remember ever going this long without a woman. I mean, since I've been old enough to need one. It's been more than three weeks now."

Hunter pulled the coffeepot from the fire. "That sounds like an earth-shattering problem, Slick."

"By God, it is a problem. I'm not used to this shit. I'll bet you a dollar that I breed somebody before I go to sleep tomorrow night."

"I sure wouldn't bet against it, old buddy. I know you too well."

After supper they sat beside the dying campfire sipping coffee. Rollins continually slapped at his neck. "These damned mosquitoes are as big as crickets, Zack. Half a dozen of 'em have already sunk their beaks in my jugular vein."

"I hear 'em buzzing," Zack said, "but none of 'em have bit me. Don't guess they will as long as you're around. They probably think you taste better than me." He had heard some of the old folks say that mosquitoes avoided certain people because of something in their blood that the insects did not like. He hoped he was one of those people. At any rate, he had never been bothered by mosquitoes.

Rollins crawled into his bedroll and covered his head. After extinguishing the fire, Hunter also went to bed.

The town of Dallas was begun when the first Anglo-American settler built a single cabin on the site in 1841. Another cabin was added two years later. Now, ten years after the Civil War, Dallas was a thriving business town and market center with an urbane air unmatched anywhere on the frontier, primarily due to several immigrations of French, German, Swiss, English and other Europeans. John Neely Bryan built the first cabin and was looked upon as the town's founder.

Though many of the town fathers were men of culture, there was a seamy side of Dallas that was beyond their control. Gunmen, gamblers, whores and thieves of every stripe were abundant, and plied their respective trades randomly. Especially during the nighttime. Saloons outnumbered churches ten to one, and drew much larger crowds. Gambling dives and pool halls, where a man could bet on almost anything, were at least tolerated by law enforcement. The bravest of the law officials were given kickbacks, while the more timid ones were simply afraid to buck the current.

Hunter and Rollins rode into town at three in the afternoon. They stabled their horses at the livery, then rented a third-story hotel room two blocks away. Rollins dropped his pack and saddlebags beside his bed, then leaned his shotgun against the wall. "The first order of business is a thick, juicy steak, Zack. That restaurant we passed down the street looked good to me."

Zack smiled. "Me, too. And you can order for both of us."

They had shaved early this morning and bathed in the Trinity River. Now Rollins unbuckled his pack and tossed a pair of jeans and a broadcloth shirt to Hunter. "I don't suppose you'll have any problem with the fit, Zack. As far as I know, we're the same size."

Hunter was soon wearing the clean jeans and cotton shirt, and the fit was fine.

They locked the pack, saddlebags and guns in the room and walked from the hotel unarmed. A short time later they were seated in the restaurant known as the Big Bull, where each man was soon served a T-bone steak, fried potatoes and a large bowl of brown beans. A pot of strong coffee sat in the middle of the table. Rollins emptied his cup quickly and poured himself another. He began to rub his hands together, eyeing the steaming meal. "Sure looks like these Texans know how to eat."

Hunter poked a large bite of steak into his mouth and spoke around it. "I imagine it would be hard to tell them anything they don't already know about beef." He said nothing else, just set about cleaning his plate.

The sun was still two hours high when they entered the dilapidated saloon on the corner. Though no name was evident on the outside of the building, a weathered sign stated that the establishment offered whiskey, poker and billiards. They walked the length of the bar and took stools on its far side. Each man ordered a beer.

"Ain't got no beer," the fat bartender said. "Beer wagon won't be here till tomorrow. Got some decent whiskey, though."

Both men ordered whiskey.

The bar was shaped like a horseshoe, with stools on three sides. There were stations for three bartenders, and Zack supposed that on busy nights that many were needed. At the moment, only the fat man was on duty.

Though the saloon was large even by Texas standards, the men could see everything in the room from their seats at the bar. A potbellied stove, which had not been fired in months, sat in the center of the room; around it were scattered tables and chairs of various shapes and sizes. Several drinkers were seated there, and occasional eruptions of laughter emanated from their conversation.

Four card tables stood in the rear of the room, along its left wall, and two poker games were in progress. Across the room, far enough away that the clacking of the balls would not unnerve the poker players, were three pool tables, none in use at the moment.

The men sat at the bar sipping their second drink, with Rollins eyeing the tables in the rear. "I think I'll take a hand in that poker game, Zack. See if I can make us a little traveling money."

Zack finished off his whiskey. "I guess I'll walk around town for a while, then. I'm sure not gonna play poker. Can't afford to lose."

Rollins inhaled his own drink and got to his feet. "You worry too much, Zack." He headed for the poker table.

Hunter walked around the town for an hour, finding nothing that held his interest. Just before sundown, he was back at the livery stable. He exchanged greetings with the hostler, a stoop-shouldered heavyweight who appeared to be about sixty years old. Zack pointed to his own animal in the corral. "Is there somebody close by that I can get to trim my horse's hooves and nail on some new shoes?"

The hostler nodded. "Ya lookin' at 'im, friend. Cain't git to it today, though. Ain't got enough daylight left. I c'n git on it early in th' mornin'."

"Tomorrow morning will be fine," Zack said, turning to leave.

"Ya c'n pick ya horse up anytime ya want to in th' mornin'," the man called after him. "I'll prob'ly be done with 'im 'fore ya git outta bed."

Zack walked the streets for another hour and returned to the saloon well after dark. He stopped halfway down the bar and leaned against a stool, for he could see that both of the poker games had broken up. A loud commotion at one of the pool tables drew his attention just in time to see Rollins punch a man in the face, knocking him to the floor. Zack was there quickly.

The man lay propped on one elbow and seemed to be in no hurry to get up. Blood trickled from one corner of his mouth. He was a snaggletoothed red-haired man about the same size and age as Rollins. "Ya ort not ta done 'at, purty boy," he said, getting to his feet slowly. "Ain't nobody never knocked Red Hilly down an' walked aroun' braggin' about it." He drew his Colt and closed the distance between himself and Rollins, waving the barrel almost under Rollins' nose. "I ain't never shot no unarmed man, an' I c'n see that you ain't holdin' nothin'.'' He poked the gun barrel even closer to Rollins' face. "I'm givin' ya ten minutes ta git a gun, mister. Do ya hear?"

Rollins nodded curtly, spun on his heel and headed for the door.

Red Hilly walked to the bar and stood facing the front door, clearly awaiting Bret's return. Every man present, including Hunter, moved to the opposite side of the bar, out of harm's way. Then all motion ceased, and the saloon was deathly quiet.

Like all the rest, Zack stood at the bar waiting. He believed that his friend's remaining lifetime might well be measured in minutes, or even seconds, for Bret Rollins would not back down. The man simply knew no fear. Hunter knew that Rollins was an excellent shot with a handgun, but doubted that he would be very quick on the draw. The quick draw was a practiced art, and Rollins had never spent much time with it.

Just as the allotted ten minutes expired, Rollins kicked the batwing doors open, and in one fluid motion, was inside the building. In his hands was a double-barreled shotgun, the barrels pointed directly at Hilly's midsection. As Rollins began to ease forward, Hilly stepped backward and held out his hand, palm forward. "Now . . . now wait a minute. I didn't say nothin' about gittin' a damn cannon." He took another step backward. "I ain't crazy, ya know." He pointed to the shotgun. "Ya thank I'm dumb enough ta go up ag'inst 'at damn thang?"

Rollins smiled and took another step forward. "Nope."

Hilly had both his palms out now. "I . . . I tell ya what," he stammered. "Let's jist forget th' whole thang. All right?"

Rollins smiled, then nodded.

Hilly gave the awesome weapon a wide berth and stumbled into several tables on his way out the door.

The saloon was quiet for several moments, then men began to speak in low tones. Rollins continued to stand his ground, the gun barrels now pointed toward the front door. Zack circled the bar and put his hand on Bret's shoulder. "Let's get out of here, Slick."

3

They were at the livery stable at sunup, and stood waiting while the hostler finished shoeing Zack's animal. "Didn't expect ya ta be gittin' up this early," the man said. "Won't take me much longer here." He dropped the horse's forefoot to the ground, then lifted one of the animal's hind legs. "I heerd all about ya little run-in with Red Hilly," he said, speaking to Rollins. "Glad ya put 'im in his place." He spat a stream of tobacco juice on a pile of horse manure. "Ain't nothin' ta Red Hilly, not unless he's got th' upper hand."

They stood in silence as the man tacked on the remaining shoes. He gave each hoof a few swipes with a file, then stepped back and removed his apron. "Guess 'at about does it. Any o' th' shoes gits loose, jist brang 'im back. Don't thank ya gon' have no problem, though."

Hunter paid the man, then saddled the animal. A short time later, they rode out of the stable and headed west, the packhorse following Rollins on a short rope.

They had ridden no more than a mile when Hunter brought up the subject of the pool game. "Was Red Hilly a good pool player?"

"Don't know," Rollins answered, guiding his horse closer. "He never did get a shot. I won the break and ran the table on him three times at five dollars a game. He didn't like losing his fifteen dollars and started raising hell.''

Hunter took a sip of water from his canteen, wiping his mouth on his sleeve. "Hilly expected you to come back with a six-gun strapped around your waist."

"Of course he did, Zack. I knew that. I try not to play another man's game unless I think I'm better at it."

"Well, I sure never saw a man's facial expression change so quick. He went totally blank when he saw that shotgun pointed at his middle."

Rollins nodded. "He knew he'd lost his advantage. Like he said, he wasn't dumb enough to try bucking two barrels of double aught."

They rode another mile. "Guess you owe me a dollar," Hunter said. "The best I recall, you bet me a dollar you'd have female company last night. Every time I looked at your bed, all I saw was you."

"And the best I recall, you refused to take the bet," Rollins said. He began to chuckle. "Anyway, there's always tonight. Tomorrow night, too."

They reached Fort Worth two hours before sundown. They stabled their horses, then ate supper at the first restaurant they saw. They chose a good hotel, and Rollins insisted that they rent separate rooms, saying that he did not intend to spend the night alone. After having two beers with Zack at the hotel bar, he said he was going hunting and stepped out into the night.

Zack bought another beer and attempted to engage the bartender in conversation. In answer to Zack's query about the local economy, the man's answer was direct. "Aw, there's a little farming goes on around here. But mostly this is cow country, mister." Then the man headed for the opposite end of the bar, where he seated himself on a stool and began laughing and talking with his drinking friends.

Hunter bought a newspaper from the desk clerk and climbed the stairs to his room. He took off his boots, then pulled the small table containing the lamp closer. Fully clothed, he lay down on the bed and began to read the paper. He dozed off in short order and the newspaper fell to the floor.

When he awoke, his internal clock told him that he had been asleep for quite some time, maybe for several hours. He had just resumed his reading when he heard a knock at the door. When Zack opened the door, Rollins gently pushed a young red-haired woman into the room. "This is Rose," he said. He handed Hunter a bottle of rum, then walked down the hall to his own room, a small blonde hanging on to his arm.

Zack stood shaking his head for a moment, then smiled and locked the door. The girl helped herself to the room's one chair, and Zack took a seat on the side of the bed. She was pretty, young, and talkative, quickly assuring him that she was of legal age. She accepted the drink he offered—right from the bottle. She soon left the chair and took a seat on the bed beside him.

They talked and sipped at the rum for the large part of an hour. The girl readily agreed to stay the remainder of the night, even after Zack explained to her that he was not the son of a wealthy banker, as she had been told by Rollins.

"Is Bret Rollins really an actor?" she asked.

Zack hid his smiling face with his hand, then slowly began to nod. "Yes, ma'am." He walked to the window and stood looking down into the lighted street. "He damn sure is." He returned to the bed and blew out the lamp, then reached for the willing redhead.

After a late start the following morning, they rode west all day. An hour before sundown, they sat their saddles beside a small spring. "Looks like a good place to camp," Zack said, pointing to a level plot of ground between two trees.

Rollins made no effort to dismount. He began to shake his head. "You know me, Zack. I always like to go first class when I can. Couldn't be more than a few miles on to the town of Weatherford. We could probably make it there by dark."

"Hotels and restaurants cost too much money, Bret. This camping spot's free."

"Aw, come on, Zack. We're not broke. Anyway, there's always a sucker around with some money."

"Like Red Hilly?" Zack asked, dismounting to relieve himself.

Rollins jumped to the ground for the same purpose. "Yeah, like Red Hilly. I got his fifteen dollars, didn't I?"

Zack chuckled. "Guess you did. But to the best of my memory, he wanted to give you something else."

"Aw, Zack. You heard that hostler say there wasn't anything to Hilly. That silly sonofabitch wasn't about to take on that double-barreled ten-gauge."

Rollins won the argument and they headed for Weatherford at a fast trot, arriving just as darkness settled in.

Weatherford originated in the 1850s, when it was designated the seat of Parker County and named for Jefferson Weatherford, a member of the Texas Senate when the county was created. In the early years, the town was the last settlement on the frontier, on the route of wagon trains operating between Fort Worth and Fort Belknap. Many of the residents built Victorian-style homes, and a two-year junior college was founded in 1869.

Like all frontier towns, however, Weatherford also had its seedy side: run-down hotels and hastily built saloons where scores of night people employed a myriad of schemes to separate the unwary cowboy, farmer or traveler from his money.

Hunter and Rollins stabled their horses and rented quarters at a nearby hotel, taking the only room the establishment had that offered two beds. Still fully clothed, Hunter stretched out immediately, fluffing his pillow. He yawned. "Thanks for talking me out of spending the night at the spring, Bret. I have to admit that this beats the hell out of sleeping on a creek bank."

"A man should go first class anytime he can, Zack. If you live like a second-class citizen long enough, you start to feel and act like one. That's not good."

Hunter nodded and said nothing. He lay on the bed watching as Rollins took his gunbelt from the pack and buckled it around his waist. Bret removed the shells from the Colt's cylinder and laid them on his bed. Then he began to practice the fast draw. Seemingly unmindful of Zack's presence, he began to experiment with different body positions, finally settling on a forward crouch, with his feet spread slightly apart.

"You planning on becoming a quick-draw artist?" Hunter asked.

Rollins emptied the holster again, whipping the Colt into firing position. "Uh-huh." He sat down on his bed. "I intend to practice till I'm the fastest man around. The world is full of men like Red Hilly, and I won't always have a shotgun close by.''

Hunter knew that Rollins would indeed become a fast gun. Everything he had ever undertaken, he had learned to do exceedingly well. And he was quick by nature. His catlike motions had always reminded Zack of some predatory animal, capable of springing at the blink of an eye. And Bret Rollins would hit his target. Zack had once seen him strike a match with a rifle, and watched him roll cans down the road with a handgun many times.

And Rollins would practice until he was the best, just as he had done with numerous other things. To a man with his reflexes and dexterity, the speed would come quickly, and he was already an expert marksman. Zack strongly believed that after Rollins had practiced the fast draw for a while, the first man to cross him would be in trouble. ''You can do anything you want to, Bret,'' Zack said, rising to his feet. ''You're a talented man.''

''Well, what I want to do right now is find something to eat.'' Bret rolled up the gunbelt and returned it to his pack. ''You about ready?''

Zack nodded, then held the door open. ''Very ready.''

At a restaurant called The Steakhouse, Rollins ordered for both men. ''Bring us two of the best beefsteaks in the house,'' he said to the smiling teenaged waiter, ''and whatever vegetables you have in the pot.'' The boy disappeared quickly.

When they had eaten, Rollins paid for the meal, then said he was going looking for some action. He invited Zack to come along. Zack declined, saying that he would walk around town for a while, then go to bed. He stood on the street watching till Rollins disappeared inside a fancy saloon, then he chose a much simpler establishment in which to have a beer.

The small saloon appeared to be the oldest building on the street and had a sawdust floor. Ten stools circled its short bar, and half as many tables were scattered around the room. No customers were in the building when Hunter entered. He took a stool directly in front of the bartender.

''I was sitting here about to doze off,'' the middle-aged

bartender said, getting to his feet. "Order up. The first drink's always on the house."

Hunter ordered a beer.

"Easy to see that you're just passing through," the man said as he slid the foamy brew in front of Zack. "Guess I know about everybody that lives around here."

Zack offered his right hand across the bar. "My name's Zack Hunter," he said, "and I guess you're right. As far as I know, I'm just passing through."

"My name's Rex Allgood," the man said, pumping Zack's hand with a firm grip. A dark-haired man with a receding hairline and a potbelly, he was broad-shouldered and of medium height. "My father-in-law owns this place." He waved his arm toward the empty tables and stools, adding, "His outdated ideas are responsible for the customers we ain't got.

"He says a man wants to drink in a quiet atmosphere. I keep telling him that it's just the opposite—drinkers want some noise and some action. A man wanting a quiet atmosphere will buy a damn bottle and go home.

"Take Bud's Place, just a block to the east. It ain't much bigger than this place, but it does ten times the business. Bud was smart enough to hire that dried-up piano player, and the house has been packed ever since. I mean, Wimpy Jones has a big following, and people will line up to listen to him play.

"I had a chance to hire Wimpy before Bud got him, but the old man wouldn't let me do it. He said drinkers wanted quiet." The bartender motioned toward the empty seats again. "Well, as you can see, we've got quiet."

Hunter nodded. "Who's the old man?"

"Clifford T. Hollingsworth," the bartender said, then refilled Zack's beer mug. "I married his daughter fifteen years ago. Cliff's a very successful cattleman, but he don't know beans about the saloon business. I think he bought this building a few years ago just so he'd have a quiet place to do his own drinking. Well, he's done got old and quit drinking, but like I say, the place is still quiet."

"He's a rancher?"

The man nodded. "Big spread called the Lazy H, ten miles north of town. He sent two herds north to the rails last year and put another one on the trail three weeks ago. He's in business, all right.''

"Sure sounds like it." Zack sipped at his beer. "Does the old man still ride horses?''

"He forks one occasionally, but he mostly gets about in a spring wagon. Don't hesitate to let the horse know he's in a hurry, either. I don't think I've seen Cliff in a good mood all year. He's frustrated 'cause he can't buy that Silver Springs property off Mrs. Lindsay. He's offered her twice what it's worth, but she won't budge.''

Hunter pushed his mug forward for a refill. "Sounds like it must be mighty important to him.''

Allgood wiped the wet bar with a sponge. "Hell, it's eating him up. It ain't but a hundred acres, but it's damn near in the middle of the ten thousand acres that Cliff claims. You see, that's where the Silver Springs are, right there in that little hollow owned by Mrs. Lindsay.

"The Lindsays were some of the first white people to settle in Parker County, and she's the last of the clan. I reckon she must be eighty years old, and she has no need in the world for that property.'' He began to laugh. "Cliff's problem is that she don't need any more money, either. She's one of the richest people in the county.

"You see, Cliff wants to turn that hundred acres into a lake, so his water problem will be solved once and for all. A dam across the lower end of that hollow is all it would take. The springs would fill it up in a few months.

"Now, the fact that Mrs. Lindsay's got lots of money ain't the only reason Cliff can't buy that property. She hates his guts, and she's told him so to his face. Cliff's always been able to buy anything he wanted, but I've told him that he may as well forget about that hundred acres. He's never going to own it.''

Zack stared at the bar for a long time, then drained his mug. "I know a man who can buy that property.''

"The hell you do!'' Allgood shook his head a few times, then added, "If this fellow's all that good, I guess he's rich too, huh?''

"Nope,'' Zack said, getting to his feet, "but he's working on it. His name is Rollins, and I'll send him around as soon as I can find him. If not tonight, maybe tomorrow night.''

"You do that,'' the bartender said as Zack headed for the door. "He can damn sure fatten up his poke if he can get that land for Cliff.''

When Zack failed to find Rollins at the fancy saloon, he began to walk the street. Peeking in one establishment after another, he finally spotted Bret playing stud poker at a run-down saloon near the livery stable. He ordered a beer and stood with his back to the bar. Watching the poker game out of the corner of his eye, he could see even at a distance that the action was slow, and that every man at the table was old enough to be Bret's father—or grandfather. Hunter drank his beer quickly; then returned to his hotel room. He undressed and stretched out on his bed, leaving the lamp burning for Rollins.

Zack was still awake when Rollins returned an hour later. Bret heaved a sigh as he sat down on his bed and dropped a boot to the floor noisily. "I played those old bastards for nearly four hours, Zack. Only made two dollars.''

"Better than losing two, ain't it?''

"Not much. You can't get them to put any money in the pot. Hell, they'll sit there all night betting on nothing but cod-lock cinches.''

Zack laughed. "I know the type; I've played 'em myself.'' He raised himself to a sitting position on the side of his bed and changed the subject. "I had a long talk with a bartender named Rex Allgood, Bret. He told me about a selling job that I know you would love. Well, it's not really a selling job; it's a buying job.''

Rollins listened quietly as Zack related as much as he knew about Clifford T. Hollingsworth and Mrs. Lindsay, and of Hollingsworth's disappointing efforts to acquire the Silver Springs property. "According to Allgood, the old man's main problem is that Mrs. Lindsay hates his guts.''

Rollins undressed and sat on his bed thinking for a long time, then finally spoke. "I wonder how much money's involved,'' he said softly, as if speaking to himself.

Hunter blew out the lamp. "Don't know,'' he said as he slid beneath the covers. "Allgood says the old man's already offered her twice as much as the property's worth."

"I'll talk with the bartender tomorrow," Rollins said, yawning. "Good night."

"Same to you."

4

Clifford T. Hollingsworth was standing on the porch two days later when Bret Rollins rode into the ranch-house yard. The Lazy H owner took the steps two at a time and walked to meet his visitor. "Something I can do for you?" he asked.

Rollins had already been told that Texans considered it bad manners for a mounted man to attempt to carry on a conversation with someone on the ground. "Do you mind if I dismount?" he asked.

The man pointed to the hitching rail. "Get down and tie up." Hollingsworth was not a big man, probably five-eight and a hundred fifty pounds. Though he moved about spryly, he had the overall appearance of an old man. His hair was milky white, and his leathery face held an unpleasant, surly expression that Rollins assumed was permanent.

Nevertheless, Rollins broadened his own perpetual smile. "I had a talk with Rex Allgood last night, sir. He says you're interested in acquiring the Silver Springs property."

"Maybe. What's that got to do with you?"

Rollins spoke softly. "I'm the man who can get it for you."

"You can get it for me?" The old man laughed aloud. "You can get it for me? Don't kid yourself, fellow. That old bitch has got half the money in this county, and she's determined to die owning Silver Springs. No, sir, you won't get it. I've sent older and more experienced men than you to deal with her and she's sent 'em all packing."

Continuing to smile, Rollins backtracked to the hitching rail. He mounted the roan, stopping abreast of the old man. "I'm sorry to have taken up your time, sir. Good day." He kicked the horse to a canter and was quickly off the premises.

In Weatherford, Bret found Zack in the small restaurant at which the two had lately begun to take their meals. "Sit down and order up," Zack said as Bret approached the table. "They've got roast beef for twenty cents today."

Bret took a seat and ordered his meal, then began to drum his fingers on the table. "I've met with Hollingsworth, Zack, and I don't like the sonofabitch any better than Mrs. Lindsay does. He's a rude old fart, even laughed at me. I mean, I've punched younger men in the mouth for treating me better than he did."

Zack chuckled and said nothing.

The waiter delivered Rollins' warmed-over meal, then walked away. Rollins began to slice the beef. "I've made up my mind about one thing, Zack: if I do figure out some way to get that property, Mister Clifford T. Hollingsworth is gonna pay through his damn nose."

Zack chuckled again. "I believe you, Bret. And I believe that he's got the money. I talked with Allgood again this morning. He says that Hollingsworth offered Mrs. Lindsay fifty dollars an acre."

Rollins struck the table lightly with his fist. "Fifty dollars an acre. Hell, that's five thousand dollars, Zack."

"I know."

"Well, by God, I intend to get that property. I don't have the faintest idea how I'll go about it, but I'll figure out a way."

Zack peeked over the rim of his coffee cup and smiled. "How about the same tactic you used on the doctor's wife?"

"Aw, shit, Zack, be serious. That woman's eighty years old."

Zack raised his eyebrows. "So?"

Bret ignored him and laid enough money on the table to pay for both meals. As they walked out onto the street, Zack laid his hand on Bret's shoulder. "Let's go to the hotel room, Slick. I want to talk to you."

They were soon sitting on their beds facing each other. "First of all," Zack began, "I want you to know that I believe you'll get the Silver Springs property, just like you've done everything else you set out to do. Just remember that Mrs. Lindsay is filthy rich and that money means nothing to her. You'll have to work from a different angle.''

"I'm aware of that," Rollins said.

Zack continued, "I believe the lady has a lot more compassion and conscience than some of the rich people you and I have known. She took in two orphan boys and raised them; put them both through college, according to Allgood.''

Ever the quick thinker, Rollins was on his feet instantly, walking around the room. He pounded his fist into his palm several times. "You just gave me the best idea I've had all week, Zack.''

Zack looked at him blankly. "Well, whatever the hell I said, I'm glad I could be of service. Anyway, I'm gonna make it easier for you to do whatever you've got in mind. You see, the two of us don't make a very good picture prowling around town together. People don't stare at us, but they certainly notice us. I'd bet that half the men in town even know where we're sleeping.

"I'm gonna take the packhorse and move back to that spring we passed east of town. I'll set up the tent and stay there till I hear from you. I also think you should move into a better hotel and buy a broadcloth suit. Whatever you plan on saying to Mrs. Lindsay, looking good sure won't hurt your case any.''

"Hell, I figured on doing all of that, Zack. I wasn't born yesterday.''

Hunter got to his feet and put his hand on Bret's shoulder. "Of course you weren't. Sorry if I spoke out of turn.'' He began to put the pack together. "My setting up camp at the spring will not only get me out of your way, it'll eliminate the expense of this hotel room and eating at the restaurant. I've got plenty of time to cook my own food. When I need meat, I'll shoot something.''

Rollins said nothing for a while, seeming less than enthusiastic about Zack's plan. "All right, we'll do it your way," he said finally, shrugging his shoulders.

Hunter reseated himself on the bed. "Hey, old buddy, I'm not leaving the country. The spring is only ten miles away.''

He began to smile. "Besides, you can visit me anytime you get lonesome. Just be sure to sing out before you ride into camp." Then he was on his feet again. "I just know that my being somewhere else is gonna help your cause, Bret. Trust me."

Leading the packhorse, Hunter rode east an hour later.

For the next three days, Rollins was a very busy man. Moving about town casually, he gathered as much information on Mrs. Lindsay as he could without appearing too anxious. He had additional talks with Rex Allgood, never telling the man that he had already met with Cliff Hollingsworth.

Since he could not visit Silver Springs for an on-site inspection without being seen by Hollingsworth, Rollins did the next best thing: he had the bartender describe the property in detail. He left the saloon with a clear mental picture, then drew himself a map when he reached his hotel room.

After a haircut, shave and a bath at the barber shop next morning, Rollins dressed himself in his new suit. He was now ready to visit Mrs. Victoria Lindsay.

The lady lived two miles south of town in a beautiful two-story home that stood a thousand yards off the main road. As Bret rode into the yard, he could see the bulldogs waiting for him at the gate. Mrs. Lindsay, who indeed appeared to be eighty years old, walked from the house and quieted the dogs. She was a tall woman, with gray hair rolled neatly into a bun and pinned at the back of her head. A short apron was tied around her waist. She reached the gate and stood there looking at him.

Rollins dismounted and flashed his best smile. "Good morning, Mrs. Lindsay. My name is Bret Rollins, and I'm hoping I can talk with you for a few minutes."

She studied him for only a moment. "If it's about that land, there ain't no use to talk."

Rollins sensed immediately that here was a down-to-earth woman who would resist high-pressure tactics till hell froze over. He must speak clearly, simply and softly; otherwise, the lady would show him the road.

Bret Rollins had been charming people all of his life and was determined that Mrs. Lindsay would be no exception. He continued to smile and leaned against the gate, deliberately letting a curl fall to his forehead. In his deepest, most resonate tone of voice, he began to speak slowly. "I did come here to talk about the land, Mrs. Lindsay, but I'm not a rancher, farmer or developer. All I ask is that you hear me out."

She looked him up and down several times. Then her stern look softened. "I don't reckon I'll deny you a chance to talk," she said, her lower lip quivering slightly. She unlatched the gate. "Come on in."

Bret tied the roan to the hitching rail, then followed her up the steps. As they entered the house, a young boy about ten years old got to his feet. "My caretaker's grandson," she said.

Rollins introduced himself and shook hands with the young man, who disappeared immediately. "Fine-looking boy," Rollins said, turning to face the woman. "Fine-looking boy."

"You don't look like much more'n a boy yourself," she told him, taking a seat in a cushioned chair.

"Everybody says I look younger than I am. Lord, I'll be thirty-two next week."

Mrs. Lindsay called to the maid, ordering tea for the two of them. "All right, Mister Rollins, what is it that you want to say?"

Rollins walked back and forth a few times, then took the tray from the maid and set it on a table. He was racking his brain as he handed a glass to Mrs. Lindsay. He knew that he would never stand in this parlor again unless he laid down a very convincing story. He cleared his throat, then plunged into the tale he had rehearsed in his mind a hundred times.

"I'm from New Orleans, Louisiana, Mrs. Lindsay. Five years ago I took a part-time job there as physical-education director at an orphanage. That job turned into what I hope will be a lifetime of dedicated work with homeless youngsters.

"To see how hard those kids try, and the happy, joyous look on their faces as they realize that for once in their lives they finally have a home, is enough to touch even the most calloused heart." Out of the corner of his eye, he could see that he had her attention.

"Two years later, my parents came to work at the orphanage when they retired. In fact, they are still working and living there, and they love those kids as they always loved their own.

"Six months ago, my folks told me that they would like to build a home for orphan boys right here in Texas. Mom and Dad would run it themselves with a minimum of hired help, and I would donate much of my time as business manager. The rest of my time would be spent helping the boys to develop strong bodies and teaching them how to become respectable men.

"That hundred acres you own at Silver Springs would be the ideal location."

The lady had not spoken since Rollins began to talk. He glanced at her expression and knew that he had her undivided attention. He knew that money would not buy the property, for he had only to look around him to know that she was rich. He must get the land for free, or he would not get it at all. He paused briefly, then continued his spiel. "I first approached a rancher named Hollingsworth with my idea, but he wouldn't even listen, said the orphans of the world are not his responsibility. I guess you know the man I'm talking about."

"Oooh, yes," she said with a sigh. "I know him all right."

Rollins continued: "Two businessmen in Dallas have agreed to bear the expense of erecting the buildings if I can get the land. Those kindhearted gentlemen are willing to help me create my vision. This, Mrs. Lindsay, is my vision: I see the Lady Lindsay Home for Boys on that Silver Springs property one year from now. I see ten acres of plowed fields, where the boys are growing much of their own food. A pasture with cattle and hogs. The second year, we would build a separate wing for girls, and change the name to indicate that.

"In three years, I see us with our own schoolteachers, so that our kids can go straight from our Home to college. Of course there's a two-year junior college right here in Weatherford. The kids could continue to live at the Home while extending their education. I see a large pond, well stocked with fish. The kids would raise their own chickens, and we would allow them to have a few dogs and cats.

"Lastly, I see on the front lawn a bronze statue of the lady who made it all possible: Mrs. Victoria Lindsay! That, dear lady, is my vision, and there will be no shortage of kids to fill it. My compassionate friends in Dallas say they will help with operating expenses till we can receive funds from the state of Texas.''

Mrs. Lindsay sat staring at the wall for quite some time as Rollins walked around looking at the numerous paintings hung about the room.

The lady finally rose from her chair. ''Would you like to stay for dinner, Mister Rollins?''

''Indeed I would, ma'am. I only had coffee this morning.''

When she had informed the cook that her guest would be present for dinner, she invited Bret to see her vegetable garden. Each row she showed him looked exactly like the ones he had grown up with and picked on his grandfather's farm. He commented on the garden. ''Being a city fellow, I've never had many opportunities to actually see the vegetables growing. This is beautiful.''

They talked of many things, but Bret was very careful not to mention the property again. When dinner had been served, she surprised him again. ''Would you like to come to supper tomorrow night?''

''Yes, ma'am. Living in hotels and eating in restaurants like I have to do, a home-cooked meal is always welcome.''

''Tomorrow night at eight, then?''

''Yes, ma'am.''

He rode out of the yard feeling that he might have scored a bull's-eye with the lady, but he also knew that he was not out of the woods yet. Given enough time, she could very easily have him and his story checked out. His only hope was to make her like and trust him so much that she would consider such a thing unnecessary. He kicked his horse toward town. He would stable the animal, then head for his hotel room, where he expected to spend most of his time in the near future. He would stay out of sight for the most part; wandering around the town now was out of the question.

Supper at Mrs. Lindsay's the following night was truly something that Rollins would remember. He told her many colorful stories about his childhood, while she talked of long-ago times when her family had first come to Texas. Neither of them mentioned the land that was the uppermost thought in Bret's mind. As he was leaving, she walked him to his horse. She was still thinking about the property, she said, and would have her caretaker contact him at the hotel when she had reached a decision.

The thought crossed Bret's mind that perhaps she was just stalling for time while she had him checked out. But she had not asked for the name of the orphanage in New Orleans or for the names of the businessmen in Dallas. Without that information, checking out his story would not be so easy. New Orleans was a big town, and there would surely be several orphanages in the area. Anyway, if Mrs. Lindsay began to cross-examine him too closely, Bret was prepared to chuck the whole idea and seek his fortune elsewhere.

He stayed in or close to the hotel for the next three days, leaving his room only to stretch his legs or get something to eat. He had just returned from the restaurant on Sunday night when the desk clerk handed him a message: Mrs. Lindsay's caretaker had come by, saying that the lady wanted to see Rollins at her home tomorrow morning. Bret put the written message in his pocket and hurried to his room.

He slept fitfully during the night and was up at the break of dawn. He ate breakfast at the restaurant, then reread yesterday's newspaper while waiting for the barber shop to open. After a bath and a shave, he dressed in his new suit and headed for the Lindsay home.

She met him at the gate, powdered and dressed expensively. "If you'll hitch up the buggy and drive me to town, we'll fix up the papers on that property."

An hour later, at the Parker County Courthouse, the lady deeded the Silver Springs property to Bret Rollins for the sum of one dollar. "I've been gauging people for eighty-one years," she said, "and I know a good man when I see one. I hadn't been around you more than five minutes before I decided that you were a man who could be depended on to do the right thing. If you need any more assistance, don't hesitate to call on me."

"Thank you, Mrs. Lindsay. The land will certainly be used for a good cause." He put the deed in his coat pocket, then drove the lady home.

Two hours later, Bret visited Rex Allgood at the saloon. "I'm the new owner of the Silver Springs property, Rex, and

I could be persuaded to part with it. Do you suppose you can get word to your father-in-law?''

Allgood nodded. ''I can send a rider out there, but why don't you just ride to the ranch yourself?''

Rollins shook his head. ''Any business I do with Mister Hollingsworth will be conducted in my hotel room. I'm at the Palace, room two-ten.''

Allgood was busy pouring himself a drink. He returned the bottle to the shelf. ''I'll get a man out there with the message this afternoon. Probably be noon tomorrow before the old man can make it, though.''

''That's fine,'' Rollins said. ''Have your rider tell him that I'll be expecting him at noon.'' He bought a shot of whiskey, then left the building.

Right on time, Rollins heard a knock at his door next day. He had put the broadcloth suit away and was now dressed in jeans and flannel shirt. ''Be with you in a minute,'' he shouted, then waited two minutes before opening the door. As he expected, Cliff Hollingsworth stood in the hall, scowling somewhat less than at their last meeting.

''Why, Mister Hollingsworth,'' Bret said, flashing a toothy smile, ''what a surprise. Won't you come in?'' He closed the door behind his visitor and reseated himself in the room's only chair, leaving the old man standing.

Hollingsworth shifted his weight from one leg to the other a few times, clearly uneasy in the younger man's element. ''My son-in-law says you've got a clear deed to the Silver Springs property,'' he said finally.

''That's correct.''

The old man shifted his feet again. ''Well, how much do you want for it?''

''Six thousand dollars, sir.'' Bret eyed the man steadily, his smile never fading. ''Cash.''

Hollingsworth began to fidget, and the scowl returned.

''That's ridiculous. You and me both know that property ain't worth no six thousand.''

''Maybe so,'' Rollins said, his expression turning serious. ''But real estate prices are rising every day. I'm a young man, I can wait. Meanwhile, I'll always have a place to take a good country shit.''

The man stared at him for several moments. "There ain't nobody in this country that needs or wants that property but me. I'll pay forty-five hundred, and that's all."

Rollins got to his feet and began to walk around the room. "Then I guess we can't do business, sir. Maybe I'll just dam up that hollow myself. You know, build my own lake and put a fence around it. The day might come when I can sell water by the barrel." He raised his eyes to meet those of Hollingsworth, his smile returning. "Or maybe by the gallon.

"The six-thousand-dollar price is firm, sir. Of course you don't have to make your decision today, you can think on it for the rest of the year. I'll be leaving for New Orleans tomorrow, should be back sometime after Christmas."

"Christmas? Hell, I was hoping to have the dam built by then."

Rollins shook his head. "If we can't do business now, we'll have to discuss it further after the first of the year. I have an appointment in Orleans Parrish that I simply cannot postpone."

Hollingsworth heaved a sigh. "All right," he said, "I'll pay your price. We'll go by the bank, then on to the courthouse."

The sun was still an hour high when Rollins rode into Zack's camp. Zack had just finished his supper and was washing his utensils at the spring. "Hey, old buddy," he said, joining Rollins under the tall oak. "I expected you to come out here before now."

Rollins dismounted, his saddlebags across his shoulder, "Load that packhorse and saddle up, Zack. We need to be making tracks." He patted the saddlebags. "I've got six thousand dollars in here."

"Six . . . did I hear you right?"

"Six thousand dollars." Rollins partially explained his recent activities as quickly as possible, adding, "We need to get the hell out of here,'cause I don't know how long it'll take for the word to get out. Mrs. Lindsay's got lots of friends, and all of them probably have guns."

Zack moved quickly. Twenty minutes later, he led both animals to the dying campfire.

Rollins sat on the ground, where he had arranged the money

in two identical stacks. He handed one of them to Zack. "Here's your half," he said.

"Half?" Zack asked. "Hell, you did all the work."

"No, Zack, you did all the work; I had all the fun. You earned your half by setting the deal up." Rollins stuffed his money in his saddlebags, then mounted the roan. Zack poured the remaining coffee over the gray coals, then bagged his own portion of the windfall. He mounted and took up the slack in the packhorse's lead rope. They would ride south till dark, then turn west, giving the town of Weatherford a wide berth.

5

They had ridden less than a mile when Hunter ordered Rollins to come clean. "It looks like we're on the run, Bret, so I want to know what the hell we're running from."

Rollins brought the roan to a halt. He sat for a moment trying to decide the best way to explain the situation. He had never lied to Zack and did not intend to do so now. He would simply leave out part of the story. He talked on and on about his exchange with Clifford T. Hollingsworth, and how he had beaten the old man at his own game. At the end of his narration, he added, "I told you I'd make the sonofabitch pay through the nose."

Hunter was still less than jubilant. "How in the hell did you get a deed to the property in the first place?"

Rollins had dreaded that question. He had first thought of letting Zack think he had romanced the lady, but he knew that Zack already knew how old she was. He decided that he would rather tell the truth than have Zack think he had bedded an eighty-one-year-old woman. He confessed the whole thing, leaving out nothing.

Zack began to drum his fingers on his kneecap. "You have no conscience whatsoever, Bret."

"Sure, I do, Zack, but that woman had no use in the world for that property. She's nearing the end of her life, and she damn sure couldn't take the place with her. You and me still have to get through this world, and though she didn't realize it, she's helped us along quite nicely."

Zack stared into the setting sun, a faint smile on one corner of his mouth.

"Anyway," Rollins continued, "Hollingsworth's the one who coughed up the money." He pointed to Zack's saddle-bags. "Do you realize that you made over four hundred dollars a day for the past week?"

Zack did not answer the question, though having more money in his saddlebag than he had ever seen before had begun to give him a feeling of security. "I guess you know that all hell's gonna break loose when the old man starts damming up that hollow," he said.

"Of course I know it, Zack, but I did nothing illegal. I paid a dollar for the property and sold it at a profit, neither of which is against the law. The story about the orphanage was all verbal. I put nothing in writing concerning my intended use for the land. In fact, the only things I signed were the deed and Hollingsworth's check. Of course Mrs. Lindsay might have some friends who will be unhappy with the transaction. That's why I was busy trying to get the hell out of this country when you started jumping on me."

Zack chuckled. He kicked his horse in the ribs and turned the animal west. "All right, Mister Rollins, let's get the hell out of this country."

A night of steady travel under a full moon brought them to the Palo Pinto Mountains at daybreak. They picketed their horses beside a spring, then prepared breakfast over a small campfire. After eating, they spread their blankets and slept soundly in the cool mountain air.

Hunter awakened at noon to find Rollins sitting on his bed studying the map. "You remember Harry Terry, Zack?" Bret asked. "He owned the pool hall back in Memphis."

Zack nodded.

"Well," Rollins continued, "he was originally from Texas,

and he was always talking about a town called Lampasas."
He thumped the map. "According to this, Lampasas is about
a hundred fifty miles directly south of here. I think I'd like to
look the town over, see if it's anything like Harry claimed."

Zack was slipping on his boots. "Lead the way," he said.

They rode all afternoon and into the night, camping at midnight on the North Bosque River. Just before going to sleep,
Zack registered a complaint: "You know, Slick, since it seems
that we have plenty of time, and since I can't hear any hoof-
beats behind us, I think we ought to start eating a little more
often. If we start riding at sunup, stop for an hour at noon,
then make camp an hour before sunset, we'll have time to eat
like normal people."

Rollins rolled up in his blanket. "No argument here, Zack.
I'm hungry, too. I'll start hunting some firewood at daybreak."

They camped on the Lampasas River Friday night and rode
into the town of the same name at noon on Saturday. They
left their horses at the livery stable on the edge of town, and
Rollins made friends with the hostler, a tall, skinny man
named Oscar Land. "Any good hotels in town?" Rollins
asked.

The liveryman pointed west. "The Hartley's the best one,
I guess. At least the folks that own it seem to think so. They
charge an arm and a leg, but they'll bring a hot bath right to
your room. Bring you a bottle of whiskey if you want it." He
smiled and winked, adding, "I've heard that a fellow can get
a little female company just by speaking up. I never have
stayed there myself; too damn rich for my blood."

With their saddlebags across their shoulders and long guns
cradled in their arms, the men walked down the street to the
Hartley, where they rented a second-story room. The hostler
had been right about the price: three-fifty a day for a room
with two beds, and another dollar for a bath. Rollins laid an
eagle on the counter, ordering two baths and a bottle of whiskey.

An hour later, after shaving, bathing and changing into
clean clothing, Hunter and Rollins sat in their room sipping
whiskey and water. Bret raised the window, mixed himself
another drink, then sat on his bed, propping his bare feet up
in a cane-bottom chair. "This is what I've been talking about,

Zack,'' he said, sipping at his drink. ''This is first class.''

Zack nodded in agreement. He pressed his hand against the springy mattress. ''I think I could get used to a bed like this mighty easy.''

''Sure you could. And we've got plenty of money to keep right on staying in places like this.''

Zack shook his head. ''We don't have to stay in a hotel to sleep on a good bed, Bret. All we have to do is find out where they buy theirs, then buy some of our own.'' He sat with his chin in his palms and his elbows propped on his knees. ''All morning we've been riding through the prettiest country I've ever seen, and I think I've traveled about as far as I want to.''

Rollins sat quietly for a few moments, then raised his eyebrows. ''You mean you want to live in this town?''

''No. I want to live in the country, and I'll bet a man could buy a piece of land around here at a reasonable price. He sure as hell never would starve; I counted nine deer that we jumped this morning.'' Zack pointed to the saddlebags. ''Besides, I'm tired of guarding that money twenty-four hours a day. I noticed when we passed the bank that it was closed. Otherwise, I'd have left my money there.''

Rollins shrugged, then began to walk around the room. ''Hell, Zack, I've always felt like I could make it anywhere. If you want to stay here, then by God, that's what we'll do. As far as the banker's concerned, I never have seen one yet that wouldn't open his door for a deposit like we'll be making.'' He sat down and began to pull on his boots. ''You just stay here with the money; I'll find the banker.'' He was quickly out of the room and down the stairway.

Zack locked the door, then fluffed up his pillow and lay down on his bed, the shotgun within easy reach. He was thinking of the beautiful country he had ridden through this morning, both east and west of the Lampasas River. Though his knowledge of the cattle business was limited, it was obvious that this area was a cattleman's dream. Grass and shade were abundant, and Zack had seen several springs and small creeks. Then there was the river, a neverending water source. A cow would probably never have to walk more than a mile in any direction to find a drink.

Hunter had no idea what it would cost to buy a section of

land in this area, but knew that the Silver Springs property could not be used as a gauge. The price of that land had been greatly inflated because of its strategic location. The fact that Hollingsworth was determined to get it, while Mrs. Lindsay was equally determined that he would not, had pushed the price up even farther. Zack believed that grazing land could be bought for a fraction of the price Hollingsworth paid for Silver Springs.

Zack was still lying on his bed when Rollins returned an hour later. "I found the banker at home," Rollins said, wiping sweat from his forehead. "Had to walk more than a damn mile."

"Oh, you poor soul," Zack said, rising to a sitting position.

Rollins ignored the remark. "Anyway, the man's name is J. Pennington McGrath, and he'll meet us at the bank in half an hour."

The banker was on time. He was a short man who weighed little more than a hundred pounds and appeared to be in his early fifties. Hatless, with thinning gray hair and a pale complexion, he introduced himself and offered Hunter an uncallused hand. Zack gripped the soft hand firmly, pumping it a few times.

McGrath unlocked the front door and led the men to his office, seating them at a huge desk. He produced a ledger, then took his own seat. A hint of a smile appeared on his face. "Welcome to Lampasas, men. I'm sure you'll find the area to your liking. You two are exactly the type of young men we need to settle this country." He opened the ledger and smiled broadly, then addressed Rollins. "What type of account did you have in mind, sir?"

They deposited their money in separate accounts. Hunter kept fifty dollars for his pocket. Rollins kept more. McGrath thanked them several times for choosing his bank, then followed them to the front door. "If you fellows decide to buy something in the area, I hope you'll check with me. I know everything that's for sale, who owns it, and what it'll cost. Good day to both of you."

"Good day to you," Hunter said. "You'll probably be seeing me again pretty soon."

Contrary to the Hartley's own interest, the desk clerk informed Hunter and Rollins that the hotel restaurant was not the best eating place in town. "Toby's T-Bone, across the street, has the best food," the balding sixty-year-old man said. "More affordable, too."

They thanked him and crossed the street. "Kind of unusual for a man to steer customers away from a business that pays his salary," Rollins said.

"It might be unusual," Zack said, reaching for the knob on Toby's front door, "but it's pretty easy to understand. The Hartley pays his salary, all right, but this place over here probably feeds him, and I'll bet he never has to pay for a meal."

"Of course not," Rollins said. "He probably hasn't paid for his dinner all year." He led the way inside the building.

The restaurant was small and exceptionally clean. A few tables were scattered throughout the room, and several stools lined the counter, behind which stood a tall, thin, middle-aged man.

"I guess you'd be Toby," Bret said as he and Zack took seats at the counter.

The man nodded. "If you fellows are hungry, you caught me between meals; supper won't be ready till about six." When neither man moved from his stool, Toby added, "I guess I could warm up some leftover stew. It was mighty tasty at dinner—I ate it myself."

Both men nodded, and Toby went through the batwing doors to the kitchen. A few minutes later, he placed a steaming bowl in front of each man. "This was supposed to be venison stew, but I didn't have enough deer meat. Had to mix in some beef. I guess it's about half and half."

Zack had already shoveled in a large bite. "I don't know which half I'm eating," he said, "but it sure is good." Toby nodded and returned to the kitchen. Both men enjoyed the stew and were served egg custard for dessert.

Their next stop was the White Horse Saloon, located on the corner at the end of the block. A large chalk replica of a white stallion stood on the roof of the building, under which was a sign reading that gambling, billiards and whiskey could be found inside.

Hunter and Rollins took stools at the far side of the horseshoe-shaped bar, where they had a good view of everything around them. A few gaming tables were set up near the back wall, and two poker games were in progress. Across the room, near the opposite wall, were two billiard tables. Nobody played the game at the moment. Several tables and chairs were located in the center of the saloon, scattered around a potbellied stove.

A dark-haired young man, whose body appeared to be about as firm and unyielding as an oak, stood behind the bar, his shirtsleeves rolled up on muscular arms. "What'll you have?" he asked, wiping the bar with a dry cloth.

Rollins ordered beer for both men. They were served quickly, then the bartender was gone to the opposite side of the bar.

They were working on their third beer when a tall, narrow-shouldered man with a thick neck walked through the door, taking a stool directly across the bar from Hunter. He ordered a drink, then decided that Zack, who thought the man looked familiar, was giving him excessive scrutiny. "Don't be settin' over there glarin' at me, feller," the man said with a snarl.

Hunter's eyes never wavered.

The man was on his feet and around the end of the bar quickly, standing beside Hunter's stool. "I guess you didn't hear me," he said, moving closer.

Zack said nothing.

Then the man turned to Rollins, who was smiling as if he knew a secret. "Don't know what you're grinnin' about," the man said. "You're gonna be next."

"Oh, no," Bret said. He laughed aloud and motioned toward Hunter. "If you manage to get by him, I'm not gonna be next; I'm gonna be running."

As if on cue, Zack went into action. In one fluid movement, he elbowed his antagonist in the midsection, slid off the stool on the opposite side, then went to work on the man's head. The fight lasted less than five seconds before the man was lying unconscious at Zack's feet. Zack had landed six devastating punches to the head and face, three of them as the man was going down. Though the man had made a few defensive movements, none had been effective.

The bartender had seen and listened to the entire exchange. "Guess that's about as quick as I've ever seen it done," he said. He poured a beer for each of the men, refusing payment.

Hunter reclaimed his stool and began to sip the foamy brew. He still had not spoken.

When the man on the floor began to stir, Zack got to his feet and stood watching. The man sat up and shook his head a few times, then pulled himself to his feet. On shaky legs, he made one step in Hunter's direction but stopped, appearing to think it over for a while. Then, shaking his head once again, he picked up his hat from the floor and left the building.

The bartender topped off Zack's beer, then stood with his elbows on the bar. "Wish there'd been more people in here to see it," he said, chuckling. "I don't believe anybody in this town's ever seen Jiggs Odom on his back before."

Zack continued to sip his beer silently.

Rollins pushed his mug toward the bartender for a refill, then shrugged. "I could have told Mister Odom that he was taking on a heavy load, but he wouldn't have listened."

"Nope," the bartender said. "Jiggs is used to getting his own way, and I doubt that he's ever run into the kind of resistance he met just now." He poured Rollins a new beer, then continued, "He's not all bad, he just likes to fight. Even after he whips a man's ass, he'll usually stake him in a poker game or something, and he's all the time buying drinks for men who don't have any money."

Hunter spoke now: "He sounds like an interesting fellow."

"He is. He'll probably apologize when he sees you again, and want to shake the hand of the only man who's ever put him on his ass."

Half an hour later, Rollins decided to take a hand in one of the poker games. Zack had no interest in gambling. He bought a newspaper and a magazine, then returned to the hotel room, where he read himself to sleep quickly.

He was awakened by Rollins at sundown. "Not much money floating around this town," Bret said, picking up the whiskey bottle that was still more than half full. He drank straight from the bottle, then wiped his mouth. "It's easy to tell how tight money is—the gamblers won't even bet more than a quarter on a pair of aces." He took another sip of whiskey, replaced the bottle on the table and sat down on his bed. "I don't know this for sure, but I believe you're gonna be surprised when you learn how cheaply land can be bought around here.''

Zack began to pull on his boots. ''I like surprises. I'll do some riding and looking tomorrow.''

Rollins was on his feet again. ''Well, I know you've always wanted a place of your own, and I want to see you get it. I think if you had a chunk of that property along the river, you'd wake up smiling every morning.''

Zack reached for his hat and changed the subject. ''I'm hungry, Bret. You want to try Toby's T-Bone again?''

''Lead the way.''

They took the restaurant's only vacant table, located in the center of the room. As they seated themselves, both men noticed that Jiggs Odom was eating supper with two men a few tables away. ''I hope to hell he don't want to fight again,'' Hunter said softly.

Rollins pulled his chair closer to the table. ''Don't worry about it, Zack,'' he said, reaching for the bill of fare. ''There ain't enough whiskey in this damn town to get him on you again.''

They had scarcely ordered T-bone steaks from a smiling waiter when Odom approached their table, stopping beside Hunter's chair. Despite the black eye, swollen cheeks and bruised lips, Odom's face held a pleasant expression. Knowing that the man standing over him now had the advantage, Zack held his breath.

Odom managed a smile. ''Hope you ain't got no hard feelin's about me,'' he said. ''Sure ain't none on my part.''

Hunter shook his head.

Odom made one step toward the front door, then stopped, turning to face Zack again. ''I sure did misjudge you, mister,'' he said, shaking his head. ''I damn sure did.'' Then he and his friends left the building.

6

On Monday morning Zack was in the banker's office discussing his desire to buy some land in the area.

"I think you should look the old Franklin Place over," McGrath said. "It's fifteen miles west of town, bordered on the west by the Colorado River. A man who intends to stay put could do right well there."

Zack scratched his chin for a moment before speaking. "What size place are we talking about?"

"Three sections. Old man Franklin never could make a go of it because the Indians kept him picked clean. All that's over with now. The last Indian battle happened three years ago, and the Indians that escaped with their lives left the area. As I said, a man could do well over there now.

"The old man died two years ago from consumption, and his children are scattered to hell and gone. I'm authorized to sell the place for a dollar an acre. In fact, I'll knock twenty dollars off the price and sell it to you lock, stock and barrel for nineteen hundred dollars.

"There's a livable four-room house that you get for nothing if you buy the land, along with a big barn and a pole corral. A small branch runs right through the corral, so your animals will always have water right under their noses. You won't have to dig a well, either. There's a good spring in the front yard that produces drinking water year-round."

Zack was getting to his feet. "I'll look it over, Mister McGrath. Can you give me directions?"

The banker pulled open a desk drawer. "I can do better than that," he said. "I'll draw you a map." He continued to talk as he drew lines on a piece of paper. "That place has changed names at least three times that I remember, and you'll probably change it again. No matter what you call it yourself, though, folks around here are still gonna call it the County Line Ranch. You see, the county line runs right through the middle of it: Lampasas County on the north, Burnet County on the south. San Saba County's right across the river.''

Zack folded the map and shoved it into his pocket. ''The Colorado borders the ranch on the west, you say?''

McGrath smiled, then nodded. ''All three sections. Water is one of the things you'll never have to worry about.''

Zack found Rollins at a poker table in the White Horse Saloon and motioned him over to the bar. Rollins pushed back his chair, asked the dealer to hold his seat, then walked to Zack's stool. ''I need to get back in that game as quick as I can,'' he said. ''I've been catching some good cards this morning.''

''I won't keep you but a minute,'' Zack said. ''I just want you to know where I'm going. McGrath told me about some land that's for sale over on the Colorado. I'm gonna take the packhorse and have a look at the place. I'll probably be gone for two or three days.''

''Take as much time as you need,'' Rollins said. ''Look me up when you get back.''

Zack nodded and left the building.

After retrieving his rifle and his Colt from the hotel, he stopped at the general store to buy bacon and matches. Then he walked to the livery stable. ''I'll be needing my bay and the packhorse, Oscar,'' he said to the liveryman.

Without a word, the hostler roped both animals in the corral, then led them to the stable. He watched as Zack saddled the bay and helped him balance the pack on the back of the packhorse. Then he spoke: ''You leaving the country?''

''Nope. I'm just gonna ride around the area for a while. Be back in two or three days.'' He began to fish around in his pocket. ''You want me to pay up now?''

The hostler shook his head. ''That won't be necessary. Not as long as you intend to be back in a few days. Where's your partner?''

Hunter smiled. ''He's trying to get rich over at the White Horse Saloon. If you decide you need some money, see him.'' He stepped into the saddle and led the packhorse west, scattering a flock of chickens that hung around the stable.

He followed what was known locally as County Line Road, though in reality it was little more than a wide, rutted trail that had obviously seen wagon traffic at one time or another. Grass grew in the ruts now, and small bushes claimed the area between. Hunter knew that if he did buy the Franklin Place, one of his first jobs would be to shape up the road.

An hour before sunset, he stopped his horses a few hundred yards east of the Colorado. He sat his saddle for a while, staring north. There, a hundred yards from the road, atop a small plateau that sloped gently down to the river, stood the house in which Ned Franklin had raised his family. Zack kneed his horse to a trot and rode into the yard. A jackrabbit bounced away from the spring and down the slope toward the river.

Zack dismounted and climbed the steps, avoiding a flimsy plank on the porch that he doubted would support his weight. The front door opened easily, and the hinges were good. He walked throughout the house, inspecting one thing and another. The fireplace was well constructed, and the firedogs had been left intact. The kitchen flue had also been left behind. A stove and two joints of pipe, and a man would be in business for cooking.

The rear door opened onto a small porch, and shelves were built along the outside wall. Several large nails had been driven halfway into the porch posts, offering places to hang things.

All four of the house's rooms were connected by doorways, but none had a door. Zack supposed the Franklin family had hung blankets to afford privacy, as he himself had done in the past.

In the yard he drank from the spring, deciding quickly that the jackrabbit had certainly known where to find the best water. Then he led his horses to the barn and fed them from the sack of grain the pack animal carried. He left the stall doors open so the horses could water themselves from the branch that ran through the corral.

The barn was in better condition than the house, and appeared to be several years newer. A wide hall, with four stalls on each side, ran the length of the building and had swinging doors on each end. The hayloft was the same length and width as the barn, and Zack saw no evidence that the roof leaked.

He spent a few minutes inspecting the corral and was pleased. The poles were good, and the cedar posts would be around for many years to come. Then, as the sun seemed to disappear into the river, he carried his pack and blankets into the house, placing them beside the fireplace. He was not hungry enough tonight to bother with fixing supper, but in the morning he would gather some wood and cook his breakfast in the fireplace. He took off his boots and with his Henry and his Colt close to hand, crawled into his blankets.

At daybreak he fed his horses, gathered an armload of wood and cooked his breakfast. He had just finished eating and was sipping his last cup of coffee when a loud voice helloed the house from the yard. With his cup in one hand and his Colt in the other, Zack stepped onto the porch. A middle-aged man of medium height stood in the yard, holding the reins of a small black mare.

"You ain't gonna be needin' that," the man said, his eyes glued to the gun in Hunter's hand. "I ain't never done nothin' to nobody. I jist seen your smoke and stopped by to see who my new neighbors is. I'm John Peabody's brother; my own name's Buster. My brother owns the spread across the river."

Hunter nodded and holstered the Colt. The man indeed looked harmless, and was unarmed. "Tie up to the rail there," Zack said. "I'll make another pot of coffee." As Peabody tied his mare and began to walk back to the porch, Hunter quickly decided that the man was mentally off center. There was a dullness in his face—no light behind his eyes—and he walked with a lumbering gait.

"Don't want no coffee," Peabody said, taking a seat on the doorstep. "Jist like to always know who my neighbors is."

Zack stepped forward and offered a handshake. "My name is Zack Hunter, and I'm not exactly a neighbor. At least not yet. I am thinking about buying the ranch, though."

Peabody began to shake his head. "This place ain't no good."

"What's wrong with it, Buster?"

"Ain't got no cows on it. You see any cows?"

Zack sat quietly for a moment, ignoring the question.

"What if I put some cows on it, Buster? Would that make it a better place?"

, "Well, yeah, if it had some cows on it. Fellow put some cows on it, I reckon it'd be a good place." He stared across the river for a few moments. "We got lots of cows over there; got lots of money, too. Yessir, my brother's got plenty."

Hunter dashed his coffee grounds into the yard. "I'm sure he does, Buster. I suppose I'll be meeting him if I buy this ranch."

Peabody was on his feet now. "I know you'll be seein' him if you move in here. John likes to visit, jist like I do. Well, gotta be goin' now." He mounted and rode down the slope, never looking back.

Hunter left his pack animal in the corral, and his pack and bedroll in the house. Mounting the bay, he crossed County Line Road to explore the south section of the ranch. He rode along the river for a while, then turned east. The short, rolling hills were separated by wide, fertile valleys that produced perennial grasses in abundance. Though tall pecan trees grew in places where moisture accumulated, most of the area was treeless, with only a few short bushes growing in the valleys.

Zack zigzagged the south section for most of the morning, then took a seat on a fallen log and allowed his horse to graze on the lush, green grass. He was pleased with everything he had seen and knew that if he was equally impressed with the northern section, he would probably buy the ranch. Three sections of prime grazing land was at least as much as he had ever dreamed of owning and he felt that he should buy it now, while he had the money.

He remounted at noon and pointed his animal toward the house. When he reached County Line Road, he encountered a man sitting astride a gray stallion a hundred yards east of the river. Tall and rangy, with most of his head poked into a high-crowned Stetson, the man had stopped his horse in the center of the road. He appeared to be in his early fifties.

"Just rode over to meet you," he said, kneeing his horse alongside Hunter for a handshake. "My name's John Peabody; I own the Circle P across the river." Zack took the man's outstretched hand and introduced himself.

"Zack Hunter, huh? Seems like I've heard your name somewhere before."

"Maybe somebody else has the same name," Zack said, " 'cause it sure wouldn't have been me you heard about. I'm new in Texas."

John Peabody nodded. "Might have just been my imagination. The older I get, the more trouble I have with names. Anyway, my brother, Buster, told me that you'd bought the Franklin Place, so I just wanted to say hello."

Zack smiled. "Your brother's a little ahead of me, Mister Peabody. I told him I was thinking about buying the ranch, just looking it over."

Peabody chuckled. "That's Buster, all right. Sure ain't the first time he's got his facts mixed up."

"No harm done," Zack said, shaking his head. "I enjoyed talking with him."

Peabody dismounted, then Hunter did likewise. They led their horses to the shade of a large pecan tree and stood talking for more than an hour. When told that Peabody's Circle P encompassed more than fifteen thousand acres west of the river, Zack was more than a little impressed. "Seems like an awful big place to me," he said.

"Maybe so, but even that ain't enough sometimes. A man has to keep a close eye on his herd. Left to their own devices, they'd overpopulate in one year, two at the most." He moved farther into the shade and leaned against the tree. "Now old Ned Franklin didn't have that problem over here; the Indians stole him blind. A few times they even stole his wife's wash right off the line."

"He didn't try to do anything about it?"

"Not much. He didn't have enough help, and I guess he was just glad they left him and his family alone. Hell, the Indians weren't about to kill him,'cause then they wouldn't have had nobody to raise beef and crops for them to steal.

"They hit me a few times when I first came here in sixty-two, but I damn sure didn't throw up my hands. Sometimes I had as many as twenty men on the payroll, hunting them down like coyotes. They treated them like coyotes when they found them, too. The Big Battle in seventy-three put a stop to it once and for all. Ain't nobody seen an Indian in these parts in ages.''

Zack changed the subject. ''How many cattle will this place support?''

''Aw, coupla hundred head wouldn't hurt it. If you start with a hundred head of cows and three bulls, it sure won't be long before you got two hundred.''

''How many men would I need?''

''If it was me, I'd put out three line riders to start with; one north, one south, and one on the east. The river'll pretty well hold the herd on the west. They can swim like fish, of course, but they don't like to. They won't cross the river unless they've got an awful good reason.''

Zack stood quietly for several moments, then continued his questioning. ''I should hire three men, then? How much should I pay them?''

''Pay scale around here runs all the way from twenty-five to thirty-five dollars and found. If it was me, I'd pay thirty-five dollars a month. You pay a man top wages, he'll stay with you. Since you don't seem to know much about ranching, I'd hire me at least one man that knows the business. I'd pay that man forty dollars a month and put him in charge of the others. Fact is, I'd hire my foreman first, let him separate the wheat from the chaff.

''It ain't just any man you run across that can carry his weight on a ranch. It's been my experience that if you hire a man in a saloon, that's where you're gonna find him the next time you start hunting him.'' Peabody moved to his horse and mounted, adding, ''If you decide you need my help in choosing a foreman, let me know. I know most of the capable men in the area.'' He turned his horse. ''Don't let that banker rob you. Ned owed less than a thousand dollars on this place.''

Hunter stopped in the ranch-house yard for a drink from the spring, then continued north. He followed the river for a mile, then turned east for about the same distance, his eyes surveying the entire area. The north section was no different from the land south of the road, with the exception that it was a little higher in elevation. And the grass was just as good.

He rode south to the road and returned to the house two hours before sunset. He fed his horses, then built a fire in the fireplace and put on a pot of beans. He would wait till his supper was done before making coffee.

He sat on the porch daydreaming, watching the setting sun creep closer to the western horizon. He had decided to buy the ranch, for he liked everything he had seen. Though he knew it would never make him wealthy, for there was only so much a man could do with three square miles, he believed he could make a living here. Anyway, he had to have a home whether he prospered or not, and this place looked as good as any.

Peabody had said that Ned Franklin owed less than a thousand dollars on the ranch, yet banker McGrath was asking almost twice as much. Asking and getting were two different things entirely, Zack was thinking. He would not speak to the banker again himself, he would let Slick Rollins close the deal.

Hunter was back in Lampasas at noon the following day. He stabled his horses, then walked to the White Horse Saloon. Failing to find Rollins there, he continued on to the hotel. He knocked on the door several times before it finally opened. Bret stood there in his bare feet, rubbing sleep from his eyes. "I played poker most of the night," he said. "Didn't get to sleep till daylight. It's good to have you back. Did you find anything you like?"

Zack took a seat on his bed. "Found something I like a whole lot, Bret. It's the old Franklin Place, over on the Colorado." He described the ranch in detail, then told Rollins of his conversation with John Peabody.

"Peabody says old man Franklin only owed a thousand dollars on it?" Bret asked.

"Said he owed less than a thousand," Zack said. "McGrath didn't say so, but I suppose his bank holds the mortgage. He did say that he was authorized to sell the ranch. Maybe he's trying to overcharge me because he figured I wouldn't know the difference."

"Of course he is, Zack. He's the typical banker. He upped the price as soon as he found out you're new in Texas and that you have some money. Tell him to kiss your ass and keep looking around till you find something reasonable."

Zack took a sip of Bret's whiskey, then placed the bottle back on the table. "I want that ranch, Bret. I'd just like to buy it at a little better price so I'll have some money left over to fix it up and stock it. On top of that, I'd have to buy furniture for the house, a team and wagon, harness, tools—''

"And a hundred other things," Rollins interrupted. He took a drink from his bottle. "You want me to go over and explain to McGrath how the goat eats the hay?"

"I was coming to that, Bret. You're awful good at putting a new light on things, and I never was much good at dickering. Even old man Davis, back home, told me I was a lousy horse trader."

Rollins put the cork back in the bottle and chuckled loudly. "The old man told you right, Zack. Arguing the price of merchandise is not one of your strong points." He began to put on his boots. "I'll talk to McGrath later this afternoon or in the morning, see if I can shake him loose from that nineteen-hundred-dollar price tag."

Rollins was in the banker's office the next morning at ten and had been talking nonstop for several minutes. "Every dollar Zack Hunter has in the world is in your bank, Mister McGrath," he was saying, pacing back and forth across the room, "so you know how much it is. And even if you cut the price of the Franklin Place in half, it'll take everything Zack has to put it in good shape and stock it. I also happen to know that Ned Franklin owed less than a thousand dollars on the ranch, and I believe you should let Mister Hunter pay off the mortgage and take charge.

"You see, Mister McGrath, Zack's been poor all his life; he's never had access to large sums of money, the way I do." The banker leaned back in his chair and folded his hands in his lap, giving Rollins his undivided attention. "I'd never be satisfied with anything as small as the Franklin Place, myself," Bret continued. "As soon as the rest of my money gets here, I intend to buy up property in all directions, build the biggest spread this area's ever seen. Might even build another good hotel; give the Hartley a little competition."

The banker was all ears. "You . . . you say you're expecting to receive more funds, Mister Rollins?"

Bret nodded. "As soon as the family business is sold. A Northern firm has agreed to buy it, and I suppose the deal might be going through even as we speak. My brother has the authority to close out the sale, then the two of us will split the proceeds. Since Pa and Ma died, neither of us boys has any desire to continue with the business.''

The banker drummed his fingers against his desk, appearing to be in deep thought. ''What kind of business are we talking about, Mister Rollins?''

''Textiles. Pa built a string of cotton mills in north Georgia, then bought three more in Tennessee. The Northern firm will be buying sixteen mills. Pa left the seventeenth to one of my cousins, and it's not for sale.''

McGrath drummed his fingers on the desk again. ''Sixteen mills,'' he said softly, as if talking to himself. Then he began to speak in a normal tone. ''You have any idea how much your share of the proceeds will amount to?''

''Of course I do,'' Rollins said, smiling. ''I was there when the price was agreed upon.''

''Of course,'' McGrath said, casting his eyes to his lap, appearing to inspect one of his fingernails. Then he was on his feet, speaking with authority. ''I'm the only banker in the area who is the sole owner of his bank, Mister Rollins. Therefore, I can offer you more services and a better rate of interest than any of the others, and none will appreciate your business more than I. If you will allow me to, I can also help you acquire the property you desire, including an ideal location for your new hotel.''

Rollins nodded. ''We'll see, but first we've got to get Zack Hunter into a home of his own at a reasonable price.''

McGrath reseated himself behind his desk. ''I had already decided to give Mister Hunter a break on the price,'' he said. ''I was looking over the records yesterday afternoon when I noticed that Ned Franklin only owed nine hundred eighty-six dollars on the ranch.'' He raised his eyes to meet those of Rollins. ''Tell Mister Hunter that he can pay off the mortgage and I'll give him a clear deed.''

Though he knew that the banker was lying about having a change of heart, Rollins shook the man's hand and left the office in search of Hunter. Right now was the time for Zack to buy.

7

Hunter bought the ranch two hours later. The old Franklin Place was no more. If the people of the area wanted to call it the County Line Ranch, Zack would do likewise. He would register his brand under that name.

At midafternoon he was at the livery stable discussing his needs with Oscar Land. "I see that wagon you've got for sale out front is already ribbed, Oscar. Do you have the canvas?"

Land nodded. "Yep. I'll put it on at no charge if you buy the wagon. I've got a good team and harness for sale, too."

Zack bought the team and the wagon within the hour, along with a turning plow and a few other things. "I guess you know that the hardware store would have charged you twice as much for a pick and shovel," Land said, dropping the tools into the wagon bed. "Yessir, you caught me on a day when my heart's right." He began to load a wheelbarrow onto the wagon, adding, "Where else in the world could you buy one of these things for ninety cents?"

Hunter paid the hostler, saying that he would return for his purchases early tomorrow morning. At the hardware store he bought an ax, saw, hoe, hammer and nails, and had the man set aside a stove and several joints of pipe. At the feed store he made arrangements for several sacks of grain and a few bales of hay. He would pick up all of these things on his way out of town tomorrow. He expected to make a round trip to the ranch every day for the next week, for the place needed almost everything. He would wait till the last day to haul out a table and chairs for the kitchen. Sometime between now and then he would buy a good bed, and some curtains for the windows.

He visited one merchant after another for most of the afternoon, buying everything from socks to cookware. Shortly after sunset he had supper at Toby's T-Bone, then headed for the hotel. As usual, Bret's unmade bed gave sign that he had slept some during the day. He was probably off at this very moment trying to shortchange somebody in a card game, Zack thought.

He read a newspaper for a while, then blew out the lamp and lay on his bed thinking. He had his own ranch now, and he owed it all to Bret Rollins. And Slick had probably saved Zack enough money on the price of the ranch to pay for stocking it. He had no idea what Rollins had said to the banker, but the man had cut the price almost in half. Zack decided that he would never ask. Rollins had his own way of doing things, sometimes ethical, sometimes otherwise.

Zack still did not approve of the tactics Bret had used on Mrs. Lindsay, but living with the deception had become easier. Maybe with a man like Rollins, certain things were excusable. He had certainly gotten the job done, and probably in the only way it could possibly have been pulled off. Who in the world but Bret Rollins would have guts enough to lay down such a story, knowing full well that he could be exposed for the imposter that he was within hours? Knowing that his friend had dozens of schemes that he had not even tried yet, and that he was surely one of the world's most believable liars, Hunter chuckled into his pillow. He was asleep quickly.

Zack spent a week moving onto the ranch and furnishing the house, then gave several days over to improving County Line Road, cutting bushes out of its center and filling in holes with pick, shovel and hoe. After the sixth day, he decided that the road would be passable for the next few years. Then he headed home to a soft bed, for he had slept in the wagon the past three nights.

Next day at noon, he had just completed an unproductive fishing trip to the river and was walking back up the hill when Rollins drove a rented wagon into the yard. Taking hold of a bridle, Zack led the team to the hitching rail. "Good to see you, Bret," he said, then pointed to the wagon's cargo. "I see you brought your bed. You gonna be around for a while?"

Rollins smiled. "Unless you run me off." He motioned toward the bed. "I hired a fellow to build that for me last week. I'll set it up in your spare bedroom if you don't mind."

"Glad to have you, Bret. I wish you'd just move out here and stay."

Rollins stepped into the yard. "I've done about as much as I can do with this thing in a hotel room," he said, patting the Colt that was buckled around his waist. "I need to practice with live ammunition, and I can't do that in town without drawing a crowd."

"I should think not," Zack said. "Plenty of room out here, though. Burn as much ammunition as you want. I'll feel better just having you around."

Rollins lowered the tailgate of the wagon. "Help me unload this bed, then I'll get the team back to Oscar. I'll ride the roan out here later tonight. Might be past midnight when I get here, so don't shoot me." They set up the bed and hung an extra blanket across the doorway to add a little privacy. Then Bret pointed the team toward Lampasas. "Sure is a nice place you have here, Mister Hunter," he said over his shoulder. "I'll be back some time before morning." Zack stood in the yard watching till the wagon disappeared, then headed for the kitchen to prepare his noon meal.

Rollins did not return during the night. It was close to noon the next day when he rode into the yard. "Met somebody who was interesting," he said, smiling broadly as he dismounted. "Decided to spend the night in town."

Zack nodded. "I figured that was the holdup," he said, motioning toward the kitchen. "There's a big pot of rabbit stew on the stove that turned out to be pretty tasty. You'll find a bowl on the shelf and a spoon in that box at the end of the table." Zack led the roan toward the corral while Bret headed for the kitchen.

After the horse had been fed and curried, Zack returned to the house and poured himself a cup of coffee, joining Bret at the table as he worked on his third bowl of stew. "This stuff is exceptionally good, Zack," Bret said, speaking around a mouthful of food. "You must have put a dozen different things in that pot."

"Put some of everything I had in it. I remember hearing

Ma say once that there weren't too many mistakes a cook could make that couldn't be cured with salt and pepper. When the time came that I had to look out for myself, I discovered a whole lot of truth in what she said.''

Rollins nodded and emptied his bowl.

Afterward, the two sat on the porch for a while, then walked down to the river, each man taking a seat on a fallen log. Rollins pointed to the river. "How deep do you think the water is right here?''

"Don't know," Zack said, shrugging. "I poked around in it with a fifteen-foot pole a couple of days ago, but I never did feel the bottom." He pointed upstream. "It's no more than a foot deep up there at that bend. I guess I'll have to put up a fence on the opposite bank after I get some cattle. Otherwise, they'll stroll right on across the river to John Peabody's grass." When Rollins said nothing, Zack added, "The cows are not likely to cross the river where the water's deep. They hate swimming.''

Bret nodded, then changed the subject. "I believe you said you'd met John Peabody. What's he like?''

"Friendly enough, looks to be about fifty years old. He came to this area more than twenty years ago and settled across the river, there." Zack pointed west. "His Circle P Ranch encompasses more than fifteen thousand acres, and I've been told that he's well-off financially. He gave me some free advice, and I suppose I'll take part of it. I won't be letting him pick my foreman, though, which is what he offered to do. I'll choose my own crew,'cause I don't know Peabody any better than I'll know the men I hire. I'll do some asking around, then follow my own hunches. Live and learn, I suppose.''

"You mean you don't trust Peabody?''

"No, that's not exactly what I meant. It's just that I didn't particularly like some of the things he said. He said that he had his men hunt the Indians down like coyotes, and implied that the cowboys shot them on sight. I don't want men like that on my little spread, Bret.''

"No Indians around here to shoot now," Bret said.

"Right," Zack said, getting to his feet. "But I can't help

remembering that Peabody was smiling when he talked about shooting them down."

An hour later, Rollins buckled his gunbelt around his waist and began to walk north. He soon disappeared into the trees, carrying five small blocks of wood that he would use as targets. A short time later, Zack heard the report of the Colt. First a single shot followed by a pause, then four more shots in quick succession.

Hunter stoked the fire in the stove and warmed up the coffee, then sat at the table sipping as he listened to the occasional eruptions of gunfire. There was no doubt in his mind that Rollins would become one of the fastest gunmen alive, for he could not even imagine a man with quicker reflexes, and Bret's hand-eye coordination was second to none. The "eye" was what had made Rollins a champion pool player, and it would also make him an expert gunman. Bret did not have to learn the speed, he had been born with it. And Zack knew that he would practice until he was the best, just as he had done with other things. Everything Bret did, he did exceedingly well, and the six-shooter would provide no exception. Zack listened to another burst of gunfire, then picked up his fishing pole and headed for the river. He fished for two hours without getting a bite.

He was sitting on the porch when Rollins walked out of the woods at sunset, complaining about the blisters on his hand. He held his right hand up for Zack to see. "I had some calluses built up, but I've been trying out a different way of doing things today. I've got blisters in some new places."

Zack could see several spots where the blisters had burst, then bled. "I've got some horse liniment," he said. "Want to try some of that?"

Rollins shook his head. "I read somewhere that the best thing for a blister is plain old water." He walked on into the yard and washed his hand in the spring's runoff, then returned to the porch, taking a cane-bottom chair. "In another week, these blisters will be new calluses."

"Sure will," Zack said. He was silent for a few moments, then asked, "Why do you want to be the fastest draw around, Bret?"

"Because it beats the hell out of being the slowest draw

around," Bret answered quickly. "You've seen enough yourself to know the game some of these Texans play. How about the way Red Hilly tried to run over me? I've seen the same thing happen several times right there in Lampasas. A man who is fast with a gun gets respect, Zack. A man who is not is likely to be mistreated by those who are." Rollins sat quietly for a while, then tapped himself on the chest with a forefinger. "Nobody is gonna run roughshod over this ass, Zack."

Zack eyed his friend for a moment, noting the look of determination on his face, then broke into soft laughter. "I believe you, Bret," he said. He pointed toward the kitchen. "Do you want some more stew for supper, or do you want to cook something yourself?"

"The stew. I don't know what in the world I'd cook anyway. I've never cooked anything in my life that tasted as good as what you've got in that pot."

They walked inside and Rollins lit a lamp, for night was coming on fast. Then Zack began to stoke the fire in the stove. They were soon enjoying a supper of hot stew, cornbread and strong coffee.

Rollins stayed on the ranch for two weeks, spending most of each day in the woods practicing the fast draw. On the last day, he demonstrated his quick hand for Zack. Rollins had decided to return to Lampasas and had just led his horse from the corral. He tied the animal to the hitching rail and stood in the yard sharing some parting words with Zack. "Guess I'll stay in town for a few days," he said. "I've been gone two weeks, long enough for some new blood to show up at the poker tables."

Zack nodded. His eyes went to the Colt that was tied to Bret's right leg. "Your speed getting better?" he asked.

"Much better."

Zack's eyes remained on the weapon. "Do you cock the hammer while you're pulling the gun from the holster?"

"Yep." Rollins walked over beside Zack. "Watch," he said. Ever so slowly, his hand closed on the handle of the Colt and began to lift it from the holster. Even as the barrel of the gun cleared leather, he was pulling the hammer back with his thumb so that when the gun was lifted into firing position, it was already cocked and ready to fire. Several times he did this as Zack watched closely.

Finally, he holstered the weapon and pointed down the slope. "Keep your eye on that little rock there by the fence post, Zack." Standing to his right and a little behind Bret, all Zack saw was a blur of movement, then the rock exploded. A split second later, Zack heard the report of the Colt. Bret stood holding the weapon at arm's length, a waft of smoke curling from its barrel.

In awe of what he had just witnessed, Zack did not speak for a while. He had not even seen Rollins draw the gun or been aware of what was happening until it was over. And Rollins had hit his target: a rock fifty feet away and no bigger than a man's fist. Zack stood shaking his head in disbelief. He was silently trying to imagine anybody being quicker than what he had just seen. Finally, he spoke: "I see," he said, offering Rollins a faint smile.

Zack stood in the yard watching till Rollins disappeared from sight, then returned to the house. A short while later he was staring at his gunbelt, which was lying atop a chest of drawers near his bed. He began to ease the Colt in and out of its holster, cocking the hammer with his thumb each time the gun cleared leather. Finally, he nodded and buckled the belt around his waist. Then he put an extra box of shells in his pocket and tied the holster to his leg. Then, more than a little impressed with what he had seen from Rollins, Zack headed for the woods. By god, if Bret could do it. . . .

8

◆───ᵈᵉ◆ᵉᵍᵃᵉ───◆

R ollins visited the ranch again two weeks later and informed Zack that he was leaving for Austin. "I've heard that there's plenty of loose money around there," he said. "I can't even get a pool game in Lampasas anymore, and the card players play for nickels and dimes. If I don't like Austin, maybe I'll try Waco. I hear there's some big money floating around that town.''

''I'm sure there is, and I suppose you'll get it, Bret.'' Zack stood at the corral watching Rollins saddle the roan. ''I hope you'll at least come back to see me occasionally.''

''Count on it, Zack. I won't be gone more than a month.'' The men shook hands, then Rollins rode away. Zack stood in his tracks watching till he was out of sight. He would miss Rollins for sure, but he would not worry. Bret knew how to take care of himself. And if there was an easy fortune to be had, he would probably find it.

An hour later, Hunter hitched his team to the wagon and headed for Lampasas. He needed food and a few other things for the kitchen, and grain and hay for the horses. It was close to noon when he arrived in town, so he stopped at the livery stable to feed and water his horses. ''I've been thinking about you for the past few days,'' Oscar Land said. ''You got the ranch up and running?''

''No, no,'' Zack said, shaking his head. ''I'm out there by myself, so I guess I'll have to find me some help before I start thinking about cattle.''

''Figured you probably needed some help, and that's what I was coming to. You see, a distant cousin of mine is in town and he's needing some work. Don't guess he'd be too particular right now, either. He's still got a good horse and saddle, but I know for a fact that he's mighty short on money. He's a good boy, Mister Hunter.''

''Boy?''

Land chuckled. ''Well, I still call him a boy, but he's actually a twenty-one-year-old man. Got more muscles than you and me put together, and he knows how to do anything you're gonna need done. He's spent his whole life on ranches, and has even made a cattle drive or two north to the rails.''

Zack stood thoughtful for a few moments, then asked the logical question: ''Why is he out of work, Oscar?''

''Said he got sick of South Texas. I don't think he liked his boss too much, either.''

Zack set a bucket of water under the nose of each of the horses, then turned to the liveryman. ''This cousin of yours staying at the hotel?''

Land shook his head. "He sleeps here at the stable, and I've been paying the freight for his meals over at Toby's. I guess he's over there right now having dinner."

Zack climbed aboard the wagon. "If your cousin happens to be around the stable later in the afternoon, I guess I'd be willing to talk to him, Oscar." He slapped the horses with the reins.

"I'll make sure he's here," Land called as Zack drove the team down the street.

All of the hitching rails in the vicinity of Toby's T-Bone were taken, for it was the noon hour. Zack tied his team a block away, then returned to the restaurant on foot. He took a table in the center of the room, ordered his meal and began to look around.

Oscar Land's cousin was easy to spot. Sitting at the counter picking at a plate of food, the youth made a handsome picture. He turned his head and gave Zack the once-over, then continued to concentrate on his plate. He had clear gray eyes and brown hair that was poked halfway into a battered Stetson. His face was the color of bronze, leaving no doubt that he spent most of his time outdoors. His jeans were faded from wear, and his boots were old and scuffed. With every movement of his body, the bulging muscles of his arms and chest threatened to rip his flannel shirt apart at the seams.

Hunter continued to eye the handsome young man as he ate his own meal. For a moment, he thought about paying for the man's dinner, but quickly decided against it. The young man was dining courtesy of Oscar Land, and Hunter had no interest in saving the liveryman the price of a meal. Zack had finished his stew and was eating a piece of cake when Oscar's cousin left the counter and headed for the front door. As he passed by, Zack decided that the man stood five-ten and weighed about two hundred pounds.

After having two drinks at the White Horse Saloon, Zack drove the team to the feed store, where he loaded the wagon with grain and hay. At the general store he bought beans, bacon, an assortment of canned goods, two dozen eggs and a smoked ham, then selected three boxes of ammunition for his Colt.

As he neared the livery stable on his way out of town, he could see Oscar Land standing out front, accompanied by the young man Zack had seen in the restaurant. He brought the horses to a halt and stepped from the wagon, nodding to both men.

Land stepped forward quickly. "I think it's about time you two met each other," he said, pointing a thumb at each man. "Zack Hunter, meet my cousin, Jolly Ross."

Hunter shook Ross's outstretched hand and was not surprised that the young man's firm grip matched his own. Ross smiled broadly, revealing rows of near-perfect teeth. "Cousin Oscar thinks you need some help," he said in a deep baritone voice, "and I was wondering if you think so, too."

Zack smiled at the young man's choice of words. "I don't know what I could put a man to doing right now," he said. "I don't have a single cow on my property."

Ross nodded, then was silent.

Not so with Oscar. "You're gonna be getting some cattle, you said so yourself. I'll tell you right now, you don't just up and drive a herd of cattle onto a ranch. You've got to get the place ready first. There are a thousand and one things to do, and you're gonna need some help getting them done." That said, the liveryman began to stare at the ground, seeming to sense that he had said enough.

Zack stood quietly staring off into space for a while, then turned to face Ross. "I'll think on it overnight, Jolly. If you don't have anything better to do tomorrow, you can ride out to the ranch and we'll talk about it further."

Ross spoke quickly: "I already know that I won't have anything better to do. I'll see you tomorrow, Mister Hunter."

"Zack," Hunter said. "Just Zack." He climbed to the wagon seat and guided the team toward County Line Road.

When Zack finished his breakfast next morning, he placed a pot of ham and beans on the back of the stove to simmer. He replaced the weak plank on the porch, then walked to the barn. He worked there for two hours doing one thing or another and was busy greasing a wagon wheel when he heard someone calling from the yard. "Come on down to the barn," Zack said loudly when he recognized the rider.

Jolly Ross rode down the slope on a large gray gelding and tied the animal to a fence post. "Sure ain't nothing wrong with this place," he said, walking toward Zack with his right hand extended.

Zack stood wiping the grease from his hand with an empty grain sack. "Thank you for coming out, Jolly," he said, then motioned toward the house. "Won't take but a few minutes to warm up the coffee." He shook hands with Ross.

Zack stoked the fire and put on the coffeepot, and the men were soon sitting at the kitchen table sipping. "I don't know for sure what I'm gonna do with this place, Jolly," Zack said after a while. "I don't even know if I can make a living with it. I bought it mainly because I have to have somewhere to live, and I don't like towns."

Ross shook his head. "I don't either." He took a sip of his coffee, then smacked his lips. "No problem making a living off this place, though. A man could grow a whole lot of what he eats." He pointed down the slope. "I noticed the perfect place for a garden down there across the road. You can fence in two or three acres with poles and split rails, but the fence has to be high enough that the deer can't jump it. Deer will destroy anything you plant if they can get to it." He motioned down the slope again. "A couple acres of corn down there would produce an awful lot of horse feed."

Zack nodded. "That would sure help, all right. Buying grain gets to be expensive." He rose and refilled both coffee cups, then reseated himself. "The ranch consists of three sections of land, Jolly. How many cattle will it support?"

"I believe I'd allow ten acres for each cow." He sipped from his cup, then began to scratch his chin. "Three sections amounts to nineteen hundred twenty acres, so that means a hundred ninety-two cows. Two hundred head would be about right." He began to smile. "Don't guess it hurts to overstock a little bit and fatten your cows on your neighbor's grass. Most ranchers won't complain as long as they see you over there every day driving your cattle home. The trick is to do that along about noon, after your cows have done most of their eating for the day."

Zack chuckled. "You talk like a man who has done that."

"Sure have. Lots of times."

They talked for the remainder of the morning. Zack put a pan of cornbread in the oven just before noon, and a short time later sat down to a meal of beans and ham with his newly hired hand.

Jolly Ross had agreed to a salary of thirty dollars a month, saying that he was happy to have a place to hang his hat after being out of work for so long. He had almost been ready to return to South Texas, he said, and had even considered asking his former overbearing boss for his old job back. Ross had paid his own way since the age of thirteen, he said, and allowing Oscar Land to buy his meals at Toby's T-Bone had put a lump in his throat. He appreciated his cousin's generosity, he said, but the food had not been easy to swallow.

Ross had been born on a ranch in the lower Rio Grande Valley in 1854. By the time he was a toddler, his father had gone west in search of gold and had never returned. His mother remarried when Jolly was eight. The following year she moved to California with her new husband, leaving the boy to be shifted back and forth between his grandfather and his aunt. During the few years he attended school, he learned to read and write well enough, and became particularly adept at working with figures. Arithmetic was easy for him right from the start, and he could solve most problems he encountered without the use of pencil and paper.

Jolly had no idea where in the world his mother and father were, and had more than once been heard to say that he did not give a damn. Shortly after his thirteenth birthday, he took a job as an errand runner and general flunky on a huge ranch in Hidalgo County. By the time he was fifteen, he was sitting his saddle beside the rest of the cowboys and was considered a top hand. He had participated in two trail drives north to Kansas, the second one being only last year.

When they had finished eating, they returned to the barn. Zack resumed his work on the wagon, while Jolly led his horse into the corral and removed the saddle. "You'll find oats in that metal bin just inside the door," Zack called. "Feed your horse in the third stall on the right every day. Pretty soon he'll know that's where he belongs."

Ross led the animal to the stall and curried it as it ate. Then, as always, he wiped its sides down with the saddle blanket. He owned a good horse, and treated it accordingly. Standing more than sixteen hands high and weighing over a thousand pounds, the animal appeared to be black when viewed from a distance. It was only when the horse moved closer that its color became a dark, speckled gray. The beautiful animal was six years old, and Jolly Ross had been its master for the past three years. The colt had been raised on the very ranch where Jolly had worked, and he had made a deal with his boss to have the price of the animal deducted from his wages.

Ross's saddle was of the same quality as his horse, and it had cost more than twice as much—which was not at all unusual. Most cowboys insisted on a good saddle, whatever the cost. A few saddlemakers, known for their fine craftsmanship, might charge a cowboy a year's pay for a saddle. Even so, the better saddlemakers usually had a long list of customers waiting. A custom-built saddle was a thing of pride for most Western men.

Ross returned to the shed to find Zack tossing pieces of lumber over the fence. "We'll use these two-by-fours and one-by-sixes to build you a bunk along the living-room wall," Zack said. "I would offer you that bed in the back room, but it belongs to my friend. No telling when he'll be needing it."

Ross walked through the gate and began to pick up the boards. "I might not be able to sleep on a soft bed anyway. I don't recall sleeping any better on the few times that I've done it. I'll just spread my bedroll on the bunk. First time I'm in town with the wagon and have some money, I'll pick up some kind of mattress."

Zack walked through the gate and shoved an eagle into Jolly's vest pocket. "Here's some money," he said. "Take the wagon into town tomorrow and get whatever you need. I'll find something to do around here while you're gone."

Ross nodded, then smiled. "I probably don't need it, but I sure would like to have a sack of smoking tobacco. Sometimes I damn near have a fit for a cigarette right after I eat."

Zack reached into his pocket, saying, "You being out of work for a while, I guess you need a lot of things." He handed the young man another eagle. "Here's ten dollars more. Just consider it a draw against your wages."

Two days later, they were on the hill half a mile north of the house, cutting wood for the stove and fireplace. They had felled half a dozen oaks, which would be sawed into blocks of different lengths. The shorter blocks would be split for the kitchen stove, while the longer ones would be used in the fireplace. Hunter had a sledge and two wedges for splitting any blocks that proved too stubborn for the ax.

"I guess we've got enough trees on the ground," he said. He laid the crosscut saw aside and began to chop limbs off the fallen tree with the ax. "Have yourself a cigarette, then we'll saw up this log and haul it to the house. I guess by then we'll both be ready for some supper."

Ross sat down on the stump and began to fashion a cigarette. "You thought any more about fencing in a plot of ground south of the road?" he asked, licking the paper and giving it a final twist.

"I sure have, Jolly. As soon as we get a winter's supply of wood cut, we'll go to work on that. The idea of having a crib full of corn for the horses seems like a good one, and I suppose I like fresh vegetables just as well as the next man. How long do you think it'll take to build the fence?"

Ross blew a cloud of smoke. "Probably a month or more. I'll lay it off with the turning plow first, then plow the topsoil under. We'll let it lie upside down all winter and turn it over again next spring. Be best to let me get the plowing done before we start on the fence."

Winter came early to Central Texas this year. It was only mid-October and already the temperature had begun to drop below the freezing point at night. Even at midday, both Zack and Jolly wore heavy coats when outside the house, and a fire burned in the fireplace most of the time.

Large piles of wood lay beside the house, with smaller stacks on the porch. The plot of ground that was to be cultivated next year had been plowed and fenced. Zack estimated it to be a little less than three acres. He would grow vegetables for the table on only a small portion of the land, with the remainder producing corn for the horses.

Last night had been another cold one, and the men had just finished their breakfast of flapjacks and sorghum syrup. Zack stood by the fireplace, a cup of coffee in one hand and the other reaching out to the heat from the fire. "I'm gonna be going into town today, Jolly. I want to get a bigger pot for the stove, and we're damn near out of food."

"Count me in," Ross said. "I need a better coat,'cause I can see that we're in for a rough winter. Need some warmer gloves and something to cover my ears, too."

Zack returned his empty coffee cup to the kitchen, placing it in a dishpan filled with water. "Bundle up as well as you can, Jolly. Then let's hitch up the team. I want to stop by the hardware store and see if they've got a middle-buster for the corn patch. I can probably buy one cheaper right now than I could next summer, when everybody else is needing one, too." He covered the fire with ashes and then the men headed for the barn.

They reached Lampasas just before noon and stopped at the livery stable to feed and water the horses. Oscar Land stood by his anvil hammering on a wagon spring. He offered the men his broadest smile. "I can see with one eye that you two make a good team." He dropped the hot spring into a metal trough filled with water, then laid the hammer aside. "What can I do for you?"

"You can feed and water the horses," Zack said. "No need to unhitch them from the wagon; we'll be using them again as soon as we make the rounds and buy a few things."

Land nodded, then spoke to his cousin: "How do you like it out on the river, Jolly?"

Ross answered quickly. "Best job I ever had," he said, then walked down the street beside Hunter.

Their first stop was the White Horse Saloon. They took seats at the bar and both men ordered whiskey. They were served by Ed Hayes, the same muscular bartender who had been on duty the day Zack fought Jiggs Odom. "Haven't seen you in a while," the young barkeep said. "Heard about you buying the old Franklin Place. You gonna run cattle on it?"

Zack nodded. "Probably get some next spring," he said, sipping at his whiskey.

Hayes refilled both men's glasses. "Where's your curly headed friend?" he asked, speaking to Zack. "I believe his name is Rollins."

"Haven't seen him in more than a month," Zack answered. "He's not living in this area at the moment."

The bartender began to shake his head very slowly. "Well, wherever this Rollins fellow is, anybody hunting trouble would damn sure be smart to walk around him."

Zack raised his eyebrows. "Why do you say that?"

Hayes placed his elbows on the bar and leaned forward. "I guess since you ain't seen him in a while, you ain't heard about the show he put on in here."

Zack shook his head.

"Let's see . . . I believe it was a month ago today," Hayes began. "Rollins and another fellow were playing pool and got into an argument. They finally decided to fight, and that other fellow didn't last no time. Rollins put him down to stay right off.

"Well, Jiggs Odom just happened to be watching, and he didn't like the way the fight went. He called Rollins 'Purty Boy,' and challenged him. Well, Rollins laid his gunbelt right up on this bar and proceeded to whip Odom's ass all over this room. Knocked him down at least five times.

"I remember the day you fought Odom, and you made short work of it, but your friend put on a show while he was doing it. Every time Odom got to his feet, Rollins would knock him on his ass again. He was laughing all the time he was doing it, too. I don't think Jiggs ever landed a single punch that hurt Rollins. I tell you, I've seen a few professionals, but I sure ain't seen nobody like him. He just does it all so quick and makes it look so damn easy."

Zack had sat nodding throughout the narration, showing no surprise at what he was hearing.

"Here I am telling you all this," Hayes said, pouring more whiskey for Zack. "I bet you've seen Rollins operate before."

Zack chuckled, then nodded. "I'm afraid so," he said. Then he headed for the outhouse to answer nature's call, leaving Jolly Ross and the bartender in conversation.

"I just went to work for Zack Hunter about a month ago," Ross said to Hayes, "and I really don't know a whole lot about him. You say you saw him whip Jiggs Odom right here in the saloon?"

"Uh-huh. He did Odom just like he'll do anybody else who

gives him any shit. He's the best I've ever seen, unless it would be his friend, Rollins. They're both from somewhere in Tennessee, you know. A fellow told me last week that every man he'd ever known from Tennessee was just like them: strong as a damn ox and quick as a cat. Must be something in the water back there.''

Ross smiled and touched a match to his cigarette. ''Maybe so,'' he said. He slid from his stool and headed toward the front door, for Zack was waiting for him there. Both men waved to the bartender as they walked out of the building.

They were soon standing in front of the hardware store. ''I'll see if they have a middle-buster and some Johnson Wings here,'' Zack said. ''Then we'll hunt up the other stuff we need. Once we get everything bought and sacked up, I'll go get the wagon.''

Two hours later, they left town with the wagon loaded. Zack whipped the horses to a trot, hoping to get home before dark.

9

Bret Rollins had spent two weeks in Austin, but found the town not to his liking. During the third week, he headed north and after riding leisurely for several days, arrived in Waco, a wide-open, hell-raising town situated on the Brazos River. Located in a rich agricultural region, Waco became home to its first white settlers around 1849. Great plantations along the river prospered for a time, until the Civil War spoiled the plantation economy and scattered the population.

The Brazos River separated Waco east from west, and the largest suspension bridge in America was built there in 1870. Much of the great Western movement passed over that bridge, as did the famous Chisholm Trail. The town quickly boomed again, attaining a state of wildness that earned it the nickname "Six-shooter Junction."

Criminals and con men of every stripe soon set up shop in Waco, using a myriad of schemes to separate the travelers and the trail drivers from their hard-earned money. Several well-known gunfighters also lived there, and though none of them showed visible means of support, all seemed to have plenty of money to spend. The town fathers tolerated the gunmen, whores and gamblers, for it was a prosperous time for all. Local lawmen also looked the other way, ever mindful of who paid their salaries.

Besides, the seamy element was largely responsible for keeping the money in circulation. While a day merchant would likely salt his profits away in the bank, that was not the case with the night people, whose "easy come, easy go" attitude kept the money moving until it found its way into the general population. Indeed, after 1870, money was a little easier to come by for every man in the area, regardless of his station in life.

Rollins rode into Waco in the middle of the afternoon. After crossing the bridge, he rode south along the river, for he could see the livery stable and its large corral. The big roan also noticed the stable and broke into a trot, sensing that he was about to be fed and pampered.

"You got someplace where you can lock up my shotgun and my bedroll?" Rollins asked, handing the roan's reins to the liveryman.

"I'll put 'em in the office," the man said. "I not only keep it locked, I sleep in it. Ain't nobody coming in there, at least nobody that expects to walk out again."

Rollins smiled and nodded. He stood watching for a while as the hostler unsaddled and cared for the roan. "Don't know how long I'll be leaving the horse here," he said. "Might be two days or two months."

The big hostler offered a toothy grin. "I like the sound of two months better," he said. "That's the way I make my living."

With his saddlebags across his shoulder and a change of clothing under his arm, Rollins headed up the street toward a hotel he had spotted earlier. When he rented a second-story room a few minutes later, he was informed by the desk clerk that a hot bath could be had at the barber shop a few doors to the north. Bret was out the door quickly; he also needed a shave and a haircut.

Having been told by both the barber and the desk clerk that the Texas Saloon served the best food in town, Rollins took a seat at a table in the establishment an hour before sunset. A dark-haired waitress was there at once. "Have you ever tried one of our broiled veal steaks, sir?" she asked, fluttering her extra-long eyelashes.

"Not until now," Bret said, winking. "Bring it on."

The girl nodded and was gone.

Though the dining area was a roped-off section close to the kitchen, Rollins nevertheless had an excellent view of the activity throughout the huge room. At the moment, two bartenders stood idly behind a forty-foot bar in the center of the building, smoking cigarettes and carrying on a conversation between themselves. No drinkers sat at the bar just now, but both bartenders would no doubt be working at a hurried pace before the night was over.

On the opposite side of the bar from the kitchen there was a large drinking and frolicking area. Though many saloons removed their heaters during the summer and returned them in the winter, the Texas did not. The large potbelly stood in the center of the room year-round. Dozens of chairs and tables of varying sizes were scattered around the stove, which had not been fired in months.

Farther toward the rear of the room was a small hardwood dance floor, and beyond that, an elevated stage where entertainers performed. Against the north wall, close to the dance floor, a steep staircase led to the second floor. A man needed little imagination to guess what went on upstairs.

The remaining area along the north wall, from the staircase to the front of the building, was devoted to gaming tables. There were six tables in all, three of them set up for poker, and Rollins could see what appeared to be a four-handed stud game in progress at one of them. There was no action of any kind at the remaining tables, and even the house dealers, who usually sat around trying to drum up a game, were noticeably absent. Rollins began to concentrate on his meal, knowing that the picture would change dramatically when the sun went down.

When he paid for his supper, he gave the waitress a quarter and another wink, then headed for the bar. "Whiskey," he said to the nearest bartender, then took a seat on a stool. His drink was served quickly. "Enjoy your supper?" the barkeep asked, his raised eyebrows and sincere tone of voice suggesting that perhaps his prosperity was directly related to the quality of food dispensed by the kitchen.

Rollins nodded. "I sure did," he said. "The food was excellent."

The bartender nodded several times, smiling broadly. "I can't think of nobody I ever asked that didn't say the same thing." He was a dark-complected man of medium height, who appeared to weigh about one-fifty. "I tell you," he continued, "the best thing old Al Foster ever did was lease that kitchen to Maggie Leafgreen. In less than a year, she's turned it into the best eating place in this town, and it's full every night.

"If you ain't never tried none of her Mexican food, you owe it to yourself. She's got two Mexican cooks back there that don't do nothing else." He topped off Bret's whiskey glass and wiped at a wet spot on the bar. "Maggie's my mother-in-law, you know."

Bret stared at his glass for a moment, then shook his head. "No," he said, "I didn't know."

"Oh, yeah. I married her daughter four years ago." He poked his arm across the bar, offering a handshake. "By the way, my name's Tim Overstreet."

Bret pumped the hand a few times. "My name's Rollins," he said, "and I'm new in the area." He took a sip of his whiskey, then spoke to Overstreet again: "You mentioned a man named Al Foster," he said. "I assume he owns this place."

"This and a lot of other things. He bought the saloon for a song back several years ago. I reckon the only money he ever spent on it was to patch the roof a little. Maybe at the time he bought it, the place wasn't worth no more'n he paid. All I know is that when they built the bridge and the travelers and the trail herds started coming through town, the Texas Saloon became a gold mine. If you'll drop back in here about ten o'clock tonight, you'll see what I mean.''

Rollins upended his glass, got to his feet and offered the bartender a parting handshake. "I'll do that, Tim. As far as I know, I'll be back about ten."

Bret walked the streets for a while, paying particular attention to the seedy buildings alongside the river. Peeking inside their open doorways, he saw that some of the run-down saloons had pool tables, with games in progress. He had no doubt that large sums of money sometimes changed hands in these out-of-the-way places, but they were also breeding grounds for violence, and he wanted to call as little attention to himself as possible. He would return to the Texas Saloon after a while. The Texas had no pool tables, but he was an excellent poker player, and he felt that a winner was more likely to get out of the Texas alive than if he played in some of the waterfront saloons.

It was not yet ten o'clock when Rollins returned to the Texas, but the place was already crowded, with men jostling each other for a position at the bar. Tim Overstreet was hard at work, as was his counterpart at the far end of the plank. Rollins stood leaning against a post for a few moments, then moved closer to the gaming tables. Many house dealers would not deal more than six poker hands at a time, and Rollins saw immediately that six players sat at each of the tables. He spoke to the dealer of a draw poker game: "I'd like to take a hand when you get an open seat."

The man gave him a quick glance, then continued to shuffle the cards. "The only way to guarantee yourself a seat is to put up some money. Then if you ain't here when a seat comes open, you'll have to pay the ante anyway. Every hand that's dealt, you'll have to pay the ante, just like you would if you was sittin' there."

Rollins shrugged. "I understand." He laid a double eagle in front of the dealer. "I won't be far away; I'll be able to see when somebody drops out of the game." Then he headed for the crowded bar to see if he could catch the eye of Tim Overstreet and get a drink. The bartender spotted Bret immediately. He motioned him to the bar and handed him a glass of whiskey, waving away his attempt to pay. Bret accepted the glass and returned to the post. Standing in the dimly lit center of the room, he had a good view of the gaming tables, and could even read the facial expressions of a few of the gamblers.

Half an hour later, a man at the poker table threw down his cards in disgust and cursed loudly, pushing his chair back. Knowing that a seat was about to become available, Rollins was there quickly. "Hope this damned chair treats you better'n it did me," the departing gambler said. "I sat there nearly two hours and won one stinkin' little pot."

Rollins smiled at the man and took the chair. "I've had my share of cold seats, too," he said. "Maybe it'll warm up after a while." The man disappeared, and Rollins laid a hundred dollars on the table.

"Table stakes with a dime ante," the dealer informed him, then began to gather up the scattered cards. "Five-card draw with nothin' wild."

"How about checks and raises?" Rollins asked. "After you've checked your hand to the man behind you, can you raise the pot if somebody else bets?"

"Damn tootin'," the dealer said, motioning to him that he should ante up. "Around here, we call it settin' a trap. If you check your hand and a man's fool enough to come bettin' into you, you can raise his ass every penny he's got in front of him. That's why we call it table stakes. You can bet a man everything he's got anytime you want to; he's got to call the bet or fold his cards."

Rollins nodded and dropped a dime in the pot. He had not needed the dealer's explanation of how the game was played. He had mentioned checks and raises mostly to plant a seed in the minds of his opponents around the table, hoping to make them wary of betting into him if he chose to check a weak hand. He had also asked the question because he had played in games before where raising after checking a hand was not tolerated. He had long ago made it his policy to ask questions before taking a hand of cards at a strange table. It simply cleared the air and left less room for arguments.

The "cold" chair the man had left Rollins did not warm up as the night wore on. When the dealer called a halt to the game at midnight, Rollins was sixty dollars in the hole. He had won only a few small pots. Several times, when he had good cards, he dragged only the ante, for everybody else folded when he opened the pot.

Rollins rose from the table and pocketed his money, offering each of the players a broad smile. "Enjoyed it, gentlemen," he said, nodding to each man individually. He was not dejected in the least, for he knew that both winning and losing streaks ran in cycles. Sometimes a man could win money blindfolded; at other times he could not even buy a pot. The trick was to weather the cold streaks by betting light, then bringing the big money into play when the good cards began to fall in your favor. Rollins never allowed a run of weak hands to dampen his spirits. He could recall many times when the cards had run against him all night long, then gotten worse after daybreak. At such times he usually stayed away from the games for a while, which was much cheaper than trying to ride out a losing streak.

He had a drink of whiskey at the bar, then walked next door to an all-night restaurant, where he ate two bowlfuls of vegetable soup. Some of the men he had played poker with were also busy eating, but Bret spoke to none of them. He had already socialized with them as much as was necessary and was hoping that the next time he spoke to any of them, he would be looking at a winning poker hand. He paid for his soup and walked to his hotel room.

Sleep was a long time coming, for as was usually the case after a night of poker, it took a while for his mind to unwind and slow down. He lay on his bed thinking of Zack Hunter and his County Line Ranch. Hunter was the best friend he had ever had, and he loved him like a brother. He also knew that although Zack would work his fingers to the bone to make a go of his ranch, the place was simply too small to offer the degree of security that Zack sought and so richly deserved. While the ranch would have been considered a large holding back home in Tennessee, in Texas it was of small consequence, barely large enough for a man to eke out a living. Rollins thought on the matter for a long time before going to sleep. What Zack needed, he decided, was more property.

Bret could see that the sun was already shining against the outside of the shaded window when he opened his eyes the following morning. Rising to a sitting position, he reached into his pants pocket and consulted his watch, which informed him that the hour was well past nine. Thinking that Zack had probably been at work for at least three hours, he began to walk toward the pan of water provided by the hotel.

He was on the street a half hour later. He had two cups of coffee at a small restaurant, but ordered no food. He had already seen today's menu at the Texas Saloon. The noontime special would be chicken and dumplings, with rice pudding for dessert, and Rollins expected to be on hand. He had literally been raised on such food, and though he seldom saw it served in a restaurant, he never passed up a chance to eat it again.

At four in the afternoon, Rollins was sitting at the bar in the Texas Saloon, talking with Tim Overstreet. "Do they ever play for big stakes over there?" Rollins asked, motioning toward the poker tables.

"Oh, yeah," Overstreet answered. "Sometimes one of the little games turns into a big one. Just 'cause they start out small don't mean they'll stay that way. After all the little fellows go broke, the big boys might bet each other a hundred dollars a card. Right after I went to work here, old Wesley Ames won over forty thousand dollars one Saturday afternoon." He pointed past his shoulder. "Right there at that table in the corner."

Rollins wet his lips with the beer he had been nursing for the better part of an hour, then got to his feet. "Forty thousand, huh?"

"Forty thousand."

When Rollins was halfway to the front door, he called over his shoulder, "Guess I'll play poker again tonight, but I intend to get an earlier start."

He returned to his hotel room and stretched out on his bed for a nap. He wanted to be fresh and well rested when he revisited the saloon. "Forty thousand dollars," Overstreet had said. The words had a nice ring. Bret fluffed up his pillow and dozed off.

He was back in the saloon at seven o'clock and played poker till the game broke up at midnight. He had won slightly more than a hundred dollars in five hours of play. The main topic of conversation around the table had been the "Big Game" that was scheduled to take place on Saturday, beginning at noon. "That sure ought to be something to watch," one player said. "It's gonna cost a thousand dollars to buy into the game, and a fellow has to put his money up first."

Rollins was listening. "Do you know who's gonna be playing?" he asked.

"Nope. Heard they got three players lined up already, though. I reckon Lonny Weeks, over at the bank, is holding the buy-in money. Anybody that wants to be guaranteed a seat has to go talk with Weeks, and take him a thousand dollars." The man continued to look at Rollins, who was rising from his chair. "Why do you ask?" he said. "You figure on getting in the game?"

Bret dropped his winnings in his pocket, then turned to leave. "Might be a little steep for me," he answered, and walked from the building.

He was up early next morning and stood in front of the little restaurant waiting for it to open. When he had eaten breakfast, he walked to the barber shop and waited for it to open. After a shave and a bath, he returned to the hotel to change his clothing. He dressed in the simplest things he owned: jeans, flannel shirt and Mexican short jacket, all of which combined had cost less than ten dollars. He only wanted to look clean, not prosperous.

Half an hour later, he was at the bank. "I'd like to speak with Lonny Weeks," he said to the bearded teller who greeted him.

"Junior or Senior?" the man asked.

"Well I . . . uh, really don't know," Rollins stammered. "I just heard that a man named Weeks is putting together a poker game for next Saturday."

The man smiled. "That would be Lonny Junior," he said, pointing to a closed door. "He's in there alone. Just knock a few times and go on in."

Rollins was soon shaking hands with a tall, lean man who appeared to be in his early thirties. Green-eyed, with a complexion that needed some sunlight, he pumped Bret's hand several times and offered the standard businessman's smile. "I'm very pleased to meet you, Mister Rollins," he said after

Bret had given his name. "Is there something I can do for you?"

Rollins matched the banker's smile. "I hear you're putting together a poker game for next Saturday," he said, "and I'd like to have a seat at the table."

Weeks began to bite his lip, then reseated himself behind his desk. He seemed to be searching for the right words. "Has . . . has anybody told you the particulars of the game? I . . . I mean about the buy-in?"

"You mean the thousand dollars up front?"

Weeks nodded. "Well, yes. That's what I meant."

Rollins took his saddlebag from his shoulder and counted out a thousand dollars, laying the money on Weeks' desk. "I'd like a receipt for that," he said, "and the names of all the men I'll be playing against."

Clearly impressed with Rollins' forthright manner, and surprised that he had come up with the cash, the banker bagged the money and wrote out a receipt. "I suppose you have a reason for wanting the names of all the other participants," he said.

"Of course I do," Bret said quickly. "It's the same reason a prize fighter has for wanting to know who's gonna be in the ring with him. He—"

"I'll make a list of the names for you," the banker interrupted, laughing. He was still smiling when he handed the names to Rollins. "You'll notice that there are five names besides your own. As of right now, it is a closed game. Nobody else can get in it now or later. When a player goes broke and drops out, we'll just deal fewer hands. It'll finally come down to only two players, and they'll butt heads till one of 'em has all the money.

"There'll probably be a lot more than six thousand dollars in the game, though. A thousand is not the most a man can put in, it's the least. A man can keep putting in new money all day if he's got it. You can't bet out of your pocket, though—the money has to be on the table. Table stakes."

Rollins folded the list and shoved it into his pocket. "I understand the game," he said, turning to leave.

Weeks stood behind his desk, nodding. "I've just got a feeling that that's an understatement," he said, only half in jest. "Good-bye, Mister Rollins, and I suppose I'll see you again on Saturday."

Bret walked the streets for a while, ending up at the livery stable. He was greeted by the big hostler, who offered him a cup of coffee. Bret accepted and leaned against the wall as he sipped the hot liquid. "How long have you had the stable?" he asked, mainly to make conversation.

"Since my daddy died, back in sixty-eight. He had it for more'n ten years, kept it open right on through the war." He motioned toward the corral. "Been meaning to ask you," he said. "You want me to put some new shoes on that roan of yours? I sure believe I heard one of 'em rattling this morning."

Rollins nodded. "He's a good horse; do whatever needs doing." He offered his right hand to the liveryman. "By the way, my name's Rollins."

"Potts," the hostler said, matching Rollins' firm grip.

Rollins drank the last of his coffee and placed the cup on a nearby table. Then he handed Potts the list of names given to him by the banker. "Know any of these men?" he asked.

Potts scanned the list with squinting eyes. "Know 'em all," he said, then returned the list to Bret.

When the liveryman said nothing else on the subject, Rollins tried again. "Can you tell me something about the nature of the men on the list?" he asked.

"I don't know nothing about the nature of 'em. All I know is that they all eat a lot higher on the hog than I do. They don't associate with working men like me. The only times any of 'em ever spoke to me was when they needed something."

Rollins shoved the list into his jacket pocket. "Thank you, Mister Potts." He turned to leave, then said over his shoulder, "Go ahead and shoe the horse; I'll see you later."

Shortly after noon, Rollins seated himself on a barstool at the Texas Saloon. He bought a beer, then handed the list of names to Overstreet. "Do you know anything about these men, Tim?"

The bartender glanced at the list, then nodded. "I guess so. What do you want to know?"

"Anything you can tell me. Just start at the top of the list."

Overstreet spent the better part of the next hour discussing the men on the list, halting only occasionally to serve a drink to a thirsty customer.

When Bret left the saloon, he had a mental picture of the men he would be facing in the poker game. He had already met Lonny Weeks, and Overstreet had supplied a good description of the other players: Wallace T. Huffstuttler was a local businessman of about sixty, who sported a milky-white beard. Rollins had already seen the man's name posted above the front door of a large hardware store.

Will Dempsey was a well-to-do rancher who lived north of Waco. He had sent two herds up the trail to Kansas last spring and according to local gossip, had profited quite handsomely. At least one man had called Dempsey's margin of profit "obscene." Will Dempsey was clean-shaven and weathered, and even with his stooped shoulders, stood well over six feet tall. He was also about sixty years old.

Johnny Shook was the owner of two saloons, both of them across the river in East Waco. He was fat, and about fifty.

Al Foster was the oldest of the lot. The bartender knew his boss's exact age, for only two months ago he had been asked to chip in some money to buy a present for Foster's sixty-third birthday. Being the owner of the establishment, Al Foster seldom played poker in the Texas Saloon. On the rare occasions when he did play, Overstreet said, he bet his cards heavily. "No skin off my ass no matter who wins the money in that game," Overstreet had said, handing the list back to Rollins, "but if you break that bunch, you damn sure won't ever have to work again."

Rollins sat in the small restaurant on the corner, picking at a piece of pie and sipping coffee. Today was Thursday, he was thinking, and two days hence he would be playing poker for more money than he had ever seen. He would also be bucking more experience than at any other time in his life: most of his opponents were more than twice his age, and he must assume that they had spent more time at a poker table. He had played old men before, however, and knew that most of them were cautious, usually sitting around waiting for a cinch before making a large bet. Rollins also knew that it was possible to milk a player dry while the man was waiting for his "cinch." An overly cautious player could be bled to death a few dollars at a time; then when he found himself deep in the hole, he would have to come out and play. He would be trying to regain lost ground, therefore at his most vulnerable, ripe for an ambush. Pleased with his thoughts, Rollins finished his coffee and got to his feet. Leaving a coin on the table for the waitress, he paid for his pie and coffee, then headed for the hotel.

At a quarter past eleven on Saturday morning, Rollins walked into the Texas Saloon and took a stool at the far end of the bar, waving away Overstreet's offer of a drink. "They're all here," the bartender said, motioning to a cluster of men who were in animated conversation beside one of the gaming tables. "Looks like you might be the only sober one in the game, too."

Rollins flashed his usual smile and said nothing, while Overstreet moved away to serve a customer. Rollins watched the men who were to be his opponents passing a bottle back and forth amid an occasional burst of boisterous laughter. He had no desire to meet any of the men till it was time to play. Nor did he intend to join them in their drinking. Today he would be serious, for he was here to take care of business. When he sat down at the table, he would be out for blood.

At five minutes to twelve, Rollins walked to the table and took the only vacant chair. The other five players were already seated. The banker had placed six stacks of poker chips around the table, each stack worth a thousand dollars. As Bret made himself comfortable, with his long legs under the table and his saddlebag across one knee, all eyes turned to the banker.

Weeks introduced the players simply by pointing to each man and calling his name, then explained the value of each of the poker chips according to its color. When each man had counted his stack, the banker spoke again: "Draw poker with nothing wild, men, and it's legal to raise after you've checked your hand. I'll deal the first hand, then the deal will revolve around the table to my left." He dealt five cards facedown to each man.

After two hours of play, Rollins was still about even but was firmly convinced that he himself was the only good poker player in the game. Time after time he had watched each of his opponents ride a hand to its conclusion when it should have been folded at the outset.

Rollins had always been amazed that most men would play poker for many years, or even for a lifetime, without ever concerning themselves with the arithmetic aspects of the game, always trusting to the "luck of the draw." Luck had nothing whatsoever to do with playing poker. It was a game of skill and percentages, nothing more, nothing less, and the pockets of the player who used patience, common sense, and bet with the percentages would always eventually jingle with the easy coin of the player who bucked the odds.

False beliefs and opinions abounded concerning the game of poker, most of them perpetuated by people who had little knowledge of the game. Rollins had long wanted to play poker with the man who coined the phrase: "Never draw to an inside straight." There was a time when a player should indeed draw to an inside straight, and that time was anytime the money odds in the pot exceeded the eleven-to-one odds against filling the hand, coupled with the fact that no other player in the pot had stood pat. Indeed, any player who consistently bet with the odds would eventually be a winner.

By midafternoon, Rollins had gauged his opponents and mentally placed each player in a separate category: Albert Shook was a blowhard. He had plenty of money and wanted to make sure everybody knew it. His style was to play every hand, usually making rash bets and unwarranted raises. Several times he had made it unnecessarily expensive for Rollins to place second in a pot in which Shook himself had placed third or fourth. Bret continued to smile good-naturedly, knowing that he would burn Shook badly when the man walked into one of his traps.

Huffstuttler was the most timid of the lot, playing as if the stakes set by this bunch were beyond his means. The fact that he was in over his head had made him too cautious. He saw traps that were nonexistent and folded too often. Bret knew that even a modest raise by Huffstuttler would indicate a powerful hand.

Will Dempsey was easy to figure. The rancher was an incessant talker who grew strangely quiet when he held good cards. Something Rollins would remember, and use.

Al Foster was the wealthiest member of the group, and the stingiest—at the table and away from it. Foster wasted no chips, keeping out of the red. He stayed only when his chances of winning the pot were excellent, and contrary to what Bret had been told by Overstreet, the man bet heavily only when he had a lock, and probably never tried to bluff. Rollins decided that Foster himself could be bluffed when he was losing.

Lonny Weeks was easygoing and likable. And though the banker appeared to take the game lightly, Rollins dared not try to bluff him, for he did not care to risk as much money as it might take to run Weeks out of a pot that Weeks thought was rightfully his. Rollins would play honest poker against the banker.

The players rested for twenty minutes at six o'clock, then continued till Al Foster called the game at midnight, amid groans by both players and spectators. "The Texas Saloon always closes at midnight," he said, "and tonight will be no exception." He motioned to the banker. "Mister Weeks will count every man's chips right now, and he'll keep them overnight. When the game resumes tomorrow at noon, each player will start with the same amount of chips he's holding now."

Rollins sat patiently while the others turned in their chips. Each time the banker finished counting a player's holdings, he would write the dollar figure in a notebook, then return the chips to the rack from whence they came. He smiled broadly as he wrote down Bret's figure. "Twenty-seven hundred and four dollars," he said. "I knew you were a good poker player before we ever turned a card. Wouldn't surprise me a bit if you end up with the whole kit and caboodle in your sock."

Rising to his feet, Rollins returned the banker's smile. "It would sure surprise me," he said. He walked to the bar quickly and spoke to the bartender: "Do I have enough time for one drink?"

Overstreet had already doffed his apron and was busy stacking glasses in a neat line along the backside of the bar. "Only if you inhale it quickly," he said, reaching for a whiskey bottle. He poured three ounces into a water glass and placed it in front of Rollins. "Spectators pretty well kept me posted on the game," he said. "I hear you've been holding your own and then some. One fellow said you were teaching the old dogs some new tricks.''

Rollins upended his glass and wiped his mouth with his sleeve, then laid a coin on the bar. "Don't believe everything you hear," he said, heading for his hotel room.

Bret was back in the saloon the next day at noon, and the poker game started on time. None of the players had changed his style from the previous day, although Albert Shook had become even more reckless with his bets. The man had put new money in the game several times, and even now had more than five thousand dollars in front of him.

Rollins had deliberately avoided pots in which Shook was his only opponent, for he did not want a showdown just yet. He was patient, content to win only a few dollars at a time until the right hand came. When the right circumstances arose, he was prepared to tap Albert Shook all the way to the poorhouse.

At midafternoon, Rollins got a good oportunity to bait Shook. The pot contained less than a hundred dollars, and he strongly believed that none of his opponents held a calling hand. When he bet four hundred dollars at a hundred-dollar pot, every man folded his hand. As Rollins raked in the pot, he "accidentally" let his low-ranking cards fall face-up in front of Shook, exposing the fact that Bret had run a bluff with a hand that held no pair at all. In fact, the highest card in the hand had been a jack. Rollins gave the players just enough time to read the cards, then grabbed them quickly, as though he was afraid his strategy might be revealed. As he returned his cards to the deck, Rollins saw Shook looking at the other players, gritting his teeth and nodding as if he had just uncovered a big secret.

Bret dealt the next hand. He folded his own cards at the outset, then watched as each of the other players did likewise. "I'm gonna quit for a while, men," he said, handing the deck to the banker. "Gotta go to the outhouse, then I'm gonna get something to eat."

Al Foster nodded and pushed back his chair. "Why don't we just halt the game for an hour?" he said. "I could stand a bite to eat, and I guess everybody needs to take a piss."

"We'll take a thirty-minute break in shifts," the banker said, "three men on each shift. That way, there'll always be three men here at the table, keeping an eye on the chips and the cards. Rollins, Dempsey and Huffstuttler, you three can go first."

The three men Weeks had named were on their feet quickly, headed in different directions. When he returned from the outhouse, Rollins had a quick meal of beans and biscuits, then took a seat at the bar. "Give me a hefty shot of the good stuff, Tim," he said to the bartender. "I feel like I need something to hold my supper down."

Overstreet complied, then leaned on his elbows against the bar. "How's the game going?" he asked. "People tell me that you're doing all right for yourself over there."

"I always make it a point not to discuss a game while it's still in progress," Bret said, taking a sip from his glass. "Every hand that's dealt creates different circumstances, and the turn of a single card can change the whole face of a game." He upended his glass, then waved away the bartender's attempt to refill it. "The only thing I can tell you, Tim, is that so far, I've managed to keep from going broke." Rollins looked at his watch, then headed for the poker table.

Dempsey and Huffstuttler had already returned and were involved in light conversation with Lonny Weeks. Bret sat down and the banker shoved the chip rack and several decks of cards in front of him. "I've been waiting for you," Weeks said. "Like I said before, there should be at least three men at the table at all times."

Bret took his watch from his vest pocket and turned its face toward Weeks so that the banker could plainly read the time. "Been gone thirty minutes," Bret said.

Weeks ignored the watch. "Guess so," he said, then took his own leave.

As was the case with most high-stakes poker games, one hand brought the Big Game to its conclusion. Rollins, seated to the left of Huffstuttler, who was dealing, peeked at his cards one at a time as they came off the deck. Then he held the cards close to his vest, making sure he had read the hand correctly. He made a conscious effort to control his demeanor, for the dealer had dealt him a lock. This was only the second time in his life that he had drawn such a hand with his original five cards. He glanced at the royal flush once more, then spoke through his usual smile: "I'll open the pot for a hundred," he said.

Shook, seated at Rollins' left, was in the pot immediately. "You don't seem very proud of whatever you've got," he said. "I'm gonna kick it three hundred." He pushed his raise into the pot.

Dempsey, who was next in line, was quiet, signifying that he held good cards. "I'll just call," he said.

Al Foster folded his hand, as did Lonny Weeks.

Huffstuttler studied his cards for a full minute. "I'll be damned if I'm gonna be run out of this pot," he said, a determined expression on his face. "Fact is, I'm gonna up it a thousand." He counted his chips into the pot, then sat twisting his beard with a thumb and forefinger. "Your opening bet's been called and raised twice," he said to Rollins. "Now you've gotta call the raise or fold."

Rollins knew, of course, that he himself was going to win the pot. His only concern right now was how to make the most money out of it. He had no doubt that Huffstuttler held the second-best hand at the table, but Shook had the most money. Rollins fought and overcame the urge to reraise the pot, for he certainly did not want to lose Shook. "I'll call both raises," he said in the most timid tone of voice he could muster.

Shook was louder now. He completely ignored Rollins and spoke to Huffstuttler. "Now we're beginning to play some poker," he said, counting out his chips. "I'm gonna call your raise, Wallace, but you didn't bet near enough. I'm gonna sweeten the pot two thousand dollars more."

Dempsey began to curse and folded his cards immediately.

Huffstuttler counted two thousand dollars' worth of chips into the pot, saying nothing.

Rollins also called, once again resisting the urge to raise.

Al Foster, who had folded with the first raise, had been paying close attention to the goings-on. He now elbowed the banker, speaking almost at a whisper, "Already somewhere around eleven thousand in that pot, and they ain't even drawed to their hands yet.''

Weeks nodded and said nothing.

Huffstuttler finally picked up the deck, prepared to replace whatever discards any player might have. "Cards to gamblers," he said. "How many you gonna draw, Rollins?"

Bret placed his hands over his cards. "I'll play these," he said.

"By God, I'm gonna stand pat, too!" Shook said loudly, beating his fist against the table and beginning to chuckle. "I guess we'll find out pretty quick whose shit don't stink, huh?"

Huffstuttler placed the deck on the table. "I won't be drawing any cards, either," he said.

"All three of 'em are standin' pat," Rollins heard one of the spectators say to another. "By God, ya don't see that very often. This oughtta be interestin'.''

It was interesting indeed. Rollins sat fiddling with his chips and reexamining his cards, hoping to appear nervous.

"You brought it, fellow," Shook said to Rollins. "Time to put up or shut up."

Rollins peeked at his cards again. "Check," he said softly.

"Naw, naw, naw," Shook said, grabbing a handful of chips. "Ain't gonna be no checking around here. I didn't come in this game checking." He pushed a stack of chips into the pot. "Bet four thousand," he said.

Rollins let out an audible sigh to give the impression that his own hand was weak. All for the benefit of Wallace T. Huffstuttler, for Bret did not want to lose the old man's four thousand dollars.

Shook had obviously counted Huffstuttler's chips, for the old man had only twenty dollars left after calling his bet.

Now Rollins was doing some counting of his own. He pushed four thousand dollars into the pot, his eyes on Shook's stack all the while. "I'm calling your bet, Mister Shook. How much more money do you have in front of you?"

Shook began to fidget. His eyes shifted from one of the idle players to the next, then returned to Rollins. "You . . . you intend to tap me?"

"Every dollar," Bret answered. "I'm raising the pot whatever you've got in front of you. Count your chips and put them in the pot, or fold and forfeit.''

"Forfeit, hell," Shook said loudly. "I've got a good hand here." All was quiet while he counted his chips. "Fifty-two hundred and nine dollars," he said, pushing the chips to the center of the table.

After Rollins had matched Shook's money, Huffstuttler began to speak: "I can't call but twenty dollars," he said. "The rest of that last bet'll have to go into a side pot."

Rollins picked up his hand and held it in front of the old man's eyes. "Save your twenty dollars, Mister Huffstuttler. You can't win."

Huffstuttler stared at Bret's cards for a moment, then threw his own hand facedown on the table. "You're damn sure right about that," he said. "Much obliged."

Judging from Huffstuttler's reaction, Shook knew by now that he himself was probably beaten. "Well, I guess, by God, you must have a gollyroster there. Old Wallace damn near fainted when he saw it. I've paid to see it, now spread it on the table."

Rollins turned his cards face-up in front of Shook: the ten, jack, queen, king, and ace of clubs. Shook bit his lip, then chuckled. "First royal flush I've ever had pulled on me," he said. "Ain't never even seen many of 'em, for that matter." He placed his losing hand in the middle of the deck without ever showing it, so that no one would ever know exactly what he had been holding.

Though no one had said so, the game was obviously over. Three of the men were already on their feet when Al Foster spoke: "I don't know about everybody else, but I've had all of this shit I want for now. Fact is, I think I hear the wife calling me." He left the table, followed by Shook and Huffstuttler.

"Forty-two thousand, eight hundred and ten dollars," the banker said when he had finished counting Bret's chips. "I can give you the money right here, or give you a receipt and keep the money in the bank overnight."

"Keep the money in the bank," Rollins said, smiling. "I might want to get drunk before the night's over."

He folded and pocketed his receipt, then stood watching as

Weeks racked up the chips and stuffed the money bag inside his shirt. Rollins knew that the banker had many thousands of dollars in that bag and silently wondered if the man intended to walk down the dark street to the bank alone. His unasked question was answered when Weeks nodded toward the door and was quickly joined by three armed men. All three wore tied-down Colts, and walking one on each side and the other behind Weeks, they escorted him from the building.

As he watched them disappear through the front door, Rollins smiled, then shook his head. He should have known. A few minutes later, he was sitting at the bar nursing a glass of expensive whiskey.

10

On the first day of November, Zack Hunter and Jolly Ross were busy building holding pens and branding chutes, a task they had undertaken more than a week ago. Using strong cedar posts, small poles and split rails, they had fenced in half an acre a quarter mile south of the house. The idea was to drive the cattle from the holding pen into the chutes singly, where they would be branded while standing, then turned out to explore their new home. Ross had suggested larger posts, heavier poles and longer nails for the chutes, saying that the cows would do most of their hard fighting there.

They had just finished a chute that both men thought would hold even the largest and the wildest of the cows when they had a visitor. The men had been sitting on a log eating ham and biscuits when the rider turned south from County Line Road. Zack was on his feet quickly, shouting and waving his hat. Bret Rollins kicked the roan to a canter and covered the remaining distance quickly. "It's not my intention to interfere with a working man," he said, dismounting.

Zack pointed to the fence. "Got most of the work done," he said, grasping Bret's hand and hugging his shoulder. "I don't mind telling you that I've been a little bit concerned about you, fellow."

"Glad to hear it," Bret said, chuckling. "Maybe your worrying is what keeps me safe and healthy."

Zack squeezed his friend's shoulder. "Can't tell you how good it is to have you back, Bret." He nodded in Ross's direction. "I've hired some help since you've been gone." Then motioning toward each man as he spoke his name, he said: "Bret Rollins, meet Jolly Ross."

With his right hand extended, Bret stepped toward the young man. "It's good to meet you, Jolly."

Ross was on his feet quickly, switching his biscuit to his left hand nervously. He had heard so much about Rollins that he was convinced the man was somebody special. "I'm glad to meet you, sir," he said.

Rollins chuckled again. "Let's forget about that sir stuff," he said, offering Ross a broad smile. "That is, unless I become a baronet or a knight. Until then, just call me Bret."

The men shook hands. "Yes, sir," Ross said.

Rollins tied the roan to a wagon wheel and took a seat on the log beside Zack, helping himself to the sack containing the ham and biscuits. After a couple of bites, he walked to his horse for his canteen, then reseated himself. "I've been in the area for nearly two weeks, Zack." He took a long swig from the canteen and continued: "I've been too busy to ride out here. Been to Llano once, and to Austin twice." He took another drink, then shoved the stopper into the mouth of the canteen. "McGrath, at the bank, did the paperwork while I did the legwork. It took more than ten days, but I believe I've put together a deal that you're gonna like." He walked to his horse and returned the canteen to his saddle, then stood beside a wagon wheel, his eyes scanning the northern horizon.

Zack stared at him for a few moments. "Dammit, Bret, you know I can't stand suspense. What the hell have you been doing?"

Rollins pushed his hat to the back of his head, then turned

to face Hunter. "I bought the property joining your place on the north," he said, pointing in that direction.

Zack was on his feet. "You did? Hey, that's nice, Bret. Did you get a whole section?"

"Nope," Rollins said, shaking his head slowly. "Bought fifteen sections."

Hunter backtracked to the log and reseated himself. "Fifteen sections," he repeated softly, then spoke louder. "Fifteen sections! Hell, Bret, that's nearly ten thousand acres."

"Right, Zack. The fifteen sections belong to you and me as equal partners. I had the deed drawn up that way. We're fifty-fifty, old buddy, and together we own eleven thousand, five hundred and twenty acres of prime ranch land, all clear and paid for. Now, don't that beat the hell out of busting our asses in Shelby County, Tennessee?"

Zack sat shaking his head. "It sure does, Bret." He stared at the ground for a few moments, then kicked at a small stone. "It damn sure does."

Rollins reseated himself on the log. "I bought the property from an old man named Hoyt Wilkerson. He's paralyzed from the waist down and can't do anything nowadays."

"I already knew about Wilkerson," Zack said, then pointed across the river. "Peabody told me."

Bret nodded. "Well, at any rate, the banker put me on to Wilkerson, and the old man wanted to sell right away. The holdup was his offspring: a son and a daughter living in Austin, who have been at each other's throat for years. They finally agreed to sell after I spent three days explaining to them that since they were neither ranchers nor farmers, selling would be in the best interest of all concerned.

"McGrath set the price, or at least wrote a letter telling them how much the land was worth, and none of them argued with it. I had no more than a small problem convincing him to set the price artificially low."

"What was the price, Bret?"

"Dollar and a nickel an acre."

Zack rounded up his tools and dropped them into the wagon box, then tethered Bret's roan to the tailgate. He spoke to Ross: "We'll quit for the day, Jolly. Take the animals and the wagon on to the barn. Bret and I will walk to the house. We've got some talking to do.''

They sat at the kitchen table drinking coffee for a while, then walked to the porch, where they took seats in cane-bottom chairs. The weather had been mild of late, and neither man wore a coat. They sat looking down the slope without speaking, watching Jolly Ross busy himself about the shed and barn. After a time, Zack broke the silence: ''I've been wondering what got you interested in ranching all of a sudden, Bret.''

''Money,'' Rollins said quickly. ''I spent two days on Will Dempsey's ranch up near Waco, looking over his operation. He was one of the men I beat in the poker game, but he seemed to hold no hard feelings. In fact, he was real friendly to me and invited me to spend a couple of days on his ranch.

''Dempsey's a big talker, but all I had to do was look around me. The man is making a lot of money, Zack, and he's doing it with longhorns. He sent two big herds up the trail to Kansas this year, and he's talking about doubling that next year. Says he's gonna sell every longhorn he's got next year and switch to Herefords.

''He believes all Texas ranchers'll quit raising longhorns in the not-too-distant future. He says Herefords produce better meat and that they'll do it in half the time.'' Rollins pounded a fist into his palm to emphasize his point. ''Half the time, Zack! Hell, that sounds to me like the difference between going broke and getting rich.''

''Might be,'' Zack said. ''But Jolly says Herefords are a lot more expensive to come by and a hell of a lot harder to raise. He says that if there is any way in the world to get in trouble or get killed in an accident, a Hereford will find it. He says longhorns are smart and that Herefords are some of the dumbest creatures on earth. Finicky eaters, too, Bret. Droughts and hard winters play hell with 'em. Jolly says he's seen blooded cattle starve to death on the same terrain that fattened longhorns. He says a longhorn'll eat anything—brush, bark or briers.''

''I've heard the same thing,'' Rollins said, getting to his feet and leaning against a post. ''I didn't mean that I think we ought to rush out and get some Herefords. I just believe it's something that we should look into. Maybe we should even consider hiring some farmers and growing some hay and grain.''

''I'll be more than glad to help you consider that, old buddy. Feeding cattle through the winter so they don't have to regain all that weight in the spring makes sense to me.'' Zack pointed north with his thumb. ''Do you know where the corners are on that land you bought?''

''Nope. But the county surveyor'll be here tomorrow to point them out. I won't be here because I'm gonna be riding around the country talking to ranchers, putting together a little book of statistics on Herefords and longhorns. The surveyor will show you the boundaries, and you can show me when I get back. By the way, the surveyor's name is Carl Odom; he's an older brother to Jiggs.''

''Older brother, huh? I wonder if he's as damn crazy as Jiggs.''

''I don't think so,'' Rollins said, laughing. ''I've talked with him a couple times and he seems pretty sane.''

Rollins rode out early next morning and the surveyor arrived two hours later, saying he had met Bret on the road to town. Odom said he was ready to show Zack the boundaries of the property and that Rollins had already paid him for the job. Zack loaded the packhorse with a tent, bedrolls and food, for Odom said the business at hand would take at least two days, maybe three. The two men rode north two hours before noon, leaving Jolly Ross to his own devices.

Rollins was gone for more than three weeks. He returned to the ranch during the last week of November, riding through a cold, steady drizzle. Though the place seemed deserted, he relaxed after he saw that the team and wagon were not there. Zack and his hired hand were somewhere in the wagon, probably gone to town for supplies. Rollins would not have met them on the road anyway. He had ridden in from the north, and only took up County Line Road half a mile east of the ranch house.

He stabled and fed his horse, then made his way to the house. He soon had a fire burning in both the fireplace and the kitchen stove, and set about heating up leftover food for his dinner. Then he put on a fresh pot of coffee and got a change of dry clothing from his bedroom. A short while later, he was washing down beans and biscuits with hot coffee and feeling better by the minute. He had been cold and hungry all day, for he had hit the trail this morning without breakfast and ridden twenty-five miles in the rain.

After eating, he sat in front of the fireplace, his hands reaching out to its warmth. Comfortable now, he began to reminisce about his recent travels. He had talked with several ranchers, one of whom owned three hundred Herefords. Then he had traveled north to the Fort Worth stockyards, where he gleaned information from growers, buyers, shippers and meat packers, none of whom made a secret of the fact that they believed longhorns would soon pass into history.

"Whoever told you that Herefords would starve to death on longhorn terrain didn't know what the hell he was talkin' about, young feller," a grizzled old rancher had said. "Now, I ain't a-sayin' that they're as tough as longhorns, but they're purty damn close, and that shit about them bein' finicky eaters is jist that: bullshit. They'll eat whatever in the hell it takes to survive, jist like a damn longhorn."

Rollins had listened to similar opinions from at least a dozen men, all of them in the cattle business. "Easterners are already beginning to demand better beef for their tables," a cattle buyer informed him, "and that means purebred cattle. Texas ranchers are not gonna buck the tide. They're gonna give the buyer what the buyer wants, and that means good-bye to the longhorn. The heavier breeds can be brought to market in half the time, and produce better beef on the same amount of feed. Now, any rancher who knows all this and still makes no effort to upgrade his herd would have to be a damn fool."

Rollins thanked the man and moved on. He was soon talking with another rancher. "All of the heavier breeds coming into Texas lately are better than longhorns," the man said, "but I think most of the stock growers will go with the Herefords. They ain't as tough as longhorns, but they're as tough as they need to be, and they'll eat whatever's handy."

Rollins spent several days in Fort Worth and left town convinced that Hereford cattle was the way to go. A dealer named Rafe Baskin had assured him that he could obtain some Hereford bulls if Rollins should ever decide to buy. Rollins wrote the man's name and address in his book, for he felt that the day would come when he would surely do some business with Mister Rafe Baskin.

Being warm and dry for the first time today, Bret dozed off in his chair after a while. He was sound asleep when Zack walked into the room. "Wake up, partner," Zack said loudly, "and I'll cook you a good supper."

"You've got a deal," Rollins said. He walked to the kitchen, where Zack was busy unloading various cans and packages of foodstuffs from a large basket. "Most of that looks mighty good," Bret said, shaking Zack's hand and patting his shoulder. "The last good meal I had was in Fort Worth."

Zack returned Bret's firm grip, then began to unwrap red meat, dumping it on a platter. "Lewis's Meat Market had sirloin steak on special for nine cents a pound today. I bought six pounds. If we don't eat it all for supper and breakfast, I'll cut the rest up for the stewpot."

"You're a good man," Bret said, lifting one of the stoves' eyes. "Let me stoke up this fire,'cause I sure hate to see a good man working under a handicap."

Throughout the late afternoon and early evening, the partners discussed the things Bret had learned on his trip. "I wrote most of the facts and figures in this," he said, handing the notebook to Zack. "If you'll read it all, I believe you'll come to the same conclusion I did. While you're thinking on it, remember that I've already got the money to put a thousand head of longhorns on this ranch, along with as many Hereford bulls as we need.

"We'll breed the longhorn strain right out of 'em, Zack. After we get a calf or two out of 'em, we'll send the longhorn cows up the trail to market. I believe we can recoup our entire investment from the sale of the longhorn cows."

Zack chuckled. "Are you saying you believe that we can end up stocking the ranch with Herefords for nothing?"

"Absolutely. Well, it won't exactly be for nothing. We'll have a few years' work invested, and we'll have to hire some ranch hands and farmers, but we can do it, Zack. I know damn well we can."

Zack nodded and sat quietly for a long time. "I guess we

should build a new house and barn closer to the center of the ranch,'' he said finally. ''Or maybe you'd rather tear down these buildings and move them up there.''

''It'll be cheaper and quicker to move these buildings, Zack. Of course we'll have to build a bunkhouse that'll sleep at least a dozen men, and we'll also need line shacks. We've got a lot of things to do, old buddy, and I think we should hire the help we need and get on with it.

''I opened an account at the bank for the H and R Cattle Company, so you can write a check for whatever you need. We have a balance of twenty-five thousand, and I believe that'll hold things together till the ranch begins to pay its own way.''

''Twenty-five thousand,'' Zack repeated. ''That sounds to me like as much as we're gonna need, Bret. We can sell the longhorn cows in the summer of seventy-eight and still have at least a thousand head of crossbreeds left on the ranch.''

''Exactly,'' Rollins said. ''Then we'll start making money.''

Hunter sat staring into the fire for a while. ''After we buy the cattle, our biggest expense is gonna be wages,'' he said. ''The payroll for half a dozen men'll add up in a hurry.''

''I think we'll need more than six men when we first bring the cattle home,'' Rollins said. ''Jolly'll know more about that than either of us.'' He pointed to the notebook, still in Zack's hand. ''Over in the back of that book you'll see Manuel Gonzalez' name and address. Will Dempsey says Gonzalez and his vaqueros will drag the longhorns out of the brakes and the Big Thicket and road-brand them for five dollars a head. The man lives just north of Beaumont, right close to the Big Thicket, and he knows where the cattle hide.

''Could be that we could get the Mexicans to rope nothing but cows. Seems like they'd be anxious to pass up the bulls anyway,'cause bulls fight so much harder. And Dempsey says that it's wise to buy a couple head of tame oxen to lead the cows away from the only home they've ever known.''

''Well, we'll worry about that problem when we come to it,'' Zack said, stretching his arms over his head and yawning. ''What I need most right now is a good night's sleep. I believe Jolly had the right idea when he went to bed more than an hour ago.'' Zack was on his feet now. ''I think we should choose a homesite, then build the bunkhouse first so we'll have somewhere to live while we're building the house and the barn. We'll need a corral up there right away, too.'' He headed for his bedroom, adding over his shoulder, ''I'll go into town tomorrow and pick up some of the things we need.''

Hunter spent a large part of the next day shopping, with Jolly Ross close at his heels. Rollins said that he himself had traveled enough lately, and chose to remain at the ranch. Zack suspected that he would spend most of the day practicing his fast draw.

Zack bought two wagons and two teams of large horses. The seller swore that although the big beasts were primarily wagon teams, they had also been trained to work in the fields and were equally resigned to pulling plows and harvesting machines. Zack was well pleased with the price and thought that the only bad part of the bargain was his having to feed the oversize animals all winter. Jolly was also impressed with the size of the horses, saying they could pull anything that could be stacked onto a wagon. ''They'll go close to fourteen hundred pounds apiece, Zack,'' he said. ''Maybe fifteen hundred.''

Zack bought a keg of nails and a variety of tools at the hardware store, along with a stove and several joints of pipe that would be needed for the new bunkhouse. And two large tarpaulins. The tarps would be attached to the tops of tall posts, with the stove, tents, table and chairs set up underneath. That would be home to all of the men until better accommodations could be constructed.

On the way out of town, they stopped at the feed store, where they finished loading both wagons with sacks of grain and bales of hay. ''These horses won't even know that the wagons are loaded,'' Ross said, seemingly awed by the size of the animals. ''As big as both these teams are, though, they're small compared to their Belgian ancestors. Their great-granddaddies probably weighed twenty-five hundred pounds apiece.''

''I believe you're right, Jolly. I'm sure it took years of careful breeding to even get 'em down to this size. I can't imagine a man wanting anything bigger.''

''Nope. Especially at feeding time.''

With a saddle horse trailing each of the wagons, the men turned west on County Line Road, knowing that the last half of their journey home would be traveled by lantern light.

At home, they stabled and fed the horses, then set about preparing their supper as quietly as possible. The blanket covered the doorway to Rollins' bedroom, and Zack assumed that Bret had gone to bed when the sun went down. Probably all tuckered out from a hard day of practicing his fast draw. Zack and Jolly ate cold beef and biscuits without speaking, then Zack went to his own bedroom, leaving Ross to blow out the lamp.

Shortly after daybreak, all three men were dining on ham, eggs, warmed-over biscuits and strong coffee. "I'm gonna be riding north this morning," Zack said, sopping up the last of his egg yolk with a biscuit. He nodded toward Rollins. "I think you ought to go too, Bret. We've got to stake out a homesite somewhere near the center of the ranch. I already spotted one place I want you to look at, saw it the day Carl Odom showed me the boundaries."

Rollins nodded. "Guess you intend to build the bunkhouse first, huh?"

"Right." Zack stepped to the stove to refill his coffee cup, then reseated himself. "I'd like to build it a little closer to the main house than most folks do. If the day ever comes when the men in the bunkhouse have to defend the ranch house, I don't want 'em to have to run a hundred yards before they can do it."

Jolly Ross put a sack of ham and biscuits in his saddlebag, and each man put a canteen on his saddle. "The place I want you to see is about eight miles north," Zack said to Bret, stepping into the saddle. "It's about three hundred yards east of the river. If we decide to use it as a homesite, I want to dig a well before we even drive a stake. If we don't like the water, we can go someplace else."

Rollins mounted, then sat for a moment looking between his horse's ears. "How deep a well do you think we'll need, Zack?" he asked, emitting an audible sigh.

Zack looked at Bret out of the corner of his eye. "No way of knowing till we hit a vein of water." He chuckled to himself, then motioned to Ross. "Jolly and I will dig the well—

wouldn't want you to mess up your gun hand.'' He laughed aloud, then added, ''Seriously, Bret, only two men can work on a well at a time. One digging and shoveling, the other hauling up dirt with a windlass.''

''Hell, I know that, Zack, but I'll certainly let you dig the well. As soon as we settle on a homesite, I'll go to town and hire some men: carpenters, if I can find them. We need to get this ranch in shape in a hurry. Three months from now, I want to order some longhorn cows and Hereford bulls.''

After two hours, Hunter halted his horse at the top of a rise. He sat quietly for a moment, then pointed down the hill to the small plateau that was a quarter mile wide. The grassy little mesa was treeless except for a few mesquite bushes that could be eliminated with a small amount of effort. It appeared to be level for the most part, the exception being the west side, where it gradually sloped down to the water's edge. Overall, the location offered a spectacular view of the surrounding area and the Colorado River.

''Hell, that's it, Zack,'' Rollins said, pointing to the west side of the mesa. ''No use wasting a lot of time looking around, that's it.''

Jolly Ross said nothing, but both Hunter and Rollins noticed that he was nodding and wore a big smile.

They rode down the hill for a closer look. Zack was soon riding up and down the mesa, pointing to one place, then another. ''We'll dig the well right here,'' he was saying ''This will be the front yard. We'll put the bunkhouse right over there, the barn and corral right down yonder, and fence in a garden spot right back there.'' He backed up a dozen steps. ''The house will be right back here, and the front porch will be right where I'm standing.'' He cleared his throat and continued. ''Now, right over here. . . .''

Rollins ate dinner at Toby's T-Bone next day. When he finished his meal, he got to his feet. ''Please give me your attention for a minute!'' he said loudly, addressing a sizable crowd of men. His deep, booming voice stopped all conversation. ''I've got some old buildings to move and some new ones to build,'' he said, ''and I need to hire two or three good carpenters.'' All was quiet. He looked around the room for a moment, then continued. ''I believe the job will last about two months, and I'll pay two dollars a day and found.''

A fork dropped into a plate noisily and a middle-aged man began to talk: ''By God, for that kind of money, I'd sure like to hear a little more about it.'' He motioned toward two young men at his table who appeared to be in their late teens. ''Me and the boys are in the middle of a job right now, but there ain't no hurry on it. We can finish it next spring.''

Rollins walked to the man's table. ''Mind if I sit?'' he asked, offering a handshake. ''My name's Bret Rollins.''

The man was on his feet quickly, grasping the hand. ''My name's Walt Dalton,'' he said, then nodded toward the boys. ''And these are my sons, Willie and Walt Junior.'' He pushed a chair toward Bret and continued to talk: ''Don't go judging the boys by their young ages, now. They grew up with hammers in their hands and they can handle any job you've got.''

Rollins smiled and shook hands with each of the young men. ''I believe you, Mister Dalton, and I'll pay your sons the same wage I'd pay any other man.''

Dalton nodded. ''Now,'' he said, ''let's hear some more about this job.''

Rollins seated himself and began to describe the situation at the ranch, making sure the men understood that they would be living beneath a tarpaulin and sleeping in tents till the bunkhouse was completed.

''Nothing we ain't done before,'' Dalton said.

''One more thing,'' Bret said, ''maybe the main thing. I don't mind spending whatever it takes to make sure everybody eats good, but I don't have a cook out at the ranch. Maybe I should start looking around, see if I can get somebody.''

''Nope,'' Dalton said, scratching at a three-day growth of stubble on his chin. ''What you need to do is hire my pappy. He's sixty years old now and he ain't gonna win no footraces, but he still gets around pretty good, plenty good enough to hold down a cooking job. He knows enough good jokes to last two months, but the main reason you ought to hire him is that he knows how to cook. He's been cooking in cow camps off and on for the past thirty years.''

''You think he'd take the job?''

"Sure he'll take it. You're paying two dollars a day, ain't you?"

"To carpenters, yes. To cooks, no. I'll pay a cook a dollar and a half a day."

Dalton scratched his beard again. "Like I say, Mister Rollins, he'll take the job. You'll have to send a wagon after him 'cause he's got a lot of stuff. Even insists on using his own pots and pans."

"Transportation is no problem," Rollins said. "I'll take care of it myself. What is your father's name?"

"Well, his name is William, but don't nobody call him nothing but Dixie. Dixie Dalton. That's all I've ever heard anybody call him."

Rollins nodded. "Dixie Dalton," he repeated. "An easy name to remember." They talked for another half hour, then Rollins headed home. It had been agreed upon that Walt Dalton and his sons would come to the ranch the day after tomorrow, and Rollins would pick up Dixie Dalton at his home on the same day.

"I'll talk to Pappy tonight," Dalton said as Bret left the restaurant. "He'll be ready and waiting on you."

11

Walt Dalton and his sons stayed on the ranch for ten weeks. Then, their project completed, they headed for their own home. The corral had been built first, then the bunkhouse, then the barn, and yesterday the workers had finished nailing the roof on the ranch house. They had also added two rooms and another fireplace, making the house both larger and warmer.

Dixie Dalton was an excellent cook and had agreed to stay on year-round. Though he was agreeable, genial and sociable, and called every man on the premises by his first name, he had nevertheless insisted on having his own private quarters built on to the cookshack so that he could shut out the world when his day's work was done.

He had come to Texas in 1848 and settled by the Lampasas River. Being a native of Florida, he was not long in acquiring the nickname "Dixie," a name that he seemed quite proud to bear. A six-footer and a little on the skinny side, he was quick to tell one and all that he stayed thin because, unlike most men he knew, he ate only as much food as his body needed. Dixie Dalton seemed happy enough with his cooking job, and was appreciated by all concerned.

Today Hunter and Rollins stood on the ranch-house porch. Neither man wore a coat, for although 1876 was only one week old, the winter thus far had been mild and the day was unseasonably warm. "This is the prettiest place I've ever seen, Bret," Zack said, his eyes cast down the slope to the river.

Rollins pulled up a chair and seated himself. "I believe it's gonna be one of the finest ranches in this part of the country, Zack. It'll be a moneymaker, too. Maybe as time goes on, we can double, triple or even quadruple the size of it."

Zack began to shake his head slowly, a faint smile forming on his lips. "A forty-thousand-acre Hereford ranch? You're making my mouth water, Bret."

"Hell, yes," Rollins said, getting to his feet and pointing north. "All we've got to do is get the land, the bulls will stock it for us in three years. I agree wholeheartedly with Will Dempsey. He says that Texas land ain't gonna stay reasonably priced much longer, that a man who intends to ranch ought to grab as much as he can right now while it's cheap."

"Makes sense," Zack said.

"Sure it does. I intend to head for Beaumont next week and get Manuel Gonzalez started rounding us up a thousand head of longhorns. I'll have to hire a crew to drive 'em back here,'cause Dempsey says the Mexicans are unwilling to give up the fiesta and the siesta for such long periods of time. They like to drink and party above all else"

Rollins walked the length of the porch, then returned to his chair. "As soon as I close the deal for the longhorns and get them lined out in this direction, I'll head for Fort Worth and put in my order with Rafe Baskin for thirty-five Hereford bulls. I should be able to hire some men to help me drive them here to the ranch.''

''You should find some riders easy, Bret. Wintertime puts an awful lot of men out of work. I'd say there are hundreds of broke and thirsty men around a place like Fort Worth.'' Zack walked down the steps and into the yard. ''I'm going to the cookshack to eat, then ride into town and order six more mattresses for the bunkhouse. We need more blankets, too.''

''Good idea,'' Rollins said, falling in beside him. ''I'll eat dinner with you, but you'll have to go into town alone. I promised Dixie I'd try to get a deer for him this evening. I want to try out that new Winchester I bought last week, anyway.''

They ate ham and beans, then talked through two cups of coffee. ''You mentioned increasing the size of the ranch, Bret,'' Zack was saying. ''After we get a calf or two out of the longhorns, we'll send the cows to market. That'll give us enough money to see if any of our neighbors are in the mood to sell.''

''If they're not, we'll buy some property somewhere else,'' Rollins said quickly.

''Right,'' Zack said, getting to his feet. ''No law against us owning more than one ranch.'' He headed for the corral, where he saddled the bay, shoved his Henry in the scabbard and headed east at a canter. He would be in Lampasas in less than two hours.

In town, Zack paid a visit to a merchant named Clyde Beers. When informed that Zack needed mattresses, Beers nodded, saying that he had any type of bedding a man might need stored in a warehouse behind his store. ''I can't take them today, Clyde,'' Zack said. ''I'm traveling on horseback. I'll just pay you for them now, then send a man back with a wagon tomorrow.'' He began to fish money out of his pocket.

Beers refused payment for the moment by shaking his head, then stepped out from behind the counter. ''Let's walk back to the warehouse, Mister Hunter. If you'll put your finger on the exact things you need, then I'll know how much to charge you. It'll also eliminate the chance of me making a mistake when I load your wagon tomorrow.''

Zack chose the things he needed, and the men laid them

aside in a separate pile. He was about to leave the building when he suddenly remembered something an old rancher had said to him in the White Horse Saloon: "Th' better ya treat yer ranch hands, th' more apt they are ta stay with ya," the old-timer had said. Zack recalled the comical picture the old rancher had made with tobacco juice dripping off his chin. Now he pointed to a shelf along the warehouse wall. "I'll take a dozen of those feather pillows, Clyde."

Zack had two drinks at the White Horse Saloon. There were only two men in the saloon that he had seen before: Jiggs Odom and the bartender, Ed Hayes. He spoke with Hayes for a few minutes, ignoring Odom, who sat at the far end of the bar talking with other drinkers. Zack was in the saloon less than twenty minutes and then headed for the livery stable.

At the stable, he watered his horse and talked with Oscar Land for a short while, then took the road home. Alternating between a canter and a fast trot, he expected to reach the ranch before sunset.

He was halfway home and had just slowed his horse to a walking gait when he heard a gunshot, the sound coming from somewhere north of the road. Somebody shooting game for the table, Zack thought, and continued on his way. He changed his mind a few steps later when he heard and felt the wind from a rifle slug pass within inches of his face, followed by the sound of another gunshot.

Hunter was out of the saddle quickly, clutching the Henry in his right hand. In the same fluid movement, he was behind a clump of short mesquite trees at the side of the road. His horse trotted off to his right for only a short distance, then stopped and began to crop grass. Crouched low to the ground, Zack peeked around the trunk of a tree, taking a long look up the slope to the north. Nothing was moving.

Trying to pinpoint the exact spot from which the shots had come was useless, for the sound had seemed to echo down the hill. Zack knew only that they had come from somewhere up that slope, on the north side of the road. There were hundreds of places up there for a man to hide, for the entire area was littered with scrubby mesquites and cedars.

Crouched behind the trees, he was relatively safe from any gunfire coming from the north side of the road, and he fully intended to stay where he was till dark. He could see for at least a mile in either direction on the road, so the chances of someone crossing to the south side and coming in behind him undetected were slim. He lay motionless, waiting for movement up the slope or for darkness, whichever came first. Then, after a time, he began to move around a little, hoping to make the shooter fire again and give away his hiding place with a telltale puff of smoke. It did not happen.

After what seemed like hours to Zack, the sun finally settled below the western horizon and darkness followed quickly. Speaking softly as he approached his horse, he caught the animal easily, mounted and headed back to Lampasas at a fast pace, his Henry held high and ready for action.

When he reached town, he tied his animal at the White Horse's hitching rail, then ran his hand along the backs and sides of the other horses tied there. All of the animals were dry. He shoved his rifle in the boot and walked inside the saloon. "Give me a beer, Ed." The bartender delivered, and Zack took a stool. "I see that Jiggs Odom is still down at the end of the bar drinking," he said, dropping a coin on the bar.

"Been at it all day long," the bartender said. "He was waiting for me when I opened up and he's been here ever since."

Zack took a sip of his beer. "You're positive that he's been here all day, Ed?"

"Of course I'm positive," Hayes said quickly. "Now, he might've walked outside to piss a few times, but he ain't never been gone more'n a coupla minutes. Hell, I've been talking to him most of the day." He wiped at the bar for a moment, then asked the logical question: "How come you're asking about Jiggs?"

Zack finished his beer and got to his feet. "No reason in particular, Ed. I just thought I saw somebody who looked like him out on the road."

"Well, there ain't no whole lot of men around here as big as Jiggs," Hayes said, shaking his head, "but it sure wasn't him you saw." The bartender was still shaking his head when Zack left the building.

Back on the street, Zack stood beside the hitching rail for a while. He could easily see that none of the horses tied there had made a hard run recently. And the bartender had said that Zack's only suspect had been inside the White Horse Saloon all day. Zack believed him.

As he lay behind the mesquite trees shortly after the rifle shot had barely missed his nose, Zack had thought immediately of Jiggs Odom. Though Odom himself had said that he held no hard feelings over the beating Zack had given him, Zack could think of no one else who would have even the slightest excuse for trying to do him in. He had no doubt that somebody wanted him dead, however, for he was thoroughly convinced that the shooter had meant business.

He mounted and rode up one side of the street and down the other, checking the hitching rails for horses that had been run hard lately. He found none.

A few minutes later, he delivered his horse to the livery stable. "Put him up and take care of him, Oscar," he said, handing the reins to the liveryman. "I'll be spending the night in town." With his Colt tucked behind his waistband, his saddlebags across his shoulder and the Henry resting in the cradle of one arm, he headed up the street at a brisk pace.

He stopped at the Hartley Hotel and after signing his name, was given an upstairs room. He locked the door and lay on the bed thinking. Who in the world would have a reason to shoot at him? Zack could think of no answer. Of one thing he was convinced: the close call had certainly been no accident, for the shooter had shot too high to be shooting at game. No, sir, the man behind the rifle had intended to kill him.

Zack's main reason for spending the night in town was to inform the sheriff that a sniper had made an attempt to end his life and that he fully intended to shoot back if and when he saw something suspicious to shoot at. Zack had decided that it was too late to go looking for the sheriff tonight, but he would be in the lawman's office tomorrow morning.

D. B. "Pete" Pope, a native of Jackson County, Mississippi, had been Lampasas County's sheriff for many years. Due to the fact that he had won two previous terms by landslide margins, he had run unopposed in the most recent election. A man of medium height and build, Pope had a weathered complexion, and hair that had long since turned to salt-and-pepper. Though his age was probably somewhere around the half-century mark, he moved about spryly, and his popularity throughout the county was reflected in the fact that nobody chose to run against him this past November.

Pope was sitting behind a scarred oak desk when Zack walked into his office the following morning. He was on his feet quickly, walking around the corner of the desk and extending his right hand. "Good morning, Mister Hunter," he said, pushing a chair out with his foot. "Have a seat."

Zack took the lawman's hand. "Kinda surprised that you know my name," he said.

The sheriff chuckled. "This is my county, Mister Hunter; it's my business to know who lives in it." He waited until Zack had seated himself, then continued, "Besides, it ain't likely that anybody's gonna buy up ten thousand acres of choice property around here without me knowing it." He moved behind his desk and reseated himself, then asked, "Something I can do for you?"

"Well, I don't really know that you can do anything about it," Zack began, "but somebody took two shots at me on County Line Road yesterday afternoon. Rifle shots, Sheriff, and if the shooter had been a better marksman by just two or three inches, I wouldn't be here. I didn't return the fire because I didn't see anything to shoot at. I took cover and waited till after dark, then rode back to town."

The sheriff had listened attentively. He leaned closer. "You saw no man or horse or powder smoke?"

"I saw nothing," Zack said. "I kept my eyes glued to that slope north of the road till dark, more than an hour. Nothing moved."

The sheriff sat thoughtfully for a few moments. "How far from town? Do you remember exactly where you were when the shooting started?"

"Of course," Zack said. "I was on that long straightaway about five miles west of town. You know where Rat Creek is?"

Pope nodded.

"Well, right past the plank bridge there's a cluster of mesquite trees, on the left-hand side of the road. I was about even with them when the second shot came, the one that came so close. I took cover behind the trees and waited till dark."

"Did you have a firearm yourself?" Pope asked.

"Had a Henry in my hand when I jumped behind the trees, and whoever was up that slope saw it. I guess the main reason he didn't fire again was because he knew I'd be shooting back if he gave away his position."

Pope nodded. "I'd say you're right about that." He stared at the window a while, then spoke again: "Can you even make a guess as to who the gunman might be, or what kind of rifle you heard?"

"I believe the shots I heard came from a Winchester, and no, I don't have the faintest idea who the sniper was. I'm new in this country. Not many people even know me, and none has a reason to want me dead."

"Could be a case of mistaken identity," the sheriff said. He sat thinking for another moment, then added, "Jiggs Odom is not the type that would do it, not just because you whipped his ass in a fistfight."

"You know about that?"

Pope chuckled. "It's like I said before, Mister Hunter; not much happens around here that I don't know about." The lawman was on his feet now, offering a parting handshake. "I'll send both of my deputies out to scout that slope for tracks this morning. Meanwhile, if you figure out who did the shooting, you have my permission to mistake the sonofabitch for a coyote."

"Thank you, Sheriff. I'll ride home by a different route, then check with you tomorrow. It might be that your deputies will learn something on the slope."

"I expect them to," Pope said, lifting his arm to wave goodbye. "They're both good trackers."

Zack rode through the woods till he reached the Colorado, then followed the river north to the ranch house, a roundabout journey that took most of the day. He released his horse in the corral and hung the bridle on a fence post, then turned to find Rollins standing beside him. After Zack explained that he had spent the night at the hotel in town, the two walked to the house, seating themselves on the doorstep.

"The sniper wasn't shooting at you," Rollins said when Zack had told him of the attempt on his life. "The bastard was shooting at me. I mean, he thought he was shooting at me.''

"That idea crossed my mind, too, Bret, and I've been wondering about it all day.''

"Well, you can stop wondering about it, and let's start figuring out how to do something about it. The sonofabitch thought he was shooting at me for sure, Zack; you don't have any enemies.'' Rollins thought for a moment, then added, "None in Texas, at least. I think the problem dates back to last summer. I believe it has followed me all the way from the town of Weatherford.''

"Are you saying you think Mrs. Lindsay has sent somebody after you?''

"Not exactly, but it is a possibility. I think it's more likely, though, that the problem is Clifford T. Hollingsworth. Maybe something went wrong with the deal. Maybe he didn't end up with the Silver Springs property after all, and I got out of town with his six thousand dollars.'' Bret scratched his chin for a moment, then added, "I hope that's the case, Zack. I wouldn't feel bad for one minute about shooting that heartless old sonofabitch.'' He smiled and got to his feet. "I'd feel a lot worse if I had to shoot Mrs. Lindsay,'' he said jokingly.

They ate venison stew in the cookshack, then walked down to the river, where they seated themselves on a fallen log and began to make plans for putting the sniper out of business. Both men believed that the shooter had seen Hunter in town, and knowing that he would return home by way of County Line Road, had ridden out and positioned himself on the north slope.

They decided that if the sniper had mistaken Hunter for Rollins, they would do nothing to correct his assumption. Zack would ride through the woods to town tomorrow and talk with Sheriff Pope. Then he would prowl around town for a while, taking in the restaurants and saloons and making sure he was seen by most of the townfolk. In the afternoon, he would ride west on County Line Road. When he could no longer be seen from town, he would turn south into the woods and return home by the same route he had used today.

Meanwhile, Rollins and Jolly Ross would be patrolling the north slope. Rollins would ride to within seeing distance of

Lampasas, then wait in the trees north of the road. Any rider who left town headed west would be under surveillance. By riding through the trees, parallel to the road, Rollins could easily keep pace with anyone on horseback.

Hunter was in the sheriff's office at ten the following morning, talking with Deputy Horace Hillman. "The sheriff won't be back till around dinnertime," Hillman said, "but I can tell you what we found out about that slope west of town. The only horse tracks anywhere up there are more'n a month old. Whoever's been shooting from that slope either walked up there or he's camping up there,'cause he damn sure ain't been riding no horse. Me and my partner went over that ridge with a fine-toothed comb."

"Thank you, Deputy," Zack said. "I appreciate it, and you've told me what I needed to know." He was out the door quickly and began to stroll around Lampasas. During the next two hours, he prowled the length of the town, up one side of the street and down the other. He drank coffee in two restaurants and had drinks in three saloons, the last one being the White Horse. He bought drinks for two men with whom he was acquainted, then talked loudly with Ed Hayes as he sipped a beer. As he was leaving the building, he stood in the doorway for a moment before calling back to the bartender, wanting to make sure every man in the saloon noticed him: "See you again tomorrow, Ed." Then he was out on the street.

He mounted the black, trotted to the end of the street and turned west on County Line Road. He held the same pace till he could no longer see the town, then turned abruptly into the woods. He would travel the same course as the day before, turning north to the ranch house when he reached the river.

Rollins had reached his surveillance position on the slope about the same time Zack reached town. Zack had been there less than an hour when Bret saw a rider come down the street headed north, then turn west on County Line Road. Rollins mounted the roan and sat behind a tall cedar till the rider was well past his own position. Then he also headed west, riding parallel to the road and keeping the rider in sight at all times.

In less than a mile, the rider guided his horse off the road and turned north, all the while in plain view of Rollins. The man kept his horse pointed west at a trot for the large part of an hour, then came to a halt behind a clump of cedars. He was now west of Rat Creek and about six miles from town. Rollins had kept pace and could plainly see the man from his own place of concealment a thousand yards farther up the slope. He sat his horse behind a cluster of mesquites.

The man dismounted behind the cedars and tied his horse to a low-hanging branch. Then, taking his rifle from the saddle scabbard, he walked west a few steps and took up a position behind a natural mound of earth that was covered with weeds and grass. He was about a hundred and fifty yards from the road—excellent shooting range for the Winchester he held.

Rollins dismounted slowly, half-hitching the roan to a small bush. Convinced that he had found the sniper, he began to creep forward, his Winchester at the ready. He had jacked a shell into the firing chamber of the rifle when the sniper came into view, long before the man was within hearing distance.

Easing himself from one hiding place to another, Rollins continued to make his way down the slope, pausing for a few minutes behind each mesquite or cedar. The man ahead of him sat very still, his eyes cast down the slope to the road. The only times he moved were when he spit tobacco juice over his shoulder.

Bret moved as silently as a breeze and after more than half an hour, only fifty feet separated him from the sniper. Off to his left, he could see the man's black horse and the big Lazy H burned into its hip. The Lazy H, Bret said to himself. Clifford T. Hollingsworth's brand.

Rollins waited no longer. He shortened the distance separating them to thirty feet, then spoke to the man: "Don't move a muscle, fellow! You'll live a little bit longer if you leave the rifle lying right where it is."

The man did as he had been told.

"Put your hands over your head and get to your feet slow and easylike." The man complied, and Rollins was now looking into the face of a man about his own age, who sported at least a month's growth of red beard. "You've been shooting at the wrong man, fellow," Rollins said, the Winchester against his shoulder and the barrel pointed directly at the redhead's chest. "You see, that's not Bret Rollins you've been stalking. You're looking at Bret Rollins."

The expression on the redhead's face told Rollins all he needed to know: the man had indeed been sent by Hollingsworth, and no doubt paid a tidy sum to do him in. Rollins commanded the man to remove his Colt from its holster. "Real easy now, with just your thumb and forefinger. Take the gun by its handle, pull it out of the holster and let it fall to the ground."

The redhead brought his right hand down very slowly. As it neared his holster, he suddenly jumped to his left, clawing frantically at the six-gun on his hip. He died instantly, drilled through the heart with a shot from Bret's Winchester.

When he searched the body, Rollins found that the man carried no identification, but he did have fifteen double eagles in his front pocket. The money was tied up in a sock. Three hundred dollars, Bret said to himself as he finished counting the money, probably about the going price for murder. He put the coins in his pocket, happy to get a chance at some more of Hollingsworth's money.

He loaded the corpse onto the sniper's own horse, then headed for the H and R ranch house. Zack should be home by now. Rollins would discuss the matter with him before deciding what to do with the body.

He had traveled only a few miles when Jolly Ross rode out of the trees and into the road. "I recognized you from up on the ridge," he said, then pointed at the corpse. "Looks like you found your man."

Rollins nodded. "It was almost too easy, Jolly. He rode straight to me, just like he'd planned it that way." Ross fell in beside Bret and they made a right turn, taking the new road to the new ranch house.

Zack was in the yard when they reached the house an hour later. After listening to part of Bret's story, he lifted the dead man's head to get a better look at his face. "Ever seen him before?"

"Nope," Rollins answered. "But I can tell you one thing for sure, Zack: he was all set to take a potshot at you when you came down the road. He was dug in about a hundred fifty yards north of the road, with a clear view. If he was any kind of marksman at all, he couldn't have missed." Rollins seated himself on the doorstep, then continued. "You see the brand on that horse's hip, Zack?" he asked, pointing. "That Lazy H is Hollingsworth's mark, so there's no doubt that the old man sent him to kill me. Either Hollingsworth didn't give him a good description or the sonofabitch forgot; he mistook you for me."

"Sounds like you're exactly right, Bret." Zack wrapped the horse's reins around the hitching rail, then leaned against the porch. "What do you plan to do with the body?"

"I plan to let you decide." Half-smiling, looking at Zack out of the corner of his eye, Bret added, "You're smarter'n me."

"First time you ever said that," Zack said, chuckling. He walked around in a small circle, then returned to his leaning post. "You don't have but two choices the way I see it: you can take the body to Sheriff Pope and tell him the story, or you can shoot the horse and bury man, horse and saddle in the same hole. If you want my suggestion, I say go to the sheriff. No offense toward Jolly there, or Dixie down at the cookshack, but four men already know that there's a dead man in this yard. That's an awful lot of people to be knowing a secret, Bret."

"You damn sure have a way of putting things," Bret said, laughing. He was on his feet now. "If we leave right away, we can probably be in Lampasas before dark." He took the reins of the dead man's horse, then mounted the roan.

They reached town a few minutes before sunset. Sheriff Pope had already left his office for the day and had to be summoned from his home, a mile west of town. When he arrived, he gave both the corpse and the Lazy H horse a lot of scrutiny, at the same time listening to Rollins describe the day's happenings. "He was dug in a hundred fifty yards north of the road, Sheriff," Bret was saying, "all set to take a shot at Mister Hunter when he rode by. I came in behind him with a Winchester and tried to disarm him. He went for the gun on his hip and I had no choice but to shoot."

The sheriff nodded and turned to Zack. "Do you think this is the man who shot at you yesterday?"

"I'm convinced of it," Zack said. "You were right when you said it could be a case of mistaken identity. The sniper was actually after Mister Rollins here and mistook me for him."

"That's mighty interesting," the sheriff said, " 'cause you two don't even resemble each other." Then he spoke to Rollins: "I guess you ought to at least have some idea about why he wanted to kill you."

"Sure do," Rollins said. He pointed to the brand on the horse's hip. "That Lazy H means that the horse belongs on Clifford Hollingsworth's spread, up near Weatherford. I bested him in a land deal last year and it's eating at him. He no doubt sent that joker to do me in."

Sheriff Pope stood quietly for several moments as he scratched his head and readjusted his hat. "Well," he said finally, "what're you gonna do with the body?"

The question caught Rollins off guard. "Well . . . uh . . . I suppose I'll do whatever you tell me."

"The undertaker's usually on twenty-four-hour call," Pope said. "I believe he charges about fifteen dollars." He walked around the horse one last time, for daylight was fading fast. "That looks like a good saddle," he said. "I suppose you can find some use for it out at your ranch. I'd keep the horse, too. If this fellow Hollingsworth ever comes after it, you can charge him as much as you want to for its keep."

"Thank you, Sheriff," Rollins said. "I'll do that."

The partners were soon headed for the undertaker's parlor, with Rollins leading the sniper's horse. "Remind me to vote for Pete Pope in the next election," he said. "I believe the sheriff is my kind of people."

12

It was now the first week in February, and central Texas had so far had the mildest winter in recent memory. Thinking it unwise to make the trip himself, Rollins had sent Jolly Ross to Weatherford to learn as much as he could about the actions of Clifford Hollingsworth. Ross had returned a week ago, saying that the old man's dam had been completed and Silver Springs Hollow was rapidly filling up with water.

Jolly had talked with Rex Allgood on several occasions, learning that Hollingsworth's health had taken a turn for the worse and that he seldom left his room nowadays. The old man had also returned to his old habit of consuming large quantities of liquor, having it delivered to the ranch house by the case. Allgood said that his father-in-law drank himself into an alcoholic stupor on a daily basis, usually before noon, and that family and friends had given up on trying to hold any kind of conversation with him. The bartender did not believe that Hollingsworth would live to see the grass turn green this year.

Rollins listened closely to Jolly's report and thought that maybe Hollingsworth was no longer a threat to him. He would remain vigilant, however, and keep an eye on his back trail, for the old man was not dead yet.

Hunter and Rollins had come to the decision just last night that it was time to contact Manuel Gonzalez about the long-horns. Zack himself decided that Rollins should be the one to make the trip. Gathering the herd and driving it to the H and R would take as long as two months, maybe three, and Zack knew that if he himself handled that chore, Rollins would get nothing whatsoever done around the ranch in the meantime. Besides, Bret was a better talker. He was also personally ac-quainted with Rafe Baskin, the man who would supply the Hereford bulls.

The partners had registered the H and R Cattle Company's brand as the HR connected, and last week Oscar Land had made up several branding irons, which Rollins would carry east on a packhorse. As the longhorns were gathered, the HR would be burned into their hides, eliminating any need for additional marking until such time as they were road-branded for the drive to the rails in Kansas. Unless the bank account reached an unacceptable low, Rollins planned to get two calves out of each of the longhorn cows before they were marketed.

Rollins must travel southeast to Saratoga, a small town in

Hardin County, only a short distance from Beaumont. There he would hunt up one Manuel Gonzalez and make a deal for a thousand head of longhorns. He had been told that Gonzalez would sometimes fill two or three orders at once. If Gonzalez had more than one buyer wanting longhorns at the same time, he simply hired more men, for he did none of the roping himself. And communication was never a problem. Though Gonzalez spoke Spanish fluently, he had been born and raised no more than a dozen miles from where he now lived and spoke English as well as did other Texans.

This morning Rollins was preparing for his journey to Saratoga. Zack followed him to the barn and stood watching as he adjusted the packsaddle on a black gelding. "I hate like hell to lead two pack animals, Zack," Rollins said, "but I just might have to. I may have to camp for a month or two while they gather the herd, and I'll be needing a lot of things. Besides, I've got to carry these branding irons."

Zack stepped under the shed and opened a metal bin, extracting a piece of rope three feet long. "I've led two horses lots of times, Bret. It's not hard to do." He handed over the rope. "Here, take this and tie one end to each of the horses' bridles. That'll keep 'em together."

"Yeah," Rollins said, "except when they decide to walk on opposite sides of a damn sapling."

Hunter laughed. "Well, I guess you should stop when that happens."

The partners spent almost two hours loading and arranging the things Bret chose to carry on the backs of two horses. A heavy bag of grain rounded out the load on the larger of the animals. In addition to a week's supply of food, Rollins carried the tent he had brought from Tennessee. He had slept in the tent through more than one downpour and knew that it would not leak. The horses also carried everything he would need in the way of cooking utensils, several changes of clothing, a good bedroll and thick blankets.

At last Rollins climbed aboard the roan. He had not taken Zack's advice on tying the packhorses' bridles together. He had tied them nose-to-tail and would lead them in single file. Hunter was quick to admit that it was a better arrangement than his own suggestion had been.

Rollins tightened up the lead rope. "Well, I guess we'll be in the cattle business pretty soon, partner." They engaged in the longest handshake of their lives, each man seeming reluctant to let go. Rollins finally pulled in his hand, then pointed east. "I figure the town of Bryan is about the halfway point. I'll try to make it there before I have to restock my supplies"

Zack nodded. "You just be careful, Bret. I'd say that there's many a man between here and Saratoga who would kill for what you're carrying. I think you should bank your money in Beaumont before you even go looking for Manuel Gonzalez."

"I'll do that, Zack. Of course I'll see if they have a bank in Saratoga before I go riding all the way to Beaumont." He waved good-bye, kicked the roan in the ribs and headed southeast, hoping to cross the Lampasas River before nightfall.

Rollins rode into Bryan at noon six days later. The sky had been overcast all day but so far, the low-hanging clouds had produced no rain. He saw several men on the street as he rode through town but made eye contact with no one. The livery stable at the end of the street looked much like a hundred others he had seen. He dismounted in the doorway.

"Howdy there, young feller," a scrawny old man said, walking into the dimly lit hall. Reaching for the roan's bridle, he continued to talk: "You look like a tard man, mister; hongry too, I bet, an' they c'n fix 'at mighty quick over at th' hotel dinin' room. If bein' 'bout dinnertime, I'd say they got a big feed on over there right now." He patted the roan's neck. "It's easy ta see 'at ya done come a right smart piece, an' I bet ya wanna rest ya animals a while. I bet—"

"Have you got someplace you can lock up my gear?" Bret interrupted.

"Why, o' course. I'll put it 'n th' office, right whur I keep muh own stuff. Ain't nobody gonna mess with nothin'."

"Good," Rollins said, beginning to unburden his pack animals. "I'm sure you're right about my horses needing rest, and I intend to leave them with you for a day or two."

"I'll shore take good care uv 'em. All uv 'em'll be awright in a coupla days." He led the animals forward and fed them in separate stalls, then turned to Bret's gear. With each man carrying a packsaddle, they soon had the equipment stored in the office. "Been here seb'm years," the old hostler said. "Ain't nobody stole nothin' out'n this office yet."

With his saddlebags across his shoulder and his rifle cradled in the crook of one arm, Rollins walked up the street to the hotel. He rented a second-story room, locked his Winchester inside, then returned to the street. He was soon sitting in a barber shop, where he requested a shave and a haircut. He was in the chair quickly, for he was the lone customer.

Unlike most barbers Rollins had known, this man was not a talker, just went about his work quietly and meticulously. When he was done, he patted Rollins on the shoulder several times, the signal that it was time to get out of the chair.

Rollins smiled as he paid the man for his work. "I guess you'd know where the best eating place is," he said.

"The hotel dining room's always treated me right," the barber said. "I eat there myself sometimes when the old lady don't make me bring something from home." He signaled a newly arrived customer to get in the chair, then turned his back to Rollins.

Bret seated himself in the dining room and noticed immediately that the bill of fare handed to him by a waitress was quite extensive. Thumbing through its three pages, he began to shake his head slowly. "Do you folks actually have everything listed here?" he asked the small, middle-aged lady.

"Most of it," she said quickly. "We pride ourselves on variety."

He pointed to the first listing on the first page. "I'll have the sirloin steak, potatoes and a bowl of those black-eyed peas." The lady nodded and headed for the kitchen.

Bret was soon served one of the tastiest meals he could remember, and he left an extra quarter on the table when he departed. He bought a bottle of good whiskey at the bar and a copy of the *Fort Worth Democrat* in the lobby, then climbed the stairs to his room.

He was soon sipping whiskey-and-water while reading the newspaper. After a while he laid the paper aside, mixed himself another drink and moved his chair to the window, where he sat looking down into the street below. Men were scampering from one place to another much like so many ants, and quite a few women were on the street, too.

All of which reminded him that he had not even seen a woman up close in weeks. Nor would he see one in the near future, for it would be a careless thing to do. He had already decided that his stay in the town of Bryan would be spent in this hotel room. He would leave the room only to eat, for prowling about town with two saddlebags full of money was out of the question. He would guard the money with his life till he could bank it in Saratoga or Beaumont. Then he would find an agreeable woman and get his ashes hauled.

When he stretched out on his bed and began reading again, he fell asleep quickly and awoke to a dark room five hours later. *Damn!* was his first thought. He struck a match and lit the coal-oil lamp, then looked at his watch. The time was a quarter past eight, probably too late to get fed in the dining room. He grabbed his saddlebags and hurried down the stairs. "Is the dining room closed?" he asked the fat desk clerk.

"About a half hour ago," the man said. "You hungry?"

Rollins nodded. "Like a wolf."

The clerk pointed to the counter. "There's a big bowl of stew and some biscuits on that tray there," he said, "and it ain't been touched. Elsie brought it to me when she closed, and I sure as hell ain't gonna eat it." He patted his belly. "I done gained more'n forty pounds this year. If you want that stew, take it right on up to your room and eat it. Won't cost you a penny."

Rollins looked at the tray a couple of times, then reached for it. "The truth is, I am mighty hungry, mister, but I'd feel better about eating it if you let me pay for it."

"Ain't gonna be no days like that," the clerk said loudly. "It'll just go to waste if you don't use it." He waved his arm toward the stairs. "Now, take it on up to your room and be done with it."

Rollins did as he had been told. The stew was neither hot nor cold. What it was, was delicious. After only one bite, he knew that the hostler and the barber had been right: the hotel cooks knew what they were doing. He continued to shovel with the large spoon until the bowl was empty. Just as had been his meal in the dining room earlier today, the stew was excellent, with exactly enough hot pepper to enhance its natural flavor.

He lay on his bed for several hours, waiting for the sleep that would not come. The long nap he had taken during the afternoon, and the large bowl of highly seasoned stew he had eaten tonight, had taken away any urge he might have had to doze off again. He was filled with energy and felt more like running a mile than sleeping.

Sitting on the side of his bed and staring into the darkness, he knew that he would be out of this room and back on the trail come morning, for being cooped up was already getting on his nerves. He knew that his horses needed rest, but he could give them that by shortening his traveling day. From now on, he would take to the trail a little later each morning and make camp two hours earlier in the afternoon. If he took his time about fixing his breakfast each morning, the animals would gain as much as three hours a day on their picket ropes, becoming better rested and better fed. Even at a slower rate of travel, he expected to be in Saratoga a week from now.

He slept soundly sometime after midnight and awoke at daybreak. When his stretching and yawning was done, he washed his face, picked up his saddlebags and headed for the stairs. In the lobby, he had to stand in line for a few minutes in order to get a seat in the dining room. Another compliment to the skills of the hotel cooks, he thought.

Rollins soon took a seat at a table already occupied by three men. One of them got to his feet and left the room just as Rollins sat down. The remaining two were apparently through eating but ordered more coffee. They nodded at Rollins, but nothing was said. Bret ordered his meal, then sat quietly. He was soon dining on ham, eggs, buttered biscuits and apple jelly, and sipping exceptionally good coffee.

The men on the opposite side of the table, who were both about Bret's size and age, were seedy-looking characters. Each man was brown-haired and had a thick beard, and each wore a battered Stetson. Just before taking his seat at the table, Rollins had noticed that each had a Colt tied to his right leg.

Neither of the men spoke to Rollins till he finished eating. "Ain't seen you before," the man directly across the table said. "Been in town long?"

Rollins said nothing, just shook his head.

The man tried again. "My name's Joe Plum," he said, his lips parting on yellow teeth, "and this here's my Cousin Billy." He pointed to the man beside him.

Sipping the last of his coffee, Rollins nodded and still said nothing.

"You don't say no helluva lot, do you?" the second man asked.

Bret shook his head again. "Nope."

A silly grin appeared on the face of the man called Billy. Turning to the man who had introduced himself as Joe Plum, he spoke softly while pointing to Rollins: "He sure is holding on to them saddlebags mighty tight, Joe. Now what in the world do you suppose he's got in 'em?" Not waiting for an answer, he turned to face Bret. "Whatcha got in them saddlebags, fellow?"

The type of man he was now facing was nothing new to Rollins. He had known dozens of them, and knew already that he might have to fight one or both of these men before the day was over. He fastened a steely stare onto the eyes of the man called Billy that quickly turned to ice. Pushing his chair back with his legs, he got to his feet quickly. Slinging his saddlebags across his shoulder, he answered the man's question: "Dynamite," he said. He paid for his breakfast and walked through the door, leaving the two men standing beside the table staring after him.

He walked to the livery stable at a fast clip, then turned to look behind him. No one was on the street. "I'll be needing my horses and my gear now," he said to the hostler, who stepped from the office yawning. "Need a sack of oats, too."

"Ain't got no oats. Ain't been able ta git none fer th' past week. Got some shelled corn."

Rollins nodded. "Put a sack of corn on that big gelding." He sat on an upended nail keg while the hostler caught up the horses. Half an hour later, having saddled the roan and arranged his gear on the pack animals, Rollins paid the man, then mounted.

He led his pack animals up the street to the Shebang, where he spent close to an hour looking over the merchandise and restocking his food supplies. The lady had hen eggs for sale and volunteered to wrap each individual egg in soft paper so it would not break. Rollins bought a dozen. He would boil them all over his first campfire anyway, eliminating any concern about breakage.

As he rode up the street to the Shebang, he had had to pass the hotel. Joe Plum and his Cousin Billy had been standing in front of the dining-room door. Now, as he repassed the hotel on his way out of town, the men were still there, looking him and his equipment over through billows of cigarette smoke. Through his peripheral vision, Rollins was looking them over also, though he made direct eye contact with neither man. He rode down the street at a fast walk and never looked back. Passing the blacksmith shop, he turned right at the livery stable and headed east.

He had traveled about a mile when he stopped at a small clearing. He sat his horse for a few moments, watching a man rearrange the earth with a turning plow pulled by two large mules. With the purple woods circling it like hungry wolves, the field did not have a look of permanence, but appeared to be no more than a shackled wilderness ready to spring back if the farmer and his plow missed so much as a single day beating it into submission. Rollins waved to the man, then circled the plowed earth and rode on.

Two hours before sunset, he camped on the east bank of the Navasota River, a few miles north of the town of the same name. He headed for the brakes immediately after fording the river, leading his animals into the cane, briers and brushwood. The horses had drunk their fill from the river, and each was soon eating shelled corn from a nose bag. There would be no grazing tonight, for though Rollins had seen no one, he had a feeling that he was not traveling alone. The horses were hidden as well as they could be, and only a man who was deliberately tracking them would ever know their whereabouts. Bret intended to discourage anybody who might be tracking the animals.

He ate sardines, cheese and crackers for his supper, then opened the pack carried by the smaller of the two horses. The double-barreled, ten-gauge shotgun he extracted was already loaded, and he put a few additional shells into his pocket. He laid his saddlebags across his shoulder and then, taking up his bedroll in one arm and the Winchester and the shotgun in the other, he began to backtrack his horses' route from the river. He had chosen his place of concealment when he passed it earlier: a large oak that the wind had uprooted on the east bank of the river. In addition to the hole in the ground, there were the dirt-clad roots of the tree itself, excellent protection against gunfire from even the heaviest of calibers.

He doffed his hat and eased himself into the hole, drawing his Colt and laying it beside his other weapons as he did so. His position offered a good view of the entire area, and he could even see a couple hundred yards past the west bank of the river. He was confident that with the moon in its three-quarter phase, nobody would sneak up on him tonight. A man moving about would not only be easy to see, he would cast a shadow ten feet long. He took a drink of water from his canteen, noting that even though the sun had not yet disappeared, the moon was already moving above the horizon.

Two hours passed, and Bret had been pinching himself to stay awake when he heard something. He leaned forward, trying to force his eyes to see deeper into the meadow across the river. Unable to identify the sound or pinpoint the direction from whence it came, he sat with his eyes glued to his back trail across the narrow river. After several minutes, the faint glow of moonlight revealed two dark clumps at the outer limits of his vision. Rollins racked his brain. Were those natural objects? Had they been there all along? The answer was no, he decided quickly. Were the objects moving? He could not tell.

Convinced now that he was looking at two horses and their riders, he sat in his hole staring around the bottom of the uprooted oak. All three of his guns lay on the ground before him, but he had touched neither. He was waiting to see how the situation developed before deciding which weapon he would need.

He no longer had to strain his eyes to see that the riders had covered half the distance between the river and the place where he had first spotted them. He had no doubt whatsoever that the men were following him and that they were up to no good. It had taken at least fifteen minutes for them to travel a hundred yards. Men not bent on mischief would have forded the river and been long gone by now.

The riders moved twenty yards closer and stopped again. Though the moon did not provide enough light for him to make out facial features, the overall physical appearance of the men told Rollins that he was once again looking at Joe Plum and his Cousin Billy. There was absolutely no doubt about what they had in mind.

The riders now sat their horses on the west bank of the river, less than forty yards from the uprooted tree on the east bank. The short distance between himself and the riders made Bret's choice of weapons obvious. He reached for the shotgun.

He knew that he himself could not be seen from the opposite side of the river, for the canopy of a nearby oak cast a dark shadow over his hiding place. The approaching riders, however, made perfect targets in the moonlight. Bret was not known for giving a man more than one chance to make a wise choice, and these two had already had their chance. Unfortunately, they had chosen to stalk and rob him, and no doubt intended to leave no witness to their deeds.

The riders continued to sit their saddles, whispering and pointing across the river. When one of them removed his hat to scratch his head, there was no problem in identifying the man called Billy. Rollins leaned over the side of his hole with his left eye closed. His right eye was sighted down the twin barrels of the ten-gauge Greener, and he was determined that neither Joe Plum nor his Cousin Billy would live to cross the river.

The riders whispered back and forth one last time. Then, with Joe Plum pointing the way, they eased their horses into the water. The animals took to the river almost eagerly, for here at the ford it was less than two feet deep. On they came: thirty yards . . . twenty-five . . . twenty . . . fifteen. The Greener spoke once, then thundered again. The big gun knocked each man from his saddle, and the horses also went down. The animals kicked a few times, but neither of the men ever moved once they hit the water. After a few moments, even the horses lay still. Rollins stood for a while watching the V formation created by the moving water as it rushed past each of the bodies. Then he headed for the cane brake and his horses, determined to put as much territory behind him as possible before daybreak.

Rollins felt no remorse whatsoever about putting Joe Plum and his cousin in the water. He did, however, feel a slight twinge of guilt about the horses. But, he reasoned with himself, he had not deliberately intended to shoot the animals. The Greener was a scattergun, and just as the name implied, the buckshot would scatter all to hell after traveling only a few yards. Predicting exactly where each of the deadly slugs would go was an impossibility, and at a distance of fifteen yards, it was inevitable that one or more of them would find the heads of the horses. It's just one of those things, Rollins said to himself, patting the neck of his nervous roan.

He was back in the saddle and headed east within the hour, grateful for the third-quarter moon that lit his way. He would travel all night and all day tomorrow, hoping to put at least seventy-five miles between himself and the scene of the shooting. The bodies were sure to be discovered sometime during the coming day, and he did not intend to be around to answer questions. He guided the roan onto the main road and kicked the animal to a fast trot. The packhorses obediently followed. He would be in another county by daybreak, and in the town of Saratoga by the end of the week.

13

It was now the middle of March, and Rollins had been gone for six weeks. Just as he had expected, Zack had heard nothing from him. He supposed it would be at least another month, maybe two months. Even then, he would probably hear the sound of bawling cattle before he heard from Rollins. He was hoping that the Hereford bulls would arrive first, for he had already built a holding pen and hauled in hay bought from a farmer in Mills County—enough hay to feed the bulls till they were turned out to fend for themselves.

Zack, Jolly Ross and the newly hired hand had spent three weeks building the two-hundred-foot-square pen out of large poles, then devoted a week to the hauling of hay from the Middleton farm twenty miles to the north. Though the distance between the two points allowed for only one round trip a day with the wagons, Abe Middleton had priced the fodder cheaply enough that Zack, recognizing a bargain, had jumped on the deal immediately. The trio had hauled twelve wagon loads to the ranch, and had promised to buy more.

The newly hired hand was a twenty-six-year-old native Texan named Bob Human. Zack knew the man's age only because Human had told him, for his appearance offered no clue. With his mouse-colored hair and beard, agate-gray eyes, hatchet chin and faint streak of a mouth, he could have been young or old. He stood more than six feet tall and was the skinniest man Zack had ever seen. He seriously doubted that Human would weigh a hundred and thirty pounds. "Don't let old Bob's appearance fool you, now," Jolly Ross had said the day he brought Human to the ranch. "He's got bark on him an inch thick, and he can do just about any damn thing that comes along."

Ross had gone to town for supplies early in the morning and when he returned in the afternoon, Human was sitting on the wagon seat beside him. A saddled, mustard-colored mustang trotted behind the wagon. Zack stood in the yard watching as the men jumped to the ground and walked forward. "I want you to meet Bob Human, Zack," Ross said by way of introduction. "The two of us worked together in South Texas, made two trail drives together."

Zack took the newcomer's outstretched hand. "Good to meet you, Bob," he said, then motioned toward the cook-shack. "You fellows go on down and eat supper so you don't keep the cook waiting. I'll unload the wagon and put up the team." He got no argument from either man, for neither of them had eaten since early morning.

Immediately after eating, Human asked Zack for a job, and was highly recommended by Jolly Ross. "He's an awful good man to have around, Zack," Jolly said. "He knows what needs doing on a ranch, and he's been up the Chisholm Trail and the Western Trail both.'' Ross was quiet for a moment, then added, ''As soon as the cows get here, we're sure gonna be needing some men like Bob.''

Zack chuckled. ''All right, Jolly, you've got me convinced. Put him on the payroll and show him his bunk.'' He stood watching the men as they walked to the bunkhouse, noticing that Human's skinny frame was as straight as a fence post. And although a full cartridge belt circled his narrow waist, his overall appearance offered no hint of the tough character described by Jolly. Ross had said that Human could handle most anything that came along, so Zack had to assume that the man would be a little handy with the Colt that was hanging on his right leg. He would discuss that with Ross when he got the chance.

His chance came the following morning while Human was gone to the outhouse. ''Is Human pretty good with that Colt, Jolly?'' Hunter asked.

Ross was busy putting the finishing touches on a cigarette. He licked the paper, then chuckled. ''He's better than that, Zack.'' He put a match to the cigarette and took a deep drag, then blew smoke through his nose and mouth at the same time. ''He's the best I've ever seen,'' he added. ''And he probably thinks he's the best in the world. Whether he is or not, I don't know, but I'll guarantee you that there ain't a sonofabitch walking that he'd back down from.''

''I see,'' Zack said, and dropped the subject. Although it would be several weeks before he learned much about the man, there was nothing complicated about his story:

Born Robert Steven Austin Human during the first week of 1850, he was the only child of John Human, a hellfire-and-brimstone preacher and part-time cattle rustler. His birthplace was a dugout on Blanco Creek, a few miles from the town of Goliad. His mother died the same night he was born, and he was consequently shifted from one relative to another for many years.

The year young Bob was four, his father was caught red-handed stealing cattle, and hung from a tall mesquite only a few minutes later. The youngster was told that his father had died in an accident, and the story was repeated often. It was only after he started school that the boy learned the truth. When his schoolmates began to taunt him, dancing around and singing little songs about his father being a cattle thief, he carried the problem to his teacher, who refused to discuss the matter.

Not so with his Aunt Bess. When the youngster confronted her, she sat him down for a long talk. She had always believed that he should be told the truth, she said, but none of the other relatives shared her opinion. To a person, his kinfolk said he was too young to understand. Bullshit! Bess Remington had said, but had refused to argue with such an overwhelming majority.

Finally, the fat lady had put the "accident" story to rest when for the first time ever, the boy asked her a direct question concerning his father: had the man been hung for cattle rustling?

Bess Remington was John Human's older sister and had known him as few people did. She hugged her nephew to her breast for a few moments, then began to answer his question: "Yes, Bob, your daddy died at the end of a rope. Now, your Aunt Bess don't want you to go feeling hard at none of the kinfolks for lying to you. Everybody just thought it was the best thing to do at the time."

She kissed the youngster's forehead and tousled his hair. "You're pretty soon gonna be eight years old, Bobby, plenty old enough to understand grown-up truth talk. Now, you just listen,'cause what I'm gonna tell you is exactly that, so help me God." She kissed his cheek.

"Your daddy was a thief, son. He stole back home in Virginia and kept right on stealing when he got to Texas. He even did some of his stealing with the Bible, carried one everywhere he went. Now, he wasn't no real preacher, just had a good strong speaking voice and learned to quote a few verses of Scripture. I've seen him stand up in a chair right in the middle of the street and shout till a crowd of people gathered, then make your mother pass a collection plate. He never failed to laugh about it when he counted the money."

Aunt Bess talked to her nephew for more than an hour, ending with a suggestion that she thought might put an end to the taunting by his classmates. In his classroom the following morning, young Robert Human stood and asked the teacher's permission to address the class. When it was granted, he walked to the front of the room. Looking as many of the children in the eye as possible, he began to speak loudly: "My daddy was a cattle rustler, and got hung. I ain't like him. I ain't no thief."

As he headed for his seat, a loud round of applause reverberated throughout the room, led by some of the same children who had been taunting him. His teacher joined in the applause, then commented about what a brave little boy he was. The taunting ended that very day, and most of his classmates began to seek him out on the playground, eager to be his friend.

The start of the Civil War was the end of Bob Human's formal schooling. With most of the men away at war, boys his age were expected to fill the void: farming, tending cattle, whatever it took to keep the homesteads afloat. Young Bob chose to go to work for wages, and paying jobs were easy to find during the first year or so. As the war continued, money became scarce, however, and few people could afford a hired hand. Many was the time when Human put in a day's work in exchange for nothing more than hot food and a bed.

The year he was thirteen he went to work on the Kettle Ranch in South Texas, and stayed there for the next five years. By that time, he was an accomplished ranch hand and could almost choose the outfit he wanted to work for. He was also an accomplished gunman who had spent half of his life around weapons, becoming especially proficient with the single-action revolver. The forty-five-caliber Colt he wore buckled around his waist nowadays was widely known as the "Peacemaker," and Human's own name became well known after he shot three gunslingers to death in South Texas a few years earlier. Talk of Human's quick hand spread rapidly, and most men who kept track of such things gave him a wide berth.

Human's first cattle drive had been up the Chisholm Trail in 1872. Oddly enough, Jesse Chisholm, the man for whom the trail was named, never traveled it. Nor did he ever work as a cowboy, or own a cow. He was a trader, and the only cattle he ever owned were the oxen that pulled his trade wagons. On occasion, he used the upper section of the trail to reach his customers: the Indians and the buffalo hunters. When the cattle herds came up from Texas to Abilene, the drovers followed Chisholm's Trail from the Cimarron River to the present-day site of Wichita, Kansas, a distance of less than a hundred and fifty miles. The entire trail, however, was given the trader's name, even as far south as San Antonio.

Traffic on the Chisholm slowed after 1873. Most drovers moved to the Western Trail, a practice that would remain constant throughout the remaining years of the trail-drive era. The well-defined and well-marked trail was followed by virtually all northbound herds for the next twenty years, for even if there had been a need to vary from the relative safety of the established trail, few men had the guts and determination of a man named Nelson Story.

In the spring of 1866, Story came into Dallas, Texas, with a thirty-thousand-dollar stake he had accumulated in Alder Gulch. He bought six hundred head of cows for ten dollars a head, then undertook the longest and most arduous cattle drive in history. With a hard-bitten crew that eventually numbered twenty-seven hired hands and himself, all equipped with the latest rapid-fire rifles, Story moved the herd through some of the most dangerous, Indian-infested country on the frontier and arrived in Virginia City with all six hundred of his cows. The cattle had traveled more than fifteen hundred miles and seemed no worse for the wear. Story sold part of the small herd for a hundred dollars a head, but kept most for breeding purposes, thus becoming one of the leading stock producers of the area. Nobody tried to duplicate Story's feat for many years, for most men continued to hang on to the conventional wisdom that said it could not be done.

Bob Human had been up the Western Trail twice, accompanied each time by Jolly Ross. Sometimes Zack would ask one of the men questions about the trail when he was out of earshot of the other, wanting to see if he got the same answers from each man. He usually did. Once when Human had just answered a question about the trail, he asked one of his own: "Do you intend to make the drive yourself when you get ready to part with the longhorns, Zack?"

Hunter did not answer for a while. He had long been interested in the cattle drives north to the rails, had even read books about them back in Tennessee. "I don't know, Bob," he said finally. "I suppose it depends on what kind of scheme Mister Rollins has on his mind when the time comes. One of us should try to stay close to the ranch at all times, but knowing Bret, I'd say that he's liable to have something entirely different going by then."

Human seemed happy enough on the ranch, and just as Ross had said, appeared to be capable of handling whatever needed doing. Zack had even discovered while cutting firewood that he was an excellent man to have on the opposite end of a crosscut saw. Though he let it be known that he preferred to work from the back of a horse, Human was not shy about exchanging his boots for work shoes and digging into whatever chore was pressing.

Hunter had decided to hire some full-time farmers. He was fully convinced that two men who were dedicated to growing things would more than pay their way. He wanted a large garden that would supply food for the cookshack, and several acres of corn for horse feed. Today he was in town to spread word of his needs. When he found his farmers, all hands would go to work fencing in the acreage that would be cultivated.

They would first tear down the fence Zack and Jolly had built down at the old home place. They would haul the poles and posts north to the new place, then go about cutting and splitting rails, for they would need much additional material. Zack intended to quadruple the size of the plot he had originally intended to cultivate. Though he had been on the ranch for only a few months, he was already tired of buying horse feed.

Shortly after noon, accompanied by Jolly Ross and Bob Human, Hunter walked into the White Horse Saloon. "Good to see you again, Ed," he said to the bartender, then motioned toward his men. "You already know Jolly, and this long-legged drink of water beside him is Bob Human."

"Bob . . . Bob Human?" A look of surprise, then of admiration, crossed the bartender's face as he extended his right hand for a shake. "I've heard the name plenty of times," he said, "and it's a pleasure to finally meet you. My name's Ed Hayes, and I'm at your service." Continuing to stare with his mouth half open, the bartender was completely awed by Human's presence, and actually seemed a bit startled when Zack spoke again.

"Give us a bottle of that good whiskey," Zack said, pointing to one of the lower shelves, "and pour the first drink for yourself." Hayes set the bottle and three glasses on the bar. Then, just as he had been told, he poured a drink for himself before serving the others.

When each man had a drink in his hand, Hayes clinked his glass against the bottle and offered a toast. "Here's to the three of you," he said, and upended the glass.

Zack picked up the bottle and got to his feet. "We'll be sitting over there at that corner table for a while, Ed. If a good man comes in that you think might want a full-time job farming, you can tell him that I might be a source of steady employment." He headed for the table, and his men followed.

They sat drinking for a while, then Ross offered his own view of the farming situation: "I don't think you're gonna find what you're looking for in here, Zack. Every farmer I've ever known who was worth a shit was a teetotaler. Men of the soil just don't hang out in saloons like us cow people do."

Zack nodded, then sipped his drink. "I suppose you're right, Jolly. I'll put out word at the hardware store, the feed store and the livery stable. Farmers patronize all of those places."

A week passed before Zack found his farmers. He was in the cookshack eating an early supper when a man helloed the building. Dixie Dalton opened the door and took a look, then turned to Zack. "Two men out there sitting on mules," he said.

Zack was in the yard quickly. The bearded men, both appearing to be somewhere around middle age, still sat their mules. "I guess you'd be Mister Hunter," one of them said.

Zack nodded.

"Well, my name's Jed Peoples," the speaker said, then motioned toward his companion, who appeared to be a few years younger, "and this is my brother, Tom. Oscar Land says you've been looking for some help."

Zack had sized the men up at a glance. Both wore faded overalls and flannel shirts topped with blue-denim jumpers. Their brogans were run-over at the heels, and their battered hats had seen better days. "If you men are farmers, Oscar Land told you right," Zack said, motioning for the men to dismount. "Get down and rest yourselves."

Neither man made a move to dismount. They sat quietly for a few moments, then Jed Peoples spoke again: "Might not be no use in us dismounting,'cause we might be heading right back down the road." He took a sack of Durham from his coat pocket and began to smooth out a cigarette paper. "You see, Tom or me neither one don't like moving around from pillar to post. What we're hunting is a year-round job where the pay and the eating and the sleeping are all decent."

Zack chuckled. "Well, we eat and sleep about as good as anybody else that I know of, and I intend to pay a decent wage, but I sure as hell ain't gonna promise you a year-round job. Somebody's gonna have the job year-round, but whether it happens to be you fellows or not depends entirely on how well your work pleases me."

Jed Peoples put a match to his cigarette and blew a cloud of smoke. "Well, I guess you made all that plain enough. How much you figure on paying?"

"Twenty-five and found."

The brothers looked at each other for a moment, then nodded. "The money's all right," the elder Peoples said, smiling for the first time, "and you sure don't look underfed. Since you say you're gonna keep some farmers year-round, I reckon me and my brother'll take the job, if you want us. You sure ain't gonna find nothing wrong with the way we work, so I guess you'd be keeping us all year."

Jed Peoples dismounted, and his brother followed suit. Zack was soon shaking hands with his new hired hands. "Come into the cookshack and eat supper," he said. "Then you can feed and take care of your mules."

"These ain't our mules," Tom Peoples said as they tied the animals to the hitching rail. "Oscar Land just loant 'em to us, and we promised to bring 'em back today. We left all of our stuff at the livery stable anyway. Got to pick it up somehow."

"I'll lend you a team and wagon in the morning," Zack said. "If Oscar wants to charge you for keeping the mules overnight, tell him I'll pay it when I see him again."

The Peoples brothers shook hands with all three of the men in the cookshack, then began to eat like there was no tomorrow. Dixie, who always cooked more food than was needed to round out a meal, just smiled and continued to dish up the vittles. "Eat up, men," he said. "If you eat it all up, you won't have leftovers for dinner tomorrow.'' The newly hired farmers took Dixie at his word and did not stop eating till the pots were empty.

When the Peoples brothers had fed and watered the mules, Jolly Ross showed them to the bunkhouse. The farmers staked out a corner immediately, pulling a small table between their cots. Then, although it was not yet dark, the men nodded their thanks, stripped off their clothing and went to bed.

Ross left the bunkhouse quietly. He supposed that the farmers had just had a long day, or perhaps they had not even slept last night. One thing was for sure, he was thinking: if they went to bed this early every night, they were in for a hard time. Even now, Ross and Human kept the lamp lit for at least two hours every night. And in the very near future, the bunkhouse would be housing a full crew, which meant loud talking and poker games that sometimes lasted till midnight. Indeed, it could be that the farmers would have to build themselves a separate shack for sleeping—which would be easy enough to do; there was plenty of material in the lumber pile, and an extra heater in the toolshed.

The Peoples brothers left the ranch shortly after sunup, driving one of Zack's wagons. They were now on the payroll, and the cook had given them money and a list of supplies he needed from town. Tom Peoples sat on the seat waving his hat as the wagon rolled out of sight, Oscar Land's mules trotting along behind.

14

Zack had turned the job of fencing the cropland over to the Peoples brothers. They had built the fence in twenty days and were now busy breaking the ground with turning plows. No planting would take place, however, till the moon was in the right phase. At that time, the brothers would plow and harrow the land again, lay off the rows and bury the seed.

Hunter, Ross and Human had been building line shacks for almost a month, and had put the roof on the fourth and final building just this morning. They had equipped each of the cabins with a small stove and cooking utensils, and had built two bunks in each of them. Usually, only one man lived in a line shack at a time, but Zack believed they would need eight men riding line till the cattle learned which areas they could graze in without being hassled by men on horseback. He would hire as many men as it took to keep the cattle on H and R property; losing a longhorn cow was one thing, losing an expensive Hereford bull was quite another.

Zack was well-pleased with his farmers. Deciding early on that the men needed no supervision, he had simply told them what he wanted done, then left them to their own devices. And he could plainly see a change in the landscape every day. In what might have been record time, the brothers had built a strong fence around the acreage that was to be cultivated and were almost ready to begin planting. They had indeed found the year-round job they had been seeking.

Today was Saturday, and the month of April was already half gone. With Ross and Human at his side, Zack had worked for almost a month without taking a day off. The nonstop schedule had been warranted, however, for it was of the utmost importance that the line shacks be in place when the cattle were delivered. Habitable cabins now stood north, south, east and west, and he expected to hear cattle bawling any day now—a sound he looked forward to eagerly.

When the three men had eaten a meal of venison steaks and sweet potatoes at the cookshack, Ross suggested that they had all earned a night at the White Horse Saloon. Both Hunter and Human agreed that a trip to Lampasas was in order. Each man bathed in cold well water and changed into clean clothing. Zack and Jolly shaved, but Human was a man who probably did not even own a razor. '

Informing the cook that they would not be around at suppertime, they saddled their horses and took to the road. They reached town an hour before sunset, and Zack stopped at the livery stable to thank Oscar Land for directing the Peoples brothers to the H and R.

"I thought you'd be satisfied with them," Land said. "I reckon they've been farming all their lives, so they ought to know something about it."

When Zack remounted and turned his horse toward the street, Land spoke again: "I hate to mention it," he said softly, "but Jed Peoples said you'd give me a dollar for them keeping my mules overnight last month."

Zack had to smile as he handed over the money. It seemed that Land should be the one paying the dollar, for Zack had furnished two feedings of oats for each of the mules. Land was also smiling. He pocketed the money, then turned his back to continue his work on a wagon wheel.

The men had to tie their horses several doors down the street from the White Horse, and Zack had never seen the saloon so crowded this early in the evening. They stepped inside and moved against the wall, waiting for their eyes to adjust to the dim lighting. Though it was not yet dark outside, the light was already beginning to fade inside, and one of the bartenders was moving about the room touching fire to the wicks of lamps.

After a while, Zack shouldered his way forward and leaned against the bar. "Give me a bottle of the good stuff and three glasses, Ed."

The bartender was quick to comply. "If you're gonna be wanting a table, you better get it now," he said, pushing the bottle and glasses toward Zack. "This place is filling up fast; that new singer we've got is pulling them in."

Zack selected one of the few unoccupied tables within ear-shot of the anticipated entertainment. A portable riser containing what appeared to be a new piano had been placed a few feet in front of the stage. A burning coal-oil lamp lit up the instrument. A large poster tacked to the riser advertised the fact that Jess Hudson, a young singer and piano player from Waco, would be entertaining at nine o'clock. Zack looked at his watch and knew that he would not be around to listen to the singer. The time was only a quarter past five, and never in his life could he recall spending four hours in a saloon at any one time. He emptied his glass and poured himself another drink.

"I've heard that singer before, Zack," Ross said, touching a match to his cigarette. "He travels all over Texas. He was in Corpus Christi last summer. I don't know much about piano playing, but his music sounded awful good to me. He's got a strong baritone voice that's easy on the ears, and he seems to know a lot of songs. I liked his singing so much that I wound up giving him nearly a dollar before the night was over."

Zack nodded. "I have no doubt that the man knows what he's doing," he said, "but I can't think of many things that I'd wait four hours for." He refilled the glasses. "What do you say we drink up and get out of here, maybe move around a little and see what's going on at some of the other places?"

"I say we should have done that already," Ross said, emptying his glass and getting to his feet. "That piano player ain't gonna be around for several hours, and I sure don't feel like sitting here that long."

Human was already on his feet. He nodded and said nothing.

Ten minutes later, the trio entered the Twin Oaks Saloon, named for the two small trees that had been transplanted on either side of its entrance. The oaks were scarcely noticeable, and would remain so for the next several years. The name of the saloon had drawn a few chuckles from the town's drinkers early on, but after the laughing was done and the jokes were told, the name was accepted by all. And business was good most of the time. Hunter, Ross and Human stood just inside the front door for a few moments waiting for their eyes to adjust.

A narrow bar ran the length of the room along the left wall, with stools lining it on three sides. Only two drinkers were seated there. The area around the potbellied stove had been left to bare earth, while the remainder of the room had a creaky floor that was covered with a thick layer of sawdust. Men sat drinking at several tables scattered about, and one poker game was in progress.

Zack walked to the bar and made his purchase. Then, with a bottle of whiskey in one hand and three glasses in the other, he led his men to a table near the back wall. They seated themselves and had not even finished their first drink when they had a visitor: a tall, slim man with a black mustache, who appeared to be about thirty years old. With his battered hat pulled low over his eyes and a Peacemaker hanging on his right hip, he stood by the table for a few moments staring, a grimace of contempt on his face. Raising his upper lip sneeringly, he spoke to Hunter: "Ain't you the fellow that jumped on my friend Jiggs Odom a while back for no reason a-tall? Ain't you the fellow that hit him in the head when his back was turned?"

"Nope," Zack said quickly. He fastened his gaze on the man's bloodshot eyes. "The only run-in I ever had with Jiggs Odom was when I defended myself after he picked a fight with me."

The man shook his head emphatically. "Naw, naw," he said. "I happen to know that you snuck up on him." He looked Hunter over for a moment, then added, "I'm just wondering why you ain't wearing no gun. Scared, maybe?"

Before Zack could answer, Bob Human was on his feet, speaking to the man softly: "Look, fellow," he said, pointing a forefinger. "We all know that you've been drinking for a while and you feel like a giant, but there ain't nobody at this table that you can whip. I'm suggesting that you take a walk while you're still healthy."

"You're suggesting?" the man asked, turning to face Human. "You're suggesting? And who might you be?"

When Human failed to answer the man's question, Jolly Ross spoke. "He's not gonna tell you who he is, fellow, but I will. I'll tell you because it just might save your life. His name is Bob Human."

The man stiffened and began to stammer. "Bob . . . Bob Human? Bob Human from the lower Rio Grande country?" When he received no answer, he continued: "Well, I certainly don't want no trouble with you, Mister Human, no, sir. What I'd really like to do is shake your hand." He pushed his right hand forward for a handshake.

Human ignored the hand. He began to shake his head, then made a quick motion with his thumb, indicating that the man should be somewhere else. "Git!" he said sternly.

"I'm leaving," the man said, beginning to move across the

room sideways. "I sure ain't looking for no set-to with a man like you." He continued walking till he was out the front door.

Human reseated himself and reached for the whiskey bottle. As he refilled his glass, Zack was paying close attention to the man's hands, noting that they were as steady as a rock. Unusual, Zack was thinking. It was hard for him to imagine a man not being at least a little bit rattled after facing down a man who was obviously a gunfighter. Zack reached for the bottle to refill his own glass, all the while remembering Jolly Ross's words the day he brought Human to the ranch for the first time. "Bob Human's a good man to have around when the going gets rough," Jolly had said. "That skinny bastard's got ice water in his veins." Zack nodded at his thoughts, then began to sip his whiskey.

Bret Rollins arrived at the ranch two days later. Zack had just eaten an early supper and stepped into the yard when he spotted Rollins riding up the hill. Seeing Zack, Rollins waved his hat, then kicked his roan to a fast trot. He dismounted in the yard a few moments later, tying the saddler and the pack-horses to the hitching rail. He grasped Zack's outstretched hand and squeezed his shoulder. "Seems like I've been gone for a year or two, partner. This place looks good." He looked farther up the hill to the large stacks of hay and the pen that had been constructed to contain the bulls. "I'm glad to see that you're prepared, Zack; we've got cattle coming.

"I left the bulls on the Loon River two nights ago, and they should be here in less than three days. The deal I made with Baskin guarantees live delivery right here at the ranch, and he sent four of his own riders to make sure that happens. They're all good men, Zack, and they certainly understand the value of the stock they're driving. They look after those bulls like they were little lambs."

Zack smiled. "I like the sound of that," he said, taking a seat on the edge of the porch. "What kind of luck did you have in getting the longhorns?"

"Bought a thousand cows for five dollars a head. When Gonzalez offered to have the herd delivered here at the ranch for an additional dollar and a quarter a head, I jumped on the deal with both feet. His men already had about two hundred head gathered and branded when I headed for Fort Worth to get the bulls. I expect the longhorns to be here within a week or two.''

Zack sat quietly for a moment, then looked his partner squarely in the eye. "I'm proud of what you've done, glad I'm gonna be a part of what's about to take place here. I've dreamed about something like this for what seems like a hundred years, and now it's about to happen." He got to his feet and waved his arm toward the eastern meadow. "We're getting the cattle at the right time, Slick. Just look at all that green grass popping through. Another week and it'll be just right."

"I noticed it right away, Zack. If we manage to get a little rain once in a while, it'll grow faster than the cattle can eat it."

Rollins untied his horses and turned toward the barn, only to have Jolly Ross lift the reins from his hand. "I'll take care of the horses," Ross said. "Welcome home. Vittles are still warm over at the cookshack, and old Dixie's dishing up some mighty good stuff today."

"Thank you, Jolly," Rollins said as Ross led the animals away. "I'm hungry enough to eat whatever he's got."

The aging cook hugged Rollins as a father would a son, then served him a platter of roast beef, potatoes and turnip greens. The Peoples brothers had planted the turnips shortly after their arrival, and one of them usually picked a mess of greens for the cook each morning.

Dixie poured a cup of hot coffee and placed it at Rollins' elbow, saying, "It's nice to see a good-looking face around here for a change. Eat up." Rollins ate two helpings of everything.

Jolly Ross and Bob Human left the ranch at sunup the following morning, headed north. It was their intention to intercept the riders driving the bulls and lead them to the holding pen, which was within seeing distance of the ranch house. "I don't think you'll have any problem finding them," Rollins said to Ross as the two men mounted their horses. "They make enough noise to wake the dead."

"That's what I'm counting on," Ross said. He kicked his gray in the ribs and left the yard at a canter.

Long after the hands had ridden out, Hunter and Rollins

were still sitting on the doorstep talking. Bret had spent more than an hour filling Zack in on the details of his trip to East Texas. "Sounds to me like you had no choice but to shoot Joe Plum and his Cousin Billy," Zack said after learning about the incident at Bryan.

Rollins smiled. "Well, I had one other choice, which was to give 'em everything I had and let 'em leave my ass in the river." He chuckled loudly. "I didn't think you'd like that." They were quiet for several minutes, then Rollins broke the silence with a different subject. "Is Jolly Ross gonna be the ranch foreman?"

"That's the way I've been thinking, Bret. What do you say about it?"

"I don't say anything, Zack. As Grandpa Rollins used to say, 'That's your red wagon.' You have the full say-so about what goes on around here, and I don't have to be consulted about anything.

"I never intended to be a rancher or a cowboy, Zack, and still don't. I only worked at putting the ranch together because that's what you've always wanted, and I know that you'll turn it into a moneymaking venture." His smile widened. "Of course, me having the security of being half owner and knowing where my next meal is coming from is something else that I considered.

"I won't be spending much time around here. Fact is, I expect to be in town looking for a woman before the day is over, and there's no telling when I'll be back."

Rollins walked to his bedroom and returned. Handing Zack a canvas poke, he said, "The money you'll be needing is in here. The bulls are bought and paid for, but you'll have to finish paying for the longhorns when they get here. I paid Gonzalez half the money up front. The receipt and the paper on the cows are in the bag with the money.

"I don't know whether any of the riders driving the longhorns will want to sign on as regular ranch hands or not, but you're certainly gonna need more men than you have. I'd say it'll take twenty men to keep the cows on our property for the first week or two."

"At least," Zack said. "Don't worry about us having a crew. You just go on about your business. Ross and I will find the riders we need. We'll start on that problem just as soon as he gets back with the bulls.''

Rollins raised his hands and opened his palms, as if dropping a heavy burden. "It's all in you hands, Zack,'cause I'm gone. As soon as I shave, bathe and put on something that smells a little better, I'll be heading for Lampasas and some female company." He began to hum softly as he headed for his bedroom.

The Hereford bulls arrived two days later. Zack heard the animals long before he saw them. He saddled a horse and rode to the holding pen, then opened the gate and waited. He checked the water troughs in the pen to determine that they were full, with no sign of leakage. With each of the three troughs holding no more than a hundred gallons, they would have to be watched closely and refilled often with water hauled from the river in barrels. The water-hauling chore would not be permanent, however, for soon the bulls would be turned out on the range so they could get to the cows. Then they could fend for themselves.

Sitting in his saddle and looking north, Zack eventually saw Jolly Ross top the rise and begin waving his hat. Only a few steps behind Ross was a line of Herefords walking two abreast, with riders on each side. Now Zack could even smell the animals, for the wind was blowing just right. It was a smell that he savored and a sight that he relished as the bulls continued down the slope toward the pen.

Zack trotted his horse to meet the herd. Then, after it became obvious that his help was not needed, he simply watched as the bulls were driven into the pen and the gate closed. A beaming Jolly Ross dismounted quickly. "What do you think, Zack? Ain't they pretty?"

Zack did not answer right away, just sat watching the beautiful Herefords jostling each other for position at the water troughs. He was thinking of bygone days and trying to imagine how many times he had dreamed of what he was now witnessing. There before his eyes was his ticket to financial security, he believed. Though it would not happen overnight, or even within the next few years, the bulls would eventually breed every single drop of longhorn blood out of the herd that should be arriving from East Texas any day now. The very thought of having a thousand head of purebred Herefords running on what was still known and referred to as County Line Ranch made his mouth water. "Yes, Jolly," he said finally. "They're the prettiest things I've ever seen."

15

Zack put out the word in Lampasas and Burnet counties that he had year-round work for experienced ranch hands and in less than a week, eight men had been hired. "Counting Bob and me, we've got ten hands now, Zack," Ross said as he rolled his after-supper cigarette. "That's all the help we're gonna need. If you can talk the drovers who bring the longhorns into staying on the ranch for a few days to give us a hand, everything'll work out just right."

Zack nodded. "I'll let the offer of money do my talking."

Ross fired his cigarette and blew a cloud of smoke. "I was gonna mention that," he said, heading for the bunkhouse.

Jolly Ross stationed three men on the ranch's eastern boundary. Though they slept in the bunkhouse, they rode out each morning at the break of dawn. Their job was to position themselves a few miles apart along the ranch's eastern line and await the arrival of the longhorns, for the drovers would have no way of knowing when they reached H and R property.

When the herd was spotted, two of Ross's riders would join the drovers, while the third rode to the ranch to deliver the news. Then all hands would join in the effort and drive the cattle to a clearing that was at least a mile wide, located almost in the center of the ranch. There the cows would be counted and their brands confirmed. Then they would be allowed to wander off as their instincts dictated. A few days later, they would be joined by the Hereford bulls.

Ross was sitting in the cookshack sipping coffee when Slim Byers, one of the men who had been riding the eastern boundary, opened the door. "The longhorns crossed the Lampasas River yesterday afternoon," Byers said. "Guess they'll be here sometime tomorrow. One of the drovers was a long way ahead of the cows, looking for the H and R Ranch. Said he'd been asking people all day, but nobody had ever heard of it." He filled a coffee cup and sat down, chuckling. "I told him he'd been asking for the ranch by the wrong name, told him if he'd asked for the County Line Ranch, most anybody could have sent him in the right direction."

"That's what this ranch has been called since statehood," Ross said, reaching for his sack of Durham, "and that's what it's gonna always be called. Me and Zack were talking about that very thing a few days ago. He says it's almost impossible to change something that has become a tradition, and that he has no intention of trying. He says he'll keep using that H and R stuff for legal documents and brand registration, but that as far as he's concerned, this place is still the County Line Ranch."

"No damn use in changing the name nohow," Dixie Dalton said, stirring the contents of a large iron pot. "It's the same damn ranch, just a lot bigger."

Ross sat quietly for a few moments, then laughed. "I'll tell Zack you said that, Dixie."

Accompanied by Jolly Ross and all nine of his riders, Hunter met the herd on the east side of the ranch two mornings later. Ross quickly took up a position in front of the point men, signaling that they should follow him to the designated clearing. Then, with little or no conversation, Ross's newly hired riders scattered themselves among the drovers on each side of the herd, with two men falling back to help those riding drag.

Even with the arrival of more men and additional shouting, the cattle had never stopped. Nor did they show any sign of skittishness, for by now they were "trail broke." Hunter rode alongside the herd knowing that his presence was completely unnecessary. He was mostly watching the cowboys that hereafter would be looking to him for a paycheck each month. Every man had no doubt done it before, and it appeared to be second nature to all of them. Pleased with the way the riders worked, he nodded. Jolly Ross had chosen the men well.

Hunter rode along at a walk, mentally counting the drovers. He counted only ten men, with two more driving the horse herd. For some reason, he had been under the impression that moving the cattle west would take at least twenty men. Perhaps it had only been his imagination, he was thinking now, for the ten drovers, two wranglers, and a cook who drove a cart with oversize wheels, had obviously brought the herd from East Texas with a minimum of difficulty. And the animals appeared to be in good shape, indicating that they had not been pushed too hard.

Zack turned his bay aside and found himself a shady spot, where he sat watching as the herd passed him by. Then he joined the men riding drag and rode beside them for the remainder of the morning.

When the leaders reached the clearing, the herd stopped and Zack rode to the front. He saw very quickly that Ross had the situation well in hand. Sitting his gray with a pencil and notebook in his hands, Jolly was barking orders loudly: "Let's cut 'em out quick, men, before that bunch down the hill there gets too nervous! Cut out about twenty head at a time, check the brands, and run 'em over the hill before they have a chance to double back." He repositioned his horse, then called out to Human: "You count 'em as they cut 'em out, Bob, then sing out the figures to me."

One of the drovers was also counting the cattle, and Zack moved out of the man's way, content to just watch and learn. One of the things he learned quickly was that it did not take men such as these all day to get something done. He had been watching for only a few minutes and already a couple hundred head had been tallied and driven over the hill. Several riders were up there now chasing back the few cows that were trying to turn around and rejoin the herd.

As each bunch was counted and driven over the hill, more cattle were pushed into the clearing to be counted, and by midafternoon, the job was done. With several riders harassing them to make sure they traveled west instead of east, the longhorns began to scatter among the short hills and grassy valleys, and in less than an hour, most were out of sight.

The drover who had been counting the cows introduced himself to Ross as Jack Singleton, head man of the outfit that had delivered the longhorns. "Nine hundred eighty-five head is my count," he said, holding up his notebook. "How about you?"

"Nine hundred eighty-four," Ross said. He smiled broadly and reached for his sack of Durham. "Shall we call it nine hundred eighty-four and a half?"

"Sounds good to me," Singleton said, his smile revealing a broken tooth. "I guess you saw that young bull in the herd. He just insisted on tagging along after his mammy." He motioned toward the large number of riders, most still sitting their saddles. "Guess there's about enough of us here to eat him; then my count would match up with yours."

Ross began to shake his head. "No, I didn't see the bull, Jack, but we need to get him out of the herd right away. We've got Herefords in the pen, and we don't want a longhorn bull anywhere near this place."

"Well, there wouldn't be no problem with this one for a long time yet. He's way too young to breed."

"He's not gonna get any older, either," Ross said. "You got somebody you can send after him?"

Singleton did not answer, just motioned one of his men over and spoke to him: "Clint, I want you and Willie to go hunt up that little old bull and drag him back here. Shouldn't be too hard to find, he always follows that big yellow cow with the broke horn." Clint spoke with Willie for a moment, then both men galloped over the hill.

Zack and Singleton were soon standing beside their horses, shaking hands. "Where's Mister Rollins?" Singleton asked. "I was told that I'd be dealing with him."

"I have no idea where he is at the moment," Zack said, "or when he'll be back. He said he was gonna take a vacation. Anyway, I'm his partner, and I'm the man with the money. We can settle up when we get to the ranch house."

Singleton shrugged, then began to nod. "Sounds all right to me. You say you're the man with the money, I reckon that makes you the man to deal with."

They stood quietly for a while, then Zack spoke again: "I've been hoping I could interest you and your riders in staying around a little longer, Mister Singleton. You see, I have only ten men, and I need more help to keep the cattle on my own property till they settle down some. You think you could talk your riders into giving us a hand?"

The thick-chested, brown-haired drover stared at the toes of his well-worn boots for a few moments, wiping the sweatband of his battered Stetson with his hand. "I guess I could talk to 'em all right," he said, raising his eyes to meet those of Zack. "Trouble is, you ain't give me nothing to say to 'em yet."

Zack chuckled softly at the drover's choice of words. "Oh, yes, of course," he said quickly. "Here's my proposition: if your bunch will lend us a hand for two weeks, I'll pay each man twenty-five dollars."

"Twenty-five dollars," Singleton repeated. "With you offering that kind of money, I don't expect to have to do much talking. That's a damn sight more'n they're making now, and I figure you just hired yourself a dozen men." He walked into the clearing and held a short conversation with a cluster of men, then returned. "Yep," he said, offering a quick glimpse of the broken tooth, "reckon we're all on your payroll now."

Pairing each of his own men with one of the drovers, Ross assigned two men to each of the line shacks. The additional members of the combined crews, bedrolls behind their saddles, would concentrate on the north, south and east boundaries of the ranch. The drovers' cook would set up a feeding station on the east boundary for half the men, and Dixie Dalton would feed the other half in the cookshack.

Long before sunset, the riders scattered to their assigned areas. The young bull had been butchered and eaten for the most part, and each of the men going to the line shacks carried along a few pounds of fresh beef. By the time the cooks had brewed up a large pot of beefstew tomorrow, it would be just as if the young bull had never existed.

With the passing of each day, the line riders had less to do. After the first week, the longhorns settled down in a grassy, five-mile area that was somewhere close to the center of the ranch, where half a dozen creeks and springs watered the landscape. For the time being, they had everything they needed right under their noses and were relatively free from the harassment of mounted men. They were unlikely to ramble any great distance until such time as they needed new graze. Even then, they would move about slowly.

Ten days after the arrival of the longhorns, Ross opened the pen and released the bulls. Then, with the help of five riders, he drove the animals north to join the herd. Shouting loudly and swinging their ropes around and around, the horsemen forced the bulls to scatter and intermingle with the cows, an arrangement that appeared to be appreciated by neither sex.

The men stayed with the herd most of the day, mainly to keep an eye on the Herefords and make sure they didn't decide to go back to Fort Worth. Two hours before sunset, Slim Byers pointed down the hill. "Guess we oughtta go home while we've still got enough daylight," he said. "These bulls ain't going nowhere."

Ross followed Slim's point with his eyes. Two hundred yards down the hill, one of the bulls had separated a cow from the herd and was already earning its keep. Ross chuckled. "I believe you're right, Slim. I can't imagine anyplace where they'd have it made like they do here. Mother Nature will keep 'em right where they are."

The last three days the drovers spent on the ranch, they worked in the rain. With the collars of their slickers turned up and their hat brims pulled low, and without a single complaint from any man, they went about their assigned duties in a steady drizzle. Today was the last day of their two-week agreement, and tomorrow the drovers would head back to East Texas. Shortly after noon, with the rain still falling, Zack paid the riders off on the ranch-house porch. Jack Singleton, the first man in the pay line, accepted his money and commented on the rain: "It gets aggravating as hell to work in it after a while, but it's sure gonna be good for your cows. They're all gonna be standing knee-deep in grass about a week from now."

Zack smiled. "That sure won't make me mad."

An hour before dark, Dixie Dalton provided the entire crew with a supper of venison steaks. Then the regular hands retired to the bunkhouse, while most of the drovers carried their bedrolls to the barn. A short time later, Jolly Ross knocked at

Zack's door. Standing beside him was a man whose name Zack could not call. The only time he had seen him up close was in today's pay line, and no conversation had taken place at that time.

"This is Bill Moon, Zack," Ross said, pointing to the man with his thumb, "and he says he ain't lost nothing in East Texas. Says he'd like to stay on with us."

Zack returned the firm grip as they shook hands. The man had an uncommomly healthy look, and Zack gauged him to be about twenty-five years old. Dark-haired, with a smooth, weathered complexion, the green-eyed Moon stood a couple of inches over six feet tall. Broad at the top and narrow in the middle, his muscular frame appeared to weigh a little more than two hundred pounds. "Good to meet you, Bill," Zack said, releasing Moon's hand. "Both of you come on in and sit by the fire. I've got hot coffee on the stove."

They sat in front of the fireplace sipping coffee for a long time, talking about one thing and another. Nothing else had been said concerning Moon's request for full-time employment on the ranch. "Where do you call home, Bill?" Zack asked finally. "I mean, where did you come from originally?" He already knew the man was a Southerner, for he spoke with an accent much like his own.

"Came from Kentucky," Moon replied quickly. "Little town called Lexington." Bill Moon had left the bluegrass country in 1866. He had been raised on a horse farm fifteen miles northwest of Lexington, with the main road to Louisville passing almost through his stepfather's front yard. Will Brown, the stepfather, had married Moon's mother when the boy was only seven years old, and Bill lived and attended school under the Brown surname.

It was only when the young man struck out on his own that his surname once again became Moon. He remembered his father clearly. Manley Moon had been a large man who raised tobacco and thoroughbred horses. He also had a small blacksmith shop behind his house, where young Bill sometimes sat for long periods of time hoping his father would let him turn the bellows.

When Manley Moon was killed by a man who owed him money, no one was more incensed than Will Brown, who owned a much larger horse farm just down the road. The two men had been friends for many years, and it was only after a respectable length of time had passed that Brown began to court young Bill's mother, eventually marrying her.

Brown treated his wife and his stepson exceptionally well, and both had many more material things than ever before. Bill was given his own horse at the age of eight, and he could usually pick and choose any animal on the place that he wanted to ride. Consequently, he was an expert horseman by the time he was a teenager and could usually tell at a glance whether or not a horse was worth its salt. In fact, his stepfather had more than once asked his opinion on a horse that he was about to buy or sell.

Bill's mother died the year he was fifteen. Though the winter had been a hard one, the family had come through it with none of them even catching a cold. Then, when spring arrived and the weather turned warm, the lady went to bed with pneumonia. Three days later, she was dead.

With his mother in the ground, Bill made up his mind quickly that he would not remain on the farm and said as much to his stepfather. "I'm gonna be heading west in a day or so, probably all the way to Texas. I hope you don't mind me taking a good horse."

Will Brown did not answer for a long time. He sat staring at the doorstep, clearly unhappy at what he was hearing. "Guess I'd mind a whole lot more if you didn't take a good horse," he said finally. "You'd better take two. You'll need one to haul the things you're gonna need to carry."

Nothing else was said for several minutes. Then Brown broke the silence: "We both know that I've never tried to tell you what to do, Bill. I've always let you grow and learn at your own pace, and you've done both very well. You're already bigger than I am. Looks like you might turn out to be as big as your daddy was, and you know near as much about horseflesh as anybody needs to know.

"I don't want you to leave, but like I say, I've always let you call your own shots." Brown rose from his seat in the porch swing and headed for the door, for it was approaching his bedtime. "Just don't run off without me knowing it," he said over his shoulder. "You'll be needing to carry enough stuff to live outdoors, and I'll make sure you've got some money to tide you over.'' He walked to his bedroom and a few minutes later, blew out the lamp.

Bill sat on the dark porch for a long time, trying to imagine what his life would be like where he was going. The things he had read and heard about Texas made the place sound like a different country—completely separate from the rest of the United States. He had also heard that a young man with a little know-how could find a job easily, for now that the war was over, cattle ranching was becoming big business.

Moon had been in Texas less than a month when he was bitten by the California bug. When he heard that a wagon master was headed west with a train that consisted of twenty families and more than forty guns, he signed on as a scout, with his only compensation the security of numbers and the food that he ate.

He spent two years in California, performing a wide assortment of jobs to sustain himself. It was during this period that he became an expert with both the long and the short gun. In the spring of 1868, he shot a well-known gunslinger dead in the middle of the street in San Francisco. The gunman had been well connected with some of the city fathers, however, and Moon was forced to leave town in the middle of the night, one jump ahead of a posse.

His diligent pursuers overtook him in Sacramento a few days later, and Moon killed one member of the posse and wounded another in the ensuing shootout. He then headed east to the Great Basin. He crossed the relatively new state of Nevada at a steady pace, then turned south into Arizona Territory.

On the same day he reached the Territory, he changed his name to Bill Barnes, a name that was also to become well known. Within a period of less than five years, Barnes outdrew and killed six men with his six-shooter, an 1860 Army Colt. Only one of the killings had been the result of a legitimate argument. All the remaining five had been gunslingers, or novices seeking a reputation.

In the fall of 1873, he left the name ''Barnes'' in Arizona and returned to Texas. Once again his name became Bill Moon. His quick hand and deadly marksmanship had earned him a reputation that he was determined to lose, and he knew that the first step was to rid himself of the big forty-four that had been riding low on his hip for more than six years.

Long before he crossed the Texas border, he rolled up his gunbelt and stowed it in his saddlebag. Never again would he walk about with the weapon on his hip, its cutaway holster tied to his right leg with rawhide. Such action was all too often viewed as an open invitation by gunslingers and novices alike. By reverting to his original name, and with no six-gun on display, Moon felt that he well might live out the remainder of his days in Texas without being involved in another gunfight.

That had been almost three years ago, and since returning to Texas, Bill Moon had been challenged by no man. Although he still owned the Colt, he kept it out of sight and always found a reason to be somewhere else when the conversations of men drifted around to gun talk.

Moon had developed into the type of ranch hand that was never out of work for long, and every time he had left an outfit, it had been of his own doing. He had gradually worked his way to East Texas and had recently signed on with Manuel Gonzalez to help deliver the longhorns to the H and R. Now that the cattle had been delivered, he was tired of traveling and on this very day had asked Jolly Ross for a steady job at County Line Ranch.

Now, sitting in front of Hunter's fireplace, Bill Moon finished his coffee and got to his feet. "Whether I work here or not, I'll be needing a good night's sleep," he said, speaking to both Zack and the young foreman. "You two talk it over, and Jolly can let me know something in the morning." Then he was gone to the barn, where his bedroll waited.

"What do you think, Zack?" Jolly asked, getting to his feet. "Do you think we should hire him?"

Zack answered quickly: "We've discussed this before, Jolly—you're the foreman. I didn't give you that job expecting to have to make your decisions for you. If you want to hire him, hire him."

"Well, I've been watching him pretty close, and he knows exactly what he's doing. He's a hand, all right."

Zack rose from his chair and carried his empty coffee cup to the kitchen. "I'll tell you one thing about Mister Bill

Moon,'' he said, dropping the cup in the dishpan. "He damn sure looks to me like a man who could plant and plow his own garden.''

Ross laughed loudly. "Ain't that the truth?'' He turned toward the doorway, adding, "I'll sign him up in the morning.''

16

By late spring of 1878, the longhorn cows had been on County Line Ranch for more than two years and most of them had already dropped a second calf. Though of mixed blood, the young cattle leaned heavily toward the appearance of their Hereford sires, and in a few cases, not a single sign of their longhorn ancestry could be detected.

Today Zack Hunter was sitting his saddle aboard the tall sorrel gelding he had bought a month ago. He had been riding the animal all morning and had just stopped in the shade two miles north of the ranch house. Beside him, Bret Rollins dismounted to relieve himself. Rollins had set up residence in Lampasas more than a year ago, and last night he had made one of his rare appearances at the ranch. Even more rare was the fact that he wanted to ride around looking at cattle all day.

Zack dismounted and tied the sorrel to a bush. "I'm gonna move the longhorns up the trail to Kansas before the summer's over, Bret,'' he said, pointing to a cluster of cattle grazing on the distant hillside. "Soon as most of them wean their calves, they're gone.''

Rollins nodded. "I guess it's time.'' He eyed the northern horizon for a few moments, then spoke again: "I know it's something you always wanted to do, Zack. You even talked about it back home.'' He raised his eyebrows and smiled. "Are you gonna go up the trail yourself?''

"No, no," Zack said quickly. "There was a time when I seriously thought about it, but I've learned a few things since then. The drive takes months to complete, and I simply don't have that kind of time. I need to stay close to home, Bret. Not a day goes by without some kind of problem cropping up.

"I'll send Jolly Ross and Bob Human to Kansas with the cows. Ross says he'll need a dozen extra men but that he already knows where to find them. I'll just give him a free hand and let him hire his own crew. I'll put Bill Moon in charge of the operation here while Jolly's gone."

"Have you been in touch with a buyer in Kansas yet?"

"Nope. Jolly says you can do just as well by taking your cows on up and talking to several buyers after you get there. Says if you're lucky, your herd might become the object of a bidding war. He says he saw the price jump three dollars a head overnight back in seventy-three. That runs into some real money when you're unloading a whole herd."

"Yep," Rollins grunted, remounting his roan. "A difference of about three thousand dollars in our case." He pointed his animal south and led the way to the ranch house.

They ate dinner at the cookshack; then Rollins informed Zack that his visit to the ranch was over. He must get back to town and take an afternoon nap, for tonight he had a high-stakes poker game scheduled that promised some new blood and, hopefully, some reckless betting. It was his custom to sleep a few hours before a big game, for he always did better when his mind was sharp and well rested.

Last summer he had leased a small cottage at the edge of town, where he now spent most of his nights and cooked a few of his own meals. He seldom saddled his horse nowadays, for the walk to town was only a few hundred yards. A small corral surrounded a shed in back of the house, where the roan spent its time getting fat on daily handouts of grain and hay.

Rollins had bought two adjoining lots a hundred yards north of the house he was leasing, but had so far made no decision to build there. He was in no hurry. The lots weren't eating anything, and would only appreciate in value. Perhaps he would build something next year, but for now, he was happy enough with the cottage. It was quiet, the rent was reasonable, and late-night visits by some of the town's respected ladies went unnoticed.

Though he had never drawn it in anger, Rollins had been wearing a tied-down Peacemaker in public for more than a year. He had long since gotten used to the extra weight on his hip and felt less than fully dressed when it was not there. He buckled the six-shooter on each morning not because he thought he might need it during the day, but because he did not intend to be caught short, as had happened at least once in the past.

On more than one occasion, Rollins had laid his gunbelt on the bar and dispatched a would-be troublemaker with his fists while a dozen or more men stood around watching. No man had ever challenged his ability with the six-gun, for it was generally assumed that he would be as quick with the weapon as he was with his fists.

And the assumption was correct. Rollins had practiced for hundreds, maybe thousands, of hours and could now put a five-shot pattern in a three-inch square at forty feet. And he could do it as quick as any man alive, or so said Jolly Ross, who had watched him practicing on the ranch last winter.

"I tell you, Zack," Ross said after Rollins had ridden back to town, "if you ain't seen it, you've missed something." He hesitated for a moment, then continued: "Guess I said that wrong. You really ain't missed seeing nothing, 'cause you can't see it. All you see is a blur, then the targets start falling."

Zack had listened to Ross's description intently and well knew the truth of what he was being told. Rollins was simply quicker by nature than normal people, and his eye was second to none. Even as a schoolboy, he had been a winner at everything he did, and it seemed that his speed only increased as he grew into manhood. Not only had nobody ever caught him in a footrace, few had ever beaten him at anything. "Do you think Bret's as fast as Bob Human, Jolly?" Zack asked.

"At least!" Ross said loudly. "I'd sure never mention it to either of them, but I believe Bret's quicker." He extracted a sack of Durham from his vest pocket and blew on a book of cigarette papers to separate them. When he had selected one and filled it, he added, "It's hard for me to believe that there's another man any damn where who's as fast as Bret Rollins."

Zack shrugged and headed for the house, believing that his young foreman just might be right in his assessment.

Rollins left the ranch at a canter and tied the roan to the White Horse Saloon's hitching rail at midafternoon. He bought a beer at the bar, then walked to the center of the building, taking a seat directly in front of the piano. As was always the case on Saturday afternoon, Jess Hudson sat on the stool waiting for someone to ask him to play.

Rollins stepped forward and dropped a coin in the ever-present cigar box atop the piano; then, without a word, he returned to his seat at the table. No conversation had been necessary, for it was Hudson's business to remember which song was each particular customer's favorite. He riffled the piano keys a few times, then began to sing "Greensleeves," an English folk song that he said was more than five hundred years old.

Rollins stared at the table as he listened to the song. It had become his favorite the first time he heard it, and Jess Hudson had sung it for him several times a week for the past year. When the song was over, Rollins finished his beer, saluted the musician and headed for the front door.

Waving to a few casual acquaintances, he rode the roan through town at a trot. Long before he reached his cottage, he spotted the white piece of paper thumbtacked to his front door. He dismounted and walked closer. The big poker game that had been planned for tonight had been canceled, the note read, and had been rescheduled for the end of next week. The location had also been changed. Instead of taking place at the White Horse Saloon as had originally been planned, the game would now be played at the Longhorn Lounge in the town of Llano. The note suggested that Rollins count on spending at least two days in Llano, and it was signed by Clyde Post, a man whom he had faced across a poker table on more than one occasion. No reason was given for rescheduling the game.

Rollins read the note twice, then folded it and placed it in his pocket. He was convinced that the note had not been written by Clyde Post, for he believed the man to be illiterate. Rollins knew him well, and knew that he had been born and raised a hundred miles from the nearest schoolhouse. Even though he was a shrewd man, intelligent enough to put together huge holdings and large sums of money, he had about as much formal education as a jackrabbit. The note was written too neatly to have come from Post's hand, and being of a suspicious nature, Rollins intended to find out who had tacked it to his door. He would ask Clyde Post that question long before he sat down at a poker table.

Thumbing the tack back into the door for future use, he led the roan to the corral and stripped the saddle. He curried the animal, then dumped two scoops of oats in the trough. He had no set schedule for feeding the roan, just did it whenever it crossed his mind. Consequently, the horse had gained a hundred pounds in less than a year. Only this morning Hunter had mentioned the fact that the roan was too heavy and cautioned Rollins about overfeeding. "Many a good horse has been ruined at the feeding trough," he said. "Getting too much is probably almost as bad as not getting enough. You should cut that roan's feed in half when he's not working, and make it a point to feed him at the same time every day."

With such an unstructured life as was led by Rollins, feeding his horse by the clock was out of the question. He had no idea when he would be home. Indeed, some days he did not come home at all, and had more than once fed the roan after midnight. "I'll do that, Zack," he lied. "I'll cut down on his oats and start feeding him every morning at sunup."

At the house, he raised his bedroom window, pulled off his boots and stretched out on the bed. He dozed off in a matter of seconds and slept soundly for more than two hours.

He awoke at dusk and touched a burning match to the wick of his lamp. He replaced the globe and carried the lamp to the kitchen. He built a fire in the stove to heat water, then laid out a change of clothing. When the water was hot, he would shave and bathe as best he could before heading for Toby's T-Bone. The fact that he was hungry was only one of the two reasons he would be going to the restaurant. The other was Shirley Doolen, a twenty-one-year-old brunette who had been working there since the first of the year.

A tall, blue-eyed young woman who was exceptionally pretty, with curly hair that hung past her shoulders, her well-turned figure was often the main topic of conversation between male patrons of the restaurant. Shirley was a native of Corpus Christi. At the age of sixteen she had married a handsome young cowboy who turned out to be a cattle rustler. He had been caught red-handed a year later by a rancher in Duval County and was shot between the eyes.

Thankful that the union had produced no children, Shirley reclaimed her maiden name and headed for Austin, where she immediately found work in a dry-goods store. She held an assortment of jobs over the next few years. When not clerking in stores, she sometimes waited tables in restaurants or saloons. She preferred restaurants over saloons, for there was almost always less hassle, and if the quality of the food was outstanding, well-fed men were usually more gracious with gratuities than were the drinkers.

Her most recent job prior to Toby's had been at a drug-and-dry-goods store in Llano, which had lasted only one month. When her fat employer informed her that in addition to her regular duties, she was expected to occasionally spend an hour on a cot with him in the storeroom, she told him off and drew her pay.

She rode her own horse to Lampasas and found work at Toby's T-Bone the same day she arrived. She sold the horse to Oscar Land, who correctly told her that the animal was worth little more than the value of its hide. He called the horse a sway-backed jughead and offered twenty dollars. Appearing to think it over for a long time, she finally accepted the twenty and walked up the street. She did not tell the liveryman that she herself had bought the animal for eight dollars.

Bret Rollins became acquainted with Shirley Doolen the second day she was in town and took her for a buggy ride a few days later. In a matter of weeks, they became fast friends, then lovers, and on more than one occasion she had accompanied Rollins in his cottage late at night.

A rendezvous at Shirley's place was out of the question, for the cabin in which she lived directly behind the restaurant belonged to her employer. Toby was at least a little bit religious, and definitely not the type of man who would buy the idea that an unmarried woman needed a man around the house. Rollins was well aware of this and kept his distance from the young woman's living quarters.

And though Rollins and Doolen were lovers, they were not necessarily in love. They were simply two people with a strong sexual attraction to each other, and neither party saw any reason not to yield to the temptation. Each of them supplied the other's physical needs completely, and of late they had been getting together about once a week.

Rollins was not the only boat on the water, however. The lady dated other men on occasion, which was pleasing to him. He wanted her to be involved with others, for he was definitely not seeking anything permanent. Nor did he believe that she was, for she had never even hinted that she was looking for a long-term arrangement. The time they spent together was immensely enjoyed by both, and each of them seemed content to leave well enough alone.

Rollins had to make his dates ahead of time like anyone else Shirley dated, and almost a week ago he had made a date for tonight. Sometime after ten o'clock, he would bring her to his cottage for the fifth time. His whole body seemed to grow warmer at the thought.

Shaved and bathed now, he dashed his used water out the back door, then carried the lamp to the bedroom. When he had changed his clothing and checked his appearance in the mirror, he buckled his gunbelt around his waist and left the building, leaving the lamp burning in the living room.

As was always the case on weekends, the restaurant was crowded almost to its capacity, and the only vacant tables were on the opposite side of the room from Shirley Doolen's station. Rollins placed his order with a forty-year-old waiter, and half an hour later, his T-bone steak was served.

He ate his meal slowly. By the time he finished, he had been in the restaurant for more than an hour but had been unable to gain Shirley's attention. She had no doubt seen him, however, for when he walked to the counter to pay for his meal, she was suddenly standing beside him, her wrist and elbow bent to level the large tray of dishes she carried.

Not a word was spoken or needed. With a look of longing in her blue eyes that could not be misread, she smiled, nodded and winked. Bret returned the smile and the wink, then headed for the street. The signal had been sent and received, and no other communication had been necessary. Just as he had done on other occasions, he would meet her at the back door of the restaurant when it closed at ten o'clock.

With more than an hour to kill, he walked around town for a while, then stopped at the Twin Oaks Saloon for a beer. He had passed up the White Horse because he was not in the mood to listen to a lot of noise. The Twin Oaks would be much quieter, for the building was never crowded. Though Jake Smith, who owned the saloon and usually tended bar at night, was a very likable man, Rollins sometimes wondered how he managed to keep the place open. Unlike the White Horse, which was located in the center of town, Smith's establishment was well off the beaten path and most of the town's drinkers passed their idle hours elsewhere. Which was the very reason Rollins stopped by the place often: when he wasn't specifically looking for action, he preferred solitude.

"I'll have a beer, Jake," Rollins said, taking a stool at the bar. His eyes swept the room quickly, resting momentarily on each of the dozen or so customers. Though he had seen most of the men around town at one time or another, he could call none by name.

"There you are," Jake Smith said, placing the beer on the bar. "Thanks for stopping in, Bret." If indeed anyone could be aptly described as "ordinary," Jake Smith was such a man: medium height, medium weight, medium build. With brown hair and eyes, his physical description probably matched that of half the men in Texas. He placed his elbows on the bar and leaned forward. "I hear that County Line Ranch is about to take a herd to Kansas."

Rollins took a long sip of his brew, then wiped the foam from his lips with his sleeve. "That's what my partner told me this morning, Jake. Has he been talking to you?"

"No, no," Smith said, seating himself on his own stool. "I don't think I've seen Zack in at least six months. Seems to me like I heard that young County Line foreman talking about it in here last week. Believe he said he was gonna be hiring some more men pretty soon, and I think I heard him promise one man a job."

"Ross?" Rollins asked.

Smith nodded. "Yeah, that's his name."

Bret upended his beer and pushed the mug forward for a

refill. "Well, Ross has the authority to hire. If he promised a man a job, I'd say the man has a job."

Smith delivered another beer and refused payment. "I'm awful glad to hear that," he said. "The fellow's name is Eldon Mays, and he certainly needs a payday for a change." He was quiet for a moment, then added with a grin, "Maybe when he gets back from Kansas, he'll pay that ten-dollar tab he owes right here at the bar."

"Maybe," Rollins said. He looked at his watch, then got to his feet. "I have to be going, Jake. There's something else I've got to do." He waved good-bye and walked through the door. A short time later, he was standing in the alley behind Toby's T-Bone.

At a quarter past ten, Shirley Doolen stepped from the back door of the restaurant and into Bret's waiting arms. He cupped his hand under her chin and brushed each of her eyes with his lips, then kissed her hard on the mouth. "Ready?" he asked.

"Oh, gosh, yes," she said, almost at a whisper. She pushed herself away from his embrace. "Stand right here till I get a different pair of shoes." She crossed the alley to her cabin and lit a lamp.

Rollins stood in his tracks for ten minutes, then leaned against the restaurant wall for half an hour. When Shirley finally reappeared, she not only wore a different pair of shoes, but had changed clothing and completely rearranged her hair, which now hung loosely about her shoulders. He kissed her again and led her from the alley. When they reached the deserted street, they turned north toward his cottage. Then, hand in hand, they quickly disappeared into the night.

They awoke at about the same time, though neither spoke for several minutes. The plan had gone awry. The plan had been for Bret to walk the lady home long before daybreak, as he had always done in the past. Lying on the bed silently, each of them could plainly see, even through a drawn window shade, that the sun was shining brightly outside. "Dammit," Rollins said finally. He pulled on his jeans, then turned to Shirley, who lay staring at the ceiling. "First time I've overslept in years," he said.

"Not me," she said, pushing the covers aside and getting

to her feet. "I oversleep all the time, but it usually doesn't matter so much what time I get up." She stood beside the bed, making no effort to cover her nakedness. After a while, she peered around the edge of the curtain, shaking her head at the bright sunshine outside. "I very well might have to leave this town, Bret, but let me tell you one thing: last night was the best it's ever been for me. Ever!"

He smiled broadly. "Thank you." He kissed her several times, then pointed to her clothes. "Get dressed while I fix us some breakfast. I'll figure out a way to get you home without people seeing you."

Making no effort to retrieve her clothing, she sat down on the bed and began to shake her head again. "It can't be done, Bret. This is Sunday morning. Everybody goes somewhere on Sunday. Even the women and kids will be walking around, going to church or wherever." Finally, she reached for her underwear. "Forget breakfast," she added. "I couldn't eat if my life depended on it."

Rollins walked to the corral and fed the roan, then returned just as Shirley finished dressing. "I've got it figured out," he said. "I'll rent a team and wagon at the livery, let you lie down in the wagon box under a blanket and drive you right up the alley to your door. When nobody's looking, you can jump out of the wagon and run inside."

"Not on your life!" she said emphatically. "I won't be jumping and running anywhere, and I'm certainly not going to lie down in a wagon." She pointed toward the front of the house. "I intend to walk right down that road out there, and I'll hold my head up all the way home."

Rollins was quiet for a while, then made another suggestion: "Why don't you just spend the day here and go home after dark?"

"It won't work, Bret. I'm scheduled to work the afternoon shift, and Toby'd have a small army of people out looking for me."

He shrugged. "Well, we have no other choice then. Let me make a pot of coffee and finish waking up. Then I'll walk you home." He headed for the kitchen.

An hour later, they stepped out onto the road and began the ten-minute walk. No one else was on the road at the moment, and they set a quick pace in order to make short work of the jaunt.

They turned east at the first street they came to, then turned south into the alley. Shirley Doolen's cabin was two blocks straight ahead. As they walked down the alley, past several buildings, Rollins walked as close to the young woman as he could in an effort to shield her from eyes that might be peering from some of the windows.

When they were within half a block of the cabin, they could see a man standing beside the small porch, leaning against one of the posts that held up the roof. Rollins slowed his pace. "Do you know that fellow?" he asked.

She stopped quickly. "Yes. His name is Al Denning, and he thinks he owns me."

Rollins thought for a moment, then began to speak sarcastically: "He does, huh? Well, well. I wonder what kind of little things you could have been doing for him to give him that idea."

"Don't talk like that, Bret. That's not the way it is at all. I've dated him a few times, but we've never actually even been alone. He certainly never has been with me like . . . like you have."

Rollins did not speak to the girl again. He was thoughtful for a moment, then began to casually walk toward the cabin. When they were forty feet from the small building, they stopped again, for Denning had left the cabin and sauntered into the alley, directly in front of them.

A couple of inches shorter and thirty pounds lighter than Rollins, Denning was a handsome man. With dark hair and eyes and a fair complexion, he appeared to be in his late twenties. Though he wore no hat or coat, he was dressed expensively. A silk shirt that buttoned at the wrists hung on his well-proportioned body as if it had been tailored, and his boots appeared to be new. Riding in a low-hanging cutaway holster that was tied to his right leg with rawhide was a forty-four-caliber 1860-model Army Colt, one of the deadliest handguns known to man. Denning stood staring at the lovers without speaking.

Rollins was a man with a short fuse, and he certainly did not intend to tolerate Denning's insolent behavior. "You want something, fellow?'' he asked, looking the man squarely in the eye.

Denning ignored the question, and without taking his eyes off Rollins, began to speak to the girl. ''Been waiting for you since way before midnight, Shirley,'' he said sneeringly. ''After a few hours, it dawned on me that whores don't come home at night.'' He forced a silly grin, then chuckled softly. ''Whores spend the nighttime hours out gathering seed. Ain't that right, Shirley?''

The girl did not answer.

Rollins pointed toward the doorstep and spoke loudly. ''Go to your cabin, Shirley, and don't look back.''

The girl took several steps, but stopped again when she heard Denning's booming voice: ''Stop right where you are, Shirley! You ain't going nowhere.'' He turned his attention to Rollins and continued to talk. ''This sonofabitch you spent the night with ain't going nowhere neither.'' He began to lean forward, his hand hovering near the butt of his Colt. ''Fact is, the bastard ain't never going nowhere else,'cause I—'' Denning never finished the sentence, for he was now doubled over, coughing out his last breath into the already crimson earth. Rollins had shot out his jugular vein.

Though no match for the quick-handed Rollins, Denning had been relatively fast on the draw, and even after taking a shot in the throat, he managed to get off a shot of his own. He did not fire in the direction of Rollins, however. As his knees buckled and he began to fall over sideways, he took a shaky aim at Shirley Doolen, prompting Rollins to put another bullet in him. Even so, he managed to squeeze the trigger as his body hit the ground. The bullet missed the girl by no more than an inch. Due to the weapon's heavy recoil, Denning had been too weak to hold on to the Colt, and it now lay several feet from his body.

Convinced that the fight was over, Rollins spoke to the girl: ''Are you all right, Shirley?''

''I think so.'' She began to run her hand up and down her arm as if feeling for a wound. ''He . . . he tried to kill me, Bret. I could feel the wind and the heat both.''

Rollins nodded. Looking up, then down, the alley, he could see men coming from both directions. Most were afoot, but at least one man was mounted. "Get in the house, Shirley!" he commanded loudly. "Get inside and stay there." She disappeared immediately.

The man on horseback, whom Rollins recognized as Bill Saxton, was the first to arrive. He halted his animal a few feet from the body and sat staring for a moment. Then his eyes met those of Rollins, who by now had taken a seat on the edge of the porch.

"He tried to gun me, Bill," Rollins said, motioning toward the corpse.

Saxton nodded. "Looks like he fell a little short." He craned his neck for a better look at the body. "Ain't that Denning?"

"It is." Rollins looked up and down the alley again. A literal mob of men was approaching from each direction. Gunfire on a Sunday morning was a rarity, and it appeared that every man within hearing distance had come to investigate. Rollins spoke again: "You seem to be the only man around with a horse right now, Bill. Could I ask a favor?"

Saxton raised his eyebrows. "Ask away," he said.

"Ride down to Sheriff Pope's house. Tell him to get here as quick as he can."

Saxton kicked his horse in the ribs and was out of the alley quickly. The ride would take only a few minutes.

More than a dozen men were approaching the scene now, and Rollins left his seat on the edge of the porch. He walked to the center of the alley and, palms forward, held out an arm in each direction. "I'm gonna have to ask you to keep your distance, men!" he said loudly. "The sheriff'll be here in a few minutes, and he'll raise hell if the area's been trampled on." The men stopped in their tracks and began to mutter among themselves.

Rollins walked backward very slowly till he reached the cabin. He leaned against a post for a few moments, then reseated himself on the porch. He sat quietly while the crowd formed a half circle several yards from the body and continued to talk among themselves. A few of the men he knew. Most, he did not.

Twenty minutes later, Sheriff Pete Pope rode into the alley, followed by Deputy Hillman and Bill Saxton. Pope stepped from the saddle before his horse came to a complete stop and was forced to take a few quick steps to keep from losing his balance. He dropped the animal's reins on the ground, glanced at the body, then walked to Rollins, who was on his feet now. "Did you do the shooting?" the sheriff asked.

Rollins nodded. "Most of it. I fired twice and Denning got off one shot." Without being asked, he handed his Peacemaker to the lawman.

Pope checked the weapon's cylinder, then spoke to his deputy, who was standing by with a pencil and writing tablet in his hands. "Two empty shell casings," he said as the deputy began to write. Pope sniffed the barrel. "And this gun's been fired recently, probably in the last few minutes." He sniffed the weapon once more, then handed it back to Rollins.

He took a few quick steps and picked up the dead man's Colt. "Still got smoke in the barrel," he called to the deputy. "Army Colt with a spent shell in the chamber." He handed the gun to Deputy Hillman, then turned to face Rollins. "Were there any witnesses?" he asked.

Rollins had dreaded the question, and as much as he hated to involve Shirley Doolen, he knew that he must. There was no telling how many pairs of unseen eyes had witnessed the shooting, and those people would eventually be talking. He pointed to the cabin. "Miss Doolen was out here beside me. She saw it all and heard every word."

The sheriff stepped up to the porch and knocked on the door, identifying himself as he did so. The door opened very quickly, and Shirley Doolen stepped forward. "I hate to bother you, Miss Doolen," the sheriff said, "but it's part of my job to ask you a few questions."

"I understand," she said softly.

The deputy moved in closer to take notes. He had not spoken since his arrival.

Sheriff Pope wiped the sweatband of his hat with his hand, then cleared his throat. "Did you see the gunfight that took place here in the alley, Miss Doolen?"

"Yes, sir."

"Want to tell me about it? Just tell me in your own words what happened."

Shirley knew that anything she told the sheriff would very

soon become public knowledge, and she had no intention of discussing her whereabouts last night. She looked the lawman in the eye. "I was right there in the alley talking with Bret when Al stepped in front of us." She pointed to the spot where they had stood.

"Al and I weren't even close enough for him to be considered a boyfriend, but he was just as jealous as could be. When he saw me standing beside Bret, he started calling me all kinds of bad names. Then he threatened Bret and went for his gun." She wiped a tear from her cheek with her hand. "Bret shot him. Al tried to kill me as he was falling, and Bret shot him again." She held out her right arm and rubbed the elbow. "I tell you, Sheriff, I could feel the wind and the heat."

Pope was quiet for a while, then cleared his throat again. "Are you saying that Denning brought it all on himself? That he went for his gun first? That Rollins was fast enough to outdraw him even after Denning had a head start?"

"That's exactly what I'm saying, Sheriff!" she said loudly. "And that's exactly what happened."

"Would you sign a sworn statement to that effect?"

"I surely would."

Pope seemed satisfied. "I'll be expecting you at my office some time tomorrow, then." He turned toward the crowd. "It's all over, men!" he shouted. "I'd appreciate it if you'd clear the alley. What happened here was a disagreement between two able-bodied men. As is usually the case, one man won the argument," he pointed to Denning's body, "and one man lost."

Within the hour, the crowd had dispersed, the body had been removed from the alley and someone had shoveled dirt over the blood.

As Rollins walked down the alley toward his own cottage, Shirley Doolen watched through her window, knowing that but for his quick action, both he and she might well be dead now. She shed a tear and turned from the window. She would go to the sheriff's office and sign her statement tomorrow, then it would all be over. She had been a good witness, and her reputation was still intact.

17

Zack Hunter and Bill Moon spent the last two weeks of June moving line shacks. Rollins had played in the big poker game in Llano and had taken Clyde Post for a ride, winning several thousand dollars in cash and almost ten thousand acres of land that bordered County Line Ranch on the east. The ranch was now nearly twice its former size, and Hunter and Moon had torn down and moved the shacks to the new property line.

Zack had been overjoyed with the additional property, and had spent two weeks in the saddle familiarizing himself with every hill and valley. Rollins, however, had ridden across it one time, returned to town, and had not been seen since.

Jolly Ross had left for Kansas with the longhorns more than a month ago and should be well on his way by now. He had hired his riders wherever he could find them, mostly in area saloons. Bob Human was the only one of the regular hands to make the drive.

Hunter was pleased that Ross had chosen to take Human. After all, the two had worked together for years and understood each other well. As to keeping order among the crew, Zack believed that Ross and Human complemented each other. Few men, even when antagonized, would attempt to physically overpower a man as muscular as Ross, and fewer still would initiate gunplay, knowing that the price of such action might be a showdown with Bob Human. Indeed, Zack expected the drive north to the rails to be a harmonious and profitable trip for all concerned.

Hunter and Moon had just finished nailing the roof on the last of the line shacks and jumped to the ground. ''Glad that's over and done,'' Zack said. ''I believe I'd rather dig ditches than drive nails.''

''Not me,'' Moon said. ''Driving nails is a little easier on a fellow's back.''

Zack gathered up a few handfuls of dry wood, then picked up the coffeepot. ''Let's move over on the creek bank to make coffee and eat dinner. We'll set up the stove in the shack after we eat.''

Moon followed and built the fire while Zack dipped a pot of water from the clear-running stream. Snaking onto the property from the northeast, the creek was known throughout the area as ''Horse Thief Creek.'' The fact that another stream a dozen miles to the south was called ''Dead Horse Thief Creek'' left little doubt as to how the two streams had come by their respective names.

After washing their beef and biscuits down with coffee, they built two bunks inside the shack, then set up the stove. At midafternoon, they harnessed the team and climbed in the wagon. The ride home would take at least three hours.

When they reached the corral, Zack jumped to the ground and headed for the cookshack, leaving Moon to put up the wagon and care for the horses. He stopped on the small porch to wash his hands, then stepped into the cook's domain. ''I hope you've got some hot coffee, Dixie,'' he said, taking a seat at one of the long tables.

''Always,'' the cook said, reaching for a tin cup and the coffeepot. He poured the coffee, then pushed the pot to the back of the stove. He took a seat at the opposite side of the table and began to munch on a porkskin. ''You being out of pocket and all, I don't suppose you've heard the latest.''

Zack sat quietly for a moment, then shook his head and raised his eyebrows. ''What is the latest, Dixie?''

''Rollins killed another man last night.''

Zack did not speak for a long time. He was wondering how the shooting came about, and how long it would be till the next one. Rollins had attained the status of ''gunfighter'' now, and as his reputation grew, so would the number of men who were anxious to test his hand. ''Do you know who he killed?'' Zack asked finally. ''Or why?''

The cook shook his head. ''Don't know much about it. One

of the hands who was in town for supplies just told me that he heard it on the street. Somebody told him that Rollins shot a man dead at the Twin Oaks Saloon last night."

Zack nodded, then pointed to the big iron pot on the stove. "Is that stuff about ready to eat?"

"It's been ready all afternoon. I've just been letting it simmer, adding a cup of water every once in a while to keep it from sticking." He was on his feet now, dishing up a large bowl of the meaty concoction. "Made some crackling bread to go with this stew," he said, placing a large slice beside the bowl. "The farmers rendered a big tub of lard and brought me a whole bucketful of cracklings."

The art of making "crackling" bread consisted of simply dumping several handfuls of cracklings into a pan of cornbread mix, stirring well, then baking it all into a solid pone. It was not one of Zack's favorite things to eat, even though his mother had served it many times during his growing years. He had eaten it then, and he would eat it now. He crumbled the bread into his bowl and mixed it with his stew.

When he finished his meal, he dropped his empty bowl in the dishpan. "I'll be leaving for Lampasas in a few minutes, Dixie. Do you need anything that's small enough to fit in a saddlebag?"

The cook shook his head. "Can't think of a thing."

Half an hour later, Zack pointed the sorrel toward town at a canter. The big gelding could maintain the pace for the entire distance, for it was an exceptionally strong animal. Now five years old, it had been bred, raised and trained by a locally renowned horseman. And though Zack had paid a stiff price, he was well pleased with the deal, for the sorrel was not only the prettiest animal on the premises, it was the best saddle horse he had ever ridden.

Zack dismounted at the livery stable a few minutes before sunset. "I want to leave my horse overnight, Oscar," he said to the liveryman, dropping the reins to the ground.

"Leave him here for a month if you want to," Land said, reaching for the animal's bridle. "I tell you, Zack, my business has been way off lately, just a fraction of what it was this time last year." He stripped the saddle from the sorrel's back, then changed the subject: "I hear you sent a herd of longhorns to Kansas."

"They've been gone five weeks, Oscar. Guess they might be about halfway there by now."

Land nodded. "Guess so. Is Jolly bossing the drive?"

"He's the ranch foreman, and he's been up the trail before. Made sense to put him in charge of the herd."

Land had wiped the sorrel's back with a feed sack and was now busy with the currycomb. "You did the right thing, Zack. That boy knows what he's doing, and he's as honest as the day is long."

Zack nodded, then brought the conversation to an abrupt halt. He turned on his heel, saying, "I'll see you sometime tomorrow, Oscar." He walked down the street to the White Horse Saloon and stepped inside. He moved away from the door and stood leaning against the wall, waiting for his eyes to adjust. After a few moments, he could see every man in the building and quickly determined that Rollins was not among them. Moments later, he was back on the sidewalk.

It was already dark when he reached the Twin Oaks Saloon. Burning coal-oil lanterns hung on metal hooks outside the front door, and two men sat on the small porch smoking cigarettes. Both nodded to Zack as he stepped up to the door, and he returned the greeting.

Jake Smith himself was behind the bar and waved hello as Zack entered the building. Zack nodded, then walked to the far side and seated himself on a barstool, putting a large post between himself and the bright light.

Smith was there quickly. "Haven't seen you in a month of Sundays, Zack," he said with his usual smile. He pushed his right hand across the bar, and Zack pumped it a few times. "I got some of the best whiskey in Texas," Smith said. "Wanna give it a try?"

Zack shook his head. "Just a beer, Jake."

Smith pushed the mug of foamy brew down the bar, refusing the coin that was offered. "I guess you heard about what happened in here last night, huh?"

"Not much," Zack said, sipping at his beer. "The cook out at the ranch just told me that he heard there was a shooting in here."

"I'll say there was. That partner of yours put more holes in Johnny Gravity than a pincushion. Gravity got his gun out all right, but Rollins put three shots into him quicker'n lightning. Every time Gravity tried to raise his shooting arm, Rollins would pop him again. I'll tell you, I've seen some fast draws in my day, but the way Bret Rollins throws a six-shooter is just about beyond description."

Zack took another sip of his beer, then nodded. "I've seen it," he said.

"Well, by God, Johnny Gravity brought it all on himself," Smith continued. "He cussed out about every man in the building, including me, then finally got around to Rollins. Rollins gave him a chance to stay alive, told him to go sit down somewhere and leave people alone.

"Even after Gravity challenged him to a gunfight, Rollins gave him another chance to come out of it alive. He suggested that the two of them lay their guns on the bar, then fight it out man to man.

"Gravity wouldn't have any part of that. He cussed Bret again and accused him of having a yellow streak down his back." Jake stood shaking his head for a moment. "That was the biggest mistake he could possibly have made. I tell you, Zack, Rollins moved away from that table and into the aisle as quick as any man alive could have done it. He didn't eyeball Johnny Gravity long, either. About one second later, all hell broke loose."

Zack pushed his mug forward for a refill. "Did Sheriff Pope come around?"

"Oh, yeah. He was questioning everybody, wanting to know exactly what they saw and heard. Hell, there wasn't anything to do but tell him the truth. Every man in here stuck up for Rollins, and Pope was gone pretty quick."

When Zack knocked on Rollins' door half an hour later, Rollins answered with a double-barreled shotgun in his hand. As Zack stepped into the room, Rollins laid the weapon on a small table. "I'm just not taking any chances, Zack. A man never knows who might be prowling around." He seated himself on the side of the bed, then pushed a cane-bottom chair toward Zack. "I guess you heard about the fracas at the Twin Oaks last night."

Zack nodded. "Jake told me. He said you did everything possible to avoid the fight, so it sounds like shooting was the only choice you had."

"There was no other choice, Zack. The man was hunting a fight, and he didn't intend to stop looking till he found one."

"Who the hell was this Johnny Gravity?" Zack asked. "Where did he come from?"

"I talked with Sheriff Pope at noon today. He says the only thing he's been able to find out is that Gravity has been around town for about two months and that he came here from Austin. Nobody seemed to know what he did for a living, but he probably wasn't in a big rush to do anything. Pope said that when he searched the man's pockets, he found almost five hundred dollars."

Zack began to shake his head. "Nope. A man walking around with that kind of money on him probably ain't looking for a job." He walked to the kitchen for a drink of water, then returned to his chair. He motioned to the shotgun. "Are you expecting some of Gravity's friends to look you up?"

Rollins shook his head. "Not necessarily. Don't even know if he had any friends, but it's like I said—I'm not taking any chances."

"I sure hope not." Zack began to fidget in his chair, then changed the subject. "I'm gonna be spending the night in town, old buddy. Have you got anything stronger than water to drink?"

"Nothing but coffee," Bret said, getting to his feet. "I quit bringing whiskey home with me, 'cause I always end up drinking too much of it." Even as he talked, he had been busy buckling on his gunbelt. That done, he reached for his hat. "Let's walk down to the White Horse for a beer," he said. "Jess Hudson will probably be singing tonight."

Zack helped himself to another drink of water, then followed Rollins out into the night.

At the saloon, Zack said hello to bartender Ed Hayes and ordered a pitcher of beer. Then, carrying the pitcher and two glasses, he walked to the table Rollins had already selected in front of the piano riser. Hudson, who sat on the stool riffling the piano keys, playing no discernible tune, nodded to both men. Then the middle-aged musician eased into the familiar strains of the only song Rollins ever requested: "Green-sleeves."

The partners sat at the table listening to the pleasing sounds of Jess Hudson till they had consumed the entire pitcher of beer, at which time Rollins suggested something to eat. "I'd like to try the food over at the Hartley Hotel, Zack. I haven't eaten there in more than a year, but I've been hearing that they've got a good cook now."

"Lead the way."

Rollins laid a coin on the piano, then headed for the front door. Once on the street, he began to walk slowly toward the hotel. Good food was not his reason for wanting to eat at the Hartley, and in reality, he had heard nothing about the establishment having a good cook. His sole reason for suggesting the hotel was to avoid Toby's T-Bone. Shirley Doolen would be waiting tables there tonight, and he was simply not in the mood to see her.

They took a table against the wall in the dining room and each man ordered a T-bone steak. They sipped coffee while their meal was being prepared; their conversation was limited to the goings-on at County Line Ranch. "Guess the long-horns'll be on a train headed east within a month or so," Zack said.

Rollins drained his coffee cup. "Do you think Ross will get a good price for 'em?"

"I think he'll get as good a price as anybody else does. He's been there before and he knows how the business works. I believe he'll even stall if he thinks it'll get him another two bits a head." Zack finished his coffee and pushed the cup aside. "You don't know Jolly like I do, Bret,'cause you haven't been around him much. You can take my word for it, though—in spite of his young age, Jolly Ross is a damn smart cookie."

Their food was delivered by a humpbacked waiter who stood around the table until he was dismissed by Rollins. "Thank you," Bret said softly after it became apparent that the man was in no hurry to leave. "That'll be all we need for now." The waiter spun on his heel and disappeared into the kitchen.

Zack ate the smaller, tender side of his steak without comment, then attacked the larger side. After several attempts to slice the meat, he pushed it aside, resigned to making a meal of his beans and potatoes. "I wonder who buys the meat for the hotel," he said, a smile appearing at the corner of his mouth. "Surely it's not that good cook you mentioned."

Rollins laughed. "Maybe the cook and the buyer are both on vacation."

Zack had intended to spend the night at the Hartley Hotel, but Rollins would not hear of it. "Hell, Zack," he said, "didn't you see two beds at my place? You're the main reason I've got two bedrooms." He was quiet for a moment, then added, "Everybody else who stays there sleeps with me."

"I can easily believe that, Bret." Zack paid for their food, then led the way to the street. He pointed in the direction of Bret's cottage. "Since you're bent on saving me the price of a hotel room, I'm gonna let you do it. Lead me to my bedroom, sir."

They talked till late in the night. Zack lay on the bed with his hands clasped behind his head, while Rollins sat in a chair a few feet away. They discussed a variety of things, including their earlier days in Tennessee, but the main topic of conversation was the H and R Cattle Company. "The ranch might not make us rich," Hunter was saying, "but it's certainly gonna make us well-off. Jolly says we can run twenty-five hundred head without being overstocked." He was quiet for a moment, then added, "That property you won from Clyde Post put us over the top, Bret."

Rollins disagreed. "We're not over the top yet, Zack, not by a long shot." He got to his feet and circled the room. "But we're gonna be!" he said loudly. "Clyde Post has gotten wealthy dealing in land and cattle, and we can do the same." He returned to his chair and began to speak more softly. "I'm not through with Clyde Post yet, Zack. The old codger owns a large part of three counties, and I intend to get some more of it.

"He's not an easy man to beat in a poker game. If you happen to doze off, he'll put you to sleeping in the streets,'cause he understands the game and plans his strategy well. As you know, I got to him pretty strong in the game at Llano, but I damn sure didn't pick up any sleep while I was doing it. Post is convinced that I just got lucky, and he's dying to try me again. I'll give him a chance before the summer's out, but I want to let him stew a while first. I intend to hit him hard, Zack. Real hard.''

Hunter lay on the bed quietly for a while, then raised himself to a sitting position. "I've been wondering about something for quite a while," he said slowly, scratching his head. "The night you won all that land and money from Post, what were you using to cover his bet?"

"I really didn't need anything, Zack. The hand I was holding was a lock.'' Bret left his chair and walked to the kitchen, where he lit another lamp and began to wash some dirty dishes.

Zack followed and leaned against the wall. "Dammit, Bret, you know that I know how the game is played. What the hell did you put up to cover the old man's bet?"

Continuing to wash the dishes, Rollins spoke over his shoulder: "I bet the ranch."

Zack had suspected as much, but hearing Rollins say it seemed to turn his stomach over. He was thoughtful for a long time, then spoke dejectedly: "Damn, Bret. I've been content for over two years now, working ten or twelve hours a day, thinking I had a good home that nobody could take away from me. Now I find out that even while I'm sleeping after a hard day's work, you're betting the very damned bed I'm sleeping in on a poker hand."

Rollins dried his hands on a towel, then turned to face his partner. "Of course I know that you understand the game. I also know that you understand what a lock is: a hand that can't possibly lose." He laid the towel aside and returned to the bedroom, reseating himself in the chair. "I had a damn lock on Clyde Post, Zack. When you get a lock, you not only bet the ranch, you bet anything under the sun that you can get some sucker to call. In that sense, I guess I didn't really bet the ranch, since there was no way for me to lose."

"Humph," Zack grunted, and stretched out on the bed.

Rollins talked him to sleep, and the only thing Zack remembered next day was that Rollins said he was going to double the size of the ranch again the next time he played poker with Clyde Post.

18

J olly Ross and Bob Human returned from Dodge
City on the tenth day of September. After stalling
for a week and dickering with several different
buyers, Ross had sold the herd to a man named Thurston Starnes for eighteen dollars a head. "I considered myself lucky to
get eighteen dollars, Zack," Ross said as he turned the money
over. "For a while, I thought I wasn't gonna be able to sell
'em at any price. All the buyers want steers, and they're sure
not falling over themselves to bid on brood cows.

"We shot some of the calves that were born on the trail,
but we allowed the stronger ones to tag along. The cattle buyers wouldn't even take the damn calves as a gift. I sold a few
of 'em to the restaurants for ninety cents a head, then gave
the rest to a Kansas farmer. He had plenty of milch cows, so
I guess he'll be able to raise 'em.

"There's a whole lot more bargaining going on up there
now than there was a few years ago. With so many cattle being
driven to Dodge City, the buyers have the upper hand and
they know it. They'll try to pick over your herd, offering about
eight dollars a head for yearlings and seven dollars for heif-
ers." He lit a cigarette, blew a cloud of smoke to the wind,
then continued: "I expect the day to come when they won't
even buy a brood cow, especially a longhorn. People back East
want better meat, and they're gonna get it. You did the right
thing, switching to Herefords.

"The longhorns are on their way out. Even now they're
being used mostly to stock the northern ranches. And the first
thing the northern ranchers'll do when they get 'em up there
is start breeding the longhorn strain right out of 'em." He blew

another cloud of smoke, then chuckled. "Ten years from now, longhorn cows'll be as scarce as hen's teeth."

When Ross paid off his crew in Dodge City, the riders scattered, with each man going his own way. A few found work locally, while others caught on with herds headed north to stock new ranches. Three of the riders had decided to accompany Ross and Human back to Texas, but made it no farther than Red River. There they met a drover who was carrying a herd to Kansas. When offered employment, the riders turned around and headed right back to Dodge City. The arrangement was pleasing to Ross, for all three men were slackers and he had no intention of taking them home to County Line Ranch.

Ross had turned over nine hundred forty-three head of cattle to Thurston Starnes and had agreed to give him the first chance to bid on the next herd he brought to Dodge City. Then, looking as if he were already mentally counting his profits, the Chicagoan wrote out a draft for sixteen thousand, nine hundred and seventy-four dollars. A local bank quickly converted the draft to cash.

Ross sold the entire herd of extra horses to a northern rancher for thirty-five dollars a head—five dollars a head more than he had paid for them at Lampasas. He had made enough profit off the animals to pay for the grub eaten by his crew on the entire drive. Even after paying off the riders and all traveling expenses, there was more than fifteen thousand dollars in the poke he handed to Zack Hunter.

The two men were still standing on the porch, with Zack commending the young foreman for a job well done, when one of the hands led Zack's saddled sorrel into the yard. Zack transferred the money to the saddlebags, then mounted. "Gotta get into town before the bank closes," he said to Ross. "I don't like the idea of leaving this much money lying around."

"I don't like the idea of you riding around by yourself with it, either," Ross said, putting a hand on the sorrel's bridle. He motioned to Bob Human, who sat his horse at the corral gate. Human rode into the yard quickly, a Winchester in his saddle scabbard and a Peacemaker around his waist. "I told Bob to ride into town with you," Ross continued, "just in case somebody wants to look in your saddlebags. You never know,

Zack; I believe that there is a certain breed of cutthroat who can actually sniff out money."

Zack nodded and smiled. "Maybe you're right, Jolly." He twisted in the saddle to face Human. "Glad to have you along, Bob. Let's go." They left the yard at a canter.

They had traveled no more than five miles when they saw four men riding down the slope from the north. When the riders reached the road, they turned west, riding to meet Hunter and Human at a slow walk. When they spread their horses out to the point that they blocked the road, Hunter and Human halted their mounts.

As the riders continued to advance, Bob Human removed his broad-brimmed hat. This to hide the fact that as he removed the hat with his left hand, he had slyly drawn his Peacemaker with his right. He now held the gun under the hat, cocked and ready.

Human had been riding on Zack's right. Just before halting the animal, he had moved his horse far to the right-hand side of the road, so that he had been able to ease his weapon out of its holster without being detected. Nor could any of the riders see that his holster was empty, for the hat blocked their view.

On the riders came. Staring at Hunter and Human coldly, they stopped their horses twenty feet away, still blocking the road. All four wore beards and had stringy hair that was badly in need of a barber. Their dirty clothing and dusty hats suggested that they had been living out of doors for a long time. Though each of the riders had a rifle on his saddle and a six gun on his hip, none had made a move toward a weapon.

At last the larger of the men, who was directly in front of Human, decided to speak. "We can do this peaceably," he said in a deep voice, his scraggly beard hiding every trace of the mouth from which the voice had come, "or we can do it the hard way, but we aim to have that money you're carryin'. Now both uv ya—" The man never finished the sentence, for Bob Human had shot out his right eye, the heavy slug knocking him completely out of the saddle.

Hunter was on the ground quickly, but even as he drew his own gun, he heard Human's Peacemaker bark twice more. Two of the remaining riders slowly fell from their saddles as

Zack brought his six-shooter to bear on the third. He held his fire, for the man had thrust his arms high above his head and begun to whine: "I didn't want no part o' this," he said, his high-pitched voice breaking. "I told 'em all that it'd prob'ly turn out this a-way.

"No, sir, I never did want ta do it, but they kep' sayin' we wuz all in it tagether, and they waren't gonna be no backin' out. I tell ya, I wuz plum' scairt,'cause them fellers wuz meaner'n a rattler. Yes, sir, I really wanted ta come tell y'all what they wuz up to, but they always watched me too close."

The man dropped his gun to the ground as ordered. Then Zack jerked him from the saddle, slapped him across the mouth several times open-handedly and slammed him to the ground. He stepped on the man's throat for a moment, then kicked him in the head. "You're alive for the moment, you sonofabitch, but I can change that very easily." He pointed to the ditch at the side of the road, where the runoff from recent rains was at least a foot deep. "I'm gonna be asking you some goddam questions, and I'd better get the right answers. Otherwise, you're gonna be breathing water instead of air."

Zack continued to stand with one foot on the man's chest. "All right now," he began. "How did you know we'd be carrying money today? Who told you?"

"One . . . one of th' han's that made th' trail drive."

"A name, fellow! I want a name!"

"Cain't remember his name. I . . . jist cain't remember."

Zack stepped on the man's throat again. "Would you know the name if you heard it?"

When the man began to make a strangling sound, Zack moved his foot. "Yes," was the answer. "Yes, I'm shore I would."

Zack spoke to Human: "Come over here and call the name of every man who was on that drive, Bob." Then to the man on the ground, he said: "Stop him when he calls the right name."

When Human began to rattle off names, he was stopped on the fourth name. "That's it," the man said. "That's it right there. Eldon Mays, that's him. I remember 'im real good now."

Hunter allowed the man, who said his name was Joe Brown,

to sit up and tell the story. It seemed that when Jolly Ross had paid off the crew in Dodge City, most of the hands, as well as Ross and Human themselves, had stayed around town for a few days of frolicky activity. Not so with Eldon Mays. Twenty minutes after receiving his pay, Mays made a beeline for Lampasas.

Showing no concern whatsoever for the well-being of his animal, he stayed in the saddle fifteen to eighteen hours a day, reaching home a full ten days ahead of Ross and Human. He lost no time in apprising Will Ballinger, a bearded outlaw of his acquaintance, that two men would be riding from Kansas to County Line Ranch with a poke full of money from selling a herd.

Ballinger immediately got in touch with Ted Peel, John Tate and Joe Brown, each man of Ballinger's own ilk. It was agreed to by all concerned that though Eldon Mays would take no part in the actual robbery, he would receive one fifth of the booty for supplying the information.

The original plan was to waylay Ross and Human several miles north of County Line Ranch, and the quartet had ridden fifty miles for that purpose. They had camped north of the ranch for almost a week before deciding that their quarry had somehow passed them by. When Ted Peel discovered the tracks of two riders and a packhorse headed straight for the ranch, the four outlaws headed south also.

Peel had been lying on the hill with a field glass trained on the ranch house when Ross turned the payment for the herd over to Zack. The outlaw watched as Zack put the money in his saddlebags and made ready to leave. Then Peel mounted and whipped his horse toward the slope where his partners were waiting, five miles to the east.

"Eldon Mays," Human said with a sigh after Joe Brown had finished the story. "That sonofabitch. Jolly had to threaten to kick his ass a time or two in order to get any work out of him, and after that happened, Mays pretty well kept to himself." He was quiet for a moment, then added, "I didn't think anything about it at the time, but now I remember Jolly talking about how quick Mays got out of Dodge City after he was paid." He shook his head a few times. "Just wait till Jolly hears about this."

None of the now dead men had moved after hitting the ground. Ballinger had been shot in the head, while Peel and Tate had been shot through the heart. Hunter pointed to the bodies and spoke to Human: "I owe you, Bob, and I won't be forgetting it."

Human shook his head. "You don't owe me anything, Zack. I acted in self-defense." He was quiet for a moment, then added, "Them sonsofbitches could have got that money if they'd gone about it right. All they had to do was hide along the road somewhere and gun us down. Like this man says, they'd just now found out that we were on the road and seen that we were about to get ahead of them.

"They didn't have time to ride ahead of us and lay an ambush, so their only chance was to ride down the slope and block the road. I don't know why and I don't know how, Zack, but I knew what the bastards were up to the second they rode out of them cedars up yonder."

"I can easily believe that," Zack said, beginning to uncoil his forty-foot rope, " 'cause you were certainly ready for them."

After cutting the rope to the necessary lengths, they tied the body of each of the dead men onto the back of his own horse, then picked up the four six-guns that still lay in the road. Joe Brown had dropped his gun when ordered to do so, and Ballinger's Colt had slid from his holster as he fell from the saddle. Peel and Tate had each drawn his own gun when the shooting started, but neither had lived to fire it.

After tying Joe Brown's hands behind him, Hunter tied his legs beneath the belly of his horse. Moments later, with each man leading two horses, Hunter and Human headed for Lampasas at a walking pace.

Two hours later, they rode down Main Street. Several men walked or rode alongside the horses asking questions, but received no answers. Refusing to make eye contact with anyone, both Hunter and Human continued to ride toward the sheriff's office.

Sheriff Pope was easy enough to find, for he was outside his office about to mount his horse when the two men rode up. As soon as Pope recognized the men from County Line Ranch and his eyes had taken in the horses carrying the dead men, he retied his mount to the hitching rail. "I can see what you've got there, Mister Hunter," he said, beginning to walk around the horses. "Now I'd like to hear the story."

Zack had not dismounted. "They tried to rob us out on County Line Road," he said, nodding toward the dead men. "Three of 'em paid a stiff price." He pointed to Brown. "This bastard here claims his name is Joe Brown. He was in on the plan right from the beginning, and he'll tell you the whole story." He turned in the saddle, looking the prisoner squarely in the eye. "You will tell the sheriff the whole story, won't you?"

Brown nodded. "Ain't got nothin' ta lose. Not now."

Pope did not speak again until he had finished walking around the horses and inspected each of the corpses. "Don't recognize but one of them," he said finally. "Ballinger's had it coming for a long time, and this certainly ain't the first time he's got it in his head to rob somebody." The sheriff untied Brown's legs and helped him from the saddle. "Come along, Mister Brown," he said, taking the man's arm and leading him up the steps toward the office. "I'm just dying to hear your tale of woe." He spoke to Zack, who had still not dismounted. "I'll be needing you and Mister Human to witness the confession, Mister Hunter."

Zack shook his head. "I'll have to do it later, Sheriff. I just sold a herd of cattle and I've got to get to the bank before it closes."

Pope smiled, then chuckled aloud. "By God, if I had that kind of money, I'd be anxious to get to the bank, too. Go ahead, we'll wait for you."

When Zack returned to the sheriff's office forty minutes later, Bret Rollins sat on the porch. "I just heard about you bringing in some dead men," he said, getting to his feet. "I was over at the White Horse shooting pool when Jim Whaley came in with the news." He pointed toward the sheriff's office with his thumb. "Bob pretty well filled me in on what happened."

Zack handed Rollins the receipt for the bank deposit. "This is what they were after, Bret. Eldon Mays sold us out."

"So I've been told," Rollins said. He glanced at the receipt, then handed it back to Zack. He stood staring down the street for a while, then spoke again: "I've seen Mays more than once lately, so he's still around town. You want me to hunt him up and kill him?"

Zack shook his head. "No, but I would like to get my hands on him before the sheriff does. Pope'll treat him too damn nice." He pointed toward the office. "We'll talk about it some more in a few minutes. Right now, I've got to witness Brown's confession."

"I already did that for you, Zack. All the sheriff wanted was a witness to what was said. Brown confessed to the whole thing, and Pope put him in leg irons and locked him in a cell. The sheriff ain't in the office right now anyway. He left Deputy Hillman in charge and trotted his horse off down the street. Deputy Morse rode off right behind him.

"I figure Pope's gone hunting Eldon Mays, and if he don't find him before Bob Human does, the grave diggers'll have one more hole to dig."

"Human's hunting Mays?"

"Didn't say so, but he sure had that kind of expression on his face when he left here."

Zack was already untying his horse's reins from the hitching rail. "Let's go," he said.

Rollins had noticed that both Pope and Human had ridden down Main Street, and he did not believe that they would find Eldon Mays there. Mays' hangout was the Twin Oaks Saloon, located well off the beaten path on a short street that nobody had bothered to name. The ride to the Twin Oaks took less than five minutes.

Only two horses were tied at the hitching rail, and both Hunter and Rollins recognized the long-legged buckskin as Mays' mount. They tied their own horses and walked through the batwing doors side by side. A man was seated alone at the far end of the bar, and Eldon Mays sat on a stool closer to the door, engaged in a conversation with owner and bartender Jake Smith.

When Mays turned his attention to the newcomers, he found that he was staring into the barrel of Rollins' Colt. Keeping the gun pointed between Mays' eyes, Rollins walked forward and jerked the man's gun out of its holster, tucking it behind his own waistband. Then he turned to Hunter, saying, "He's all yours, Zack."

Hunter handed his own Colt to Rollins, then jerked Mays off the stool, elbowing him in the mouth at the same time. Mays fell over a table but regained his feet quickly. Then he began to give a fair accounting of himself, proving very quickly that he was a much better fighter than Rollins had suspected. Nevertheless, Rollins was confident of the outcome. He turned his back to the fight, took a seat on a stool and ordered a beer, knowing that the conflict would end just like all the rest of the fights in which Zack Hunter was involved.

The tussle ended just as suddenly as it had begun, and Rollins turned his head to see Zack standing over the unconscious Mays. Then Zack walked to the bar. He had one shaded eye, a few bruises around his chin, and a single drop of blood fell from the corner of his mouth. "Give me a beer, Jake," he said. When the bartender complied, Zack walked across the room and took a seat at a table beside the unconscious man. He began to sip his beer and appeared to be waiting for Mays to regain consciousness so he could beat him some more.

Zack's full intent would never be known, for at that moment, Sheriff Pope and Deputy Morse walked through the door. Pope spotted Mays' feet and legs, which were well out into the aisle and in plain view. He was there quickly. "I see you found your man before I could, Mister Hunter. Is he still alive?"

Zack nodded. "Think so."

The sheriff was soon bathing Mays' face with a wet towel. Twenty minutes later, aboard his own buckskin, Eldon Mays was being led to jail, charged with attempted murder and attempted robbery.

After Rollins had filled Smith in on the day's happenings, the saloon owner set a bottle of his best whiskey on the bar. Hunter and Rollins were later joined by Bob Human, and the three sat drinking till late in the night.

19

When the Twin Oaks Saloon closed at midnight, Bob Human headed for the ranch, insisting that he preferred riding during the last few hours before daybreak. Not so with Hunter. He followed Rollins home, loosed his horse in Rollins' corral, then helped himself to the extra bed.

He could see daylight around the edges of the window shade when he opened his eyes next morning. He sat on the side of the bed stretching and yawning for a while, then walked to the kitchen. He kindled a fire in the stove, put on the coffeepot and reseated himself on the bed to await the coffee.

It was then that Zack noticed a large envelope lying on the small table next to the bed. He absentmindedly picked it up and read its face, then laid it back down with a chuckle. He sat shaking his head, wondering what kind of scheme Rollins was up to this time. The oversized letter had come from a Chicago firm and was addressed to ''Doctor'' Bret Rollins.

Zack was still sitting on the bed when Rollins, already fully dressed, walked into the room. After a cheerful greeting, Rollins moved the table farther away from the bed, as if to get it out of Zack's way. Then he quickly picked up the letter and carried it to his bedroom.

Though Zack knew that he himself would get a good laugh out of knowing what was in the letter, he would never mention it to Bret. The obvious fact that Bret had some kind of scheme going in which it was advantageous to pass himself off as a doctor surprised Zack not in the least. It had long been that way with Bret; even as a schoolboy, he had always had something in the works.

And whether that something was honest or dishonest had

been of little concern to young Bret. Zack knew of one incident in particular when a deputy sheriff had collared him on the school playground and carried him home to his grandfather. Bret and one of his young friends had recently canvassed farmhouses all over the area, soliciting cash donations to buy flowers for a well-known lady who had supposedly been confined to the local hospital for more than a week. The boys' pockets soon jingled with coin, and they laughed a lot.

Their scheme came to an abrupt halt when they told their story to a woman who had talked with the lady in question only two days before and knew her to be as healthy as a horse. The county sheriff was notified at once, and he quickly dispatched the deputy to the schoolhouse. Bret was easy to find, especially since the woman making the complaint had identified one of the culprits as "that blond-haired Rollins kid."

Zack walked to the corral and fed the horses while Bret busied himself making breakfast. As they sat down to the table a short time later, Zack discovered why Bret had volunteered to make breakfast instead of eating at one of the restaurants, as they usually did. Bret had wanted to show off his newly acquired skill at making biscuits. Zack eyed the pan with appreciation, knowing that Toby's T Bone turned out none better. He dumped some jelly onto his plate, then buttered himself a few of the hot biscuits. "Now that you've learned to cook this good, I don't suppose you'll ever get married."

"Aw, I suppose I will someday," Rollins said, speaking around a mouthful of ham. "I sure won't be getting married till after you do, though."

Zack chuckled and took a sip of his coffee. "Why in the world do you say that, Bret?"

"Why?" Rollins dropped his fork in his plate. "Hell, Zack, look at how many years we've been running loose together. A man don't take that lightly, my friend."

Zack stared at his plate for a moment. "No," he said, "I guess not." He knew that Bret Rollins might very well be the only true friend he had in the world; that aside from Bret's rough edges and the fact that their ideas of morals and scruples were worlds apart, Rollins loved him like a brother and would not hesitate to lay his life on the line if Zack were in trouble. Indeed, Zack suspected that most men lived and died without ever having a friend who would side them when the chips were truly down, and he knew that he had such a friend in Bret.

Zack finished his breakfast and carried his empty plate to the dishpan. "I've had an idea for several months now, Bret," he said, reseating himself at the table. "I think we should fence the ranch with barbed wire. Not only will it save us money on the payroll, but with some cross-fencing, it'll completely eliminate overgrazing."

Rollins spoke quickly: "I've thought of the same thing, Zack, and I believe you're right on both counts." He got to his feet and began to walk around the room. "But I think we should wait till next spring. You see, County Line Ranch is gonna be a whole lot bigger by then. Clyde Post is chomping at the bit to have at me in another poker game, and I intend to nail his ass to the cross long before springtime. Each time he's asked me about another game, I've begged off, wanting to let him stew a while longer.

"I saw him last week and told him I was ready to play, but he had to attend a cattle auction in Fort Worth. I won't rush it, Zack; my time will come. After the fall roundup is over, there won't be much else to do but play poker." He poured a cup of coffee and reseated himself at the table. "I'll tangle with Post in a no-limit game before the winter's over. The game might last a week, but I'll wait however long I have to for just the right hand. When I get him where I want him, I'll show no mercy. When I get done with Clyde Post, the H and R Cattle Company will be the biggest thing in this part of Texas."

Zack listened attentively and noted the tone of finality in Bret's declaration. "Sounds good, Bret," he said, rising to his feet, "but you know that I've never been one to count my chickens before they hatch." He walked to the back door and stood with his hand on the knob. "The farmers have got the last cutting of hay started, so I'll get on back to the ranch and help them out."

Rollins followed Zack to the corral and stood by while he saddled the sorrel and mounted. They said their good-byes and as Zack headed toward the road, Rollins called after him:

"The chickens should be hatching off sometime between now and Christmas, Zack!"

Zack spent a few hours in town taking care of business. One of the places he visited was the hardware store, where he inquired as to the cost and availability of barbed wire. Although there was more than one man in town who sold hardware, Zack had conducted the bulk of his business over the past two years with Casey Bagwell, a transplanted Tennessean whose establishment was advertised by nothing more than a tiny sign attached to a wooden stake that had been driven into the ground in front of the building. "Bagwell's Farm and Ranch Supplies," the sign read, although the grass was usually too high for the lettering to be seen.

Bagwell spent more than an hour arriving at an estimated cost of fencing County Line Ranch, and assured Zack that he could get the wire through his supplier in Dallas. "Glidden and Vaughn invented a machine a few years ago that spits out barbed wire mighty fast," he said. "Now I'm not saying that I can get it overnight,'cause they're probably selling it faster than they can make it. But I sure don't believe we'd have to wait very long, especially on a big order like you'd be making."

Zack had been studying a diagram and reading a description of the wire. He laid those aside now. "It's like I said, Casey. I won't be undertaking the job right away, but I definitely intend to fence the ranch next summer. I won't have to buy any posts, got a million cedars right there on the ranch. The more of 'em I cut, the better the grass will grow."

As he left the building, Bagwell called after him: "Let me know as quick as you can, Zack. Might take me two or three months to get the wire."

Zack took County Line Road and headed home at a canter. When he rode into the yard more than two hours later, Jolly Ross and Bill Moon stood by the porch holding the reins of their saddled horses. A small gray mule was tied at the hitching rail, and a bedraggled, middle-aged man sat on its back. One glance at the stranger told Zack that the man had not been eating on a regular basis. He did not appear to be sickly, but rather had a gaunt, hollow-eyed, hungry look. One knee protruded through a hole in the leg of his trousers, and the brogans on his feet were old and worn. He sat on the mule without the benefit of a saddle.

Ross motioned toward the man. "We were just about to take him to the sheriff, Zack. We caught him up near the line with a dead calf on that mule's back."

"The calf wore our brand?"

"No brand at all," Bill Moon said, "but we didn't need to see any markings to know that the little critter belonged to the H and R. We heard a cow bawling from more than a quarter mile away and went to have a look. We saw what the problem was as soon as we topped the rise: the old cow was taking on because this fellow had her calf on the back of his mule, shot right through the head."

"I shot that calf 'cause it had a broke leg!" the man on the mule volunteered loudly. "Bone stickin' plumb through th' hide."

Zack stood quietly for a while, then spoke to Ross: "Did you bring the calf home with you?"

Ross pointed down the slope to the tree that grew beside the cookshack. "I gutted it and hung it on a limb down there. Dixie said he'd skin it out and cut it up for the pot as soon as he gets around to it."

Zack walked to the tree and examined the carcass, which hung from the limb by its hind legs. When he returned, he took a seat on the edge of the porch. He motioned toward the prisoner and spoke to Moon. "Untie his hands and bring him over here, Bill."

Moon complied, and Zack pointed to the doorstep. "Have a seat there," he said to the man. "I want to hear your side of the story."

The man took a seat and began to rub his wrists. "Ain't done nothin' nobody else wouldna done," he said. "Whatcha gonna do when ya find a calf with a broke leg? Ya cain't jist leave it ta die, not when ya got folks at home that ain't et lately." His voice trailed off and he sat staring toward the river.

"How did the calf break the leg?" Hunter asked.

"I don't righteous know. Coulda stepped in a hole er sump'm. All I know is that it had been broke fer a while, 'cause th' blood had already caked and dried where th' bone popped through th' hide. Weren't no holes around nowhere close that the critter coulda stepped in, neither. It had prob'ly been a-draggin' that leg fer a day er two. I shore did't break that calf's leg. How'n th' worl' could I break that leg? I ask you that, mister."

Zack did not answer, just made a motion like a man breaking a limb over his knee for a campfire.

The prisoner read Zack's actions correctly. "No, no," he said, "not me. You might be strong enough ta do that, but I shore as hell ain't."

Zack could easily believe that part of the story, for he had been silently wondering how the emaciated man, who probably weighed less than a hundred thirty pounds, had ever managed to get the calf on the mule's back. Indeed, Zack guessed the little red Hereford now hanging from the tree limb would weigh at least two-fifty. Two hundred fifty pounds of deadweight. "Maybe you're stronger than you want us to believe," Zack said. "You got that calf on the mule's back, didn't you?"

"Took ever'thang in me," the man said with a sigh. "I drug th' calf over ta a little cutbank an' put th' mule on th' downhill side. Didn't hatta lift it very high." He took a tobacco sack from his pocket and began to roll a cigarette. "I shot th' calf jist as quick as I seen it had a broke leg. Had ta git it outta its misery, ya know. If I had cattle o' my own, I reckon I'd want another man ta do th' same thang ter me.

"Now I ask ya, what I wuz s'posed ta do? Wuz I s'posed ta ride off an' leave all that meat ta rot? Leave it fer th' coyotes? I've got a sister back at my dugout that's hungry, mister. Got a kid a-suckin' on 'er that's near 'bout four years old. She cain't wean 'im 'cause she ain't got nothin' ta feed 'im." He lit his cigarette and blew a cloud of smoke to the wind.

Zack had listened attentively. The man had told his story convincingly and had asked for no special treatment. Zack knew that the next decision was his alone, that he himself must make judgment and pass sentence. "What is your name?" he asked, "and what were you doing on my property?"

"Name's Wilf Berryhill, an' I wuz out hopin' ta git a shot at a deer. Didn't have no way o' knowin' whose property I wuz a-huntin' on."

"This dugout you mentioned, where is it located?"

" 'Bout three miles north o' where I shot th' calf is what I'm a-thankin'."

Hunter sat quietly for a long while, then spoke to Ross: "Cut the calf down and put it back on the mule, Jolly. Mister Berryhill and I are going to take a ride." When Ross had untied the mule and led it toward the tree, Zack spoke to Moon: "Put my saddle on a fresh horse, Bill, and saddle that little black mare for Mister Berryhill." Then when Zack crooked his finger at Berryhill and began to walk toward the cookshack, the man followed obediently.

Dixie Dalton stood by the stove stirring the big iron pot, which contained a concoction of beef, beans, onions, tomatoes and finely diced chili peppers. He pushed the pot to the back of the stove to simmer as the men walked in. "This stuff's about as done as it's gonna get," he said. "You fellows want some?"

Zack nodded and pulled out the bench for Berryhill. The cook placed a steaming bowl in front of each man, along with a thick slice of cornbread. Zack filled two tin cups with coffee and placed one beside Berryhill's plate. Then each man sat blowing into his bowl and his coffee cup, for the contents of both were too hot for consumption.

"Lordy, Lordy," Berryhill said after he had taken his first bite. "If this ain't some good eatin', I'd shore pay fer lyin'. Lordy."

The cook smiled his appreciation for the comment. "Eat all you want," he said. "I've got more than enough to go around."

When they finished eating, Zack spoke to the cook: "I heard you say you had more of that stuff than you needed, Dixie. Can you put enough of it to feed two people in something that's easy to carry?"

"Got some empty syrup buckets, and I saved the lids."

"A syrup bucket'll be just right," Zack said, handing him part of last week's newspaper, "and wrap up some of that cornbread."

Berryhill had stood by listening. "I 'preciate ya feedin' me, Mister Hunter, an' I c'n see whatcha doin' now. Esther's gonna be mighty beholdin' to ya."

Zack handed the bucket and the bread to Berryhill. "Let's go," he said.

When they walked into the yard, Ross called Zack aside. "I ain't gonna let you ride off to that dugout by yourself, Zack. I'm gonna send somebody with you."

Zack looked toward the yard, where Bill Moon sat on the doorstep. "Bill's already got his horse saddled," he said. "He can ride up with me."

"No," Ross said quickly. "I want to send somebody who knows how to use a gun." He headed to the bunkhouse to get Bob Human. What Jolly Ross did not know, and would never know, was that Bill Moon himself was the fastest and deadliest gunman on the premises.

Five minutes later, riding the mare and leading the mule bearing the carcass of the calf, Berryhill led off toward his dugout, the syrup bucket hanging by its handle from the saddlehorn and the cornbread tucked under his arm. Zack Hunter and Bob Human followed close behind. Zack carried Berryhill's rifle across his own saddle.

Berryhill led on for more than two hours, seldom looking at the men following. When he crossed the northern border of County Line Ranch, he pointed northeast and turned his mule in that direction. After another half hour, he stopped and pointed again.

The "dugout" was not really a dugout at all, although Berryhill had dug away part of the hillside to erect his dwelling. After driving several posts in the ground and framing a roof with small poles, the man had merely used an oversize tarpaulin to cover the top and three sides. The front side consisted of several different kinds of brush, and a blanket had been hung over the doorway. The fact that it was almost flush against the hillside protected the hut from the north wind, and Berryhill had dug shallow ditches above and on both sides to divert rainwater.

A cart with oversize wheels was parked in the yard, its shafts pointed downhill and dug into the ground. The box of the vehicle was covered with a small tarp. A knotted rope with a notched board at the bottom hung from a nearby tree limb, obviously a swing for the youngster to play on.

Zack sat beside Berryhill, his eyes taking in the place. "Do you think your sister's home?" he asked.

"O' course she is. She ain't got nowheres else ta go." He cupped his hands around his mouth. "Esther!" he called at the top of his lungs.

The blanket was pulled aside immediately and a tall, slender woman walked through the doorway. She stopped just outside the hut and stood with her arms folded. A small boy with his thumb in his mouth peered from behind her, his other hand hanging on to her ankle-length cotton dress.

Zack dismounted and walked toward the lady. Though deep lines creased her face and her dark hair had turned salt-and-pepper, he could see that she had once been an attractive woman. The sun, wind, rain and otherwise harsh life she lived had taken their toll. As he drew near, she smiled and began to speak: "I saw y'all a-comin' up th' hill, but I jist stayed inside a-purpose. Women ain't got no business bein' aroun' when menfolks is a-talkin'."

"Well, I don't know about that," Zack said. "Anyway, I just wanted to talk with you for a little while. My name's Zack Hunter, and—"

"My name's Esther Berryhill," she interrupted. "I used ta be a Martin, but I took my ol' name back when my husban' run off."

"I see. How long have you been here?" He pointed to the ground. "I mean right here?"

"Four weeks, maybe five. Been 'bout six months since we left Arkansas, though."

He nodded. "What did you do in Arkansas?"

"Farmed. At least we tried ta farm. Ya cain't raise nothin' on no rocky clay hillside where ever' bit o' th' moisture runs down ta th' rich man's bottomland. We fin'ly jist quit fightin' it, but thangs shore ain't got no better since we been on th' move." She pushed a strand of hair away from her face. "Ya said what ya name wuz, but ya didn't say why ya been askin' me all these questions."

"I just met your brother a little while ago. I own a ranch a few miles south of here, and he convinced me that you need some meat. We brought you a calf."

She looked down the hill, shading her eyes from the sun

with one hand. "I saw sump'n on th' mule, thought it wuz a deer. That's what Wilford said he wuz goin' after, so how come he's got a calf?"

Seeing that the lady was smiling now, Zack offered a broad smile of his own. "He couldn't find a deer," he said. "Anyway, a calf is easier to catch."

She nodded. "Well, we can shore use th' beef aroun' here,'cause it's been a right smart while since we eeb'm seen any." She pointed to the cart. "I've got jars enough ta put up th' biggest part o' that calf fer another day. Shore don't know how ya expect us ta ever pay fer it, though."

"I don't need any pay, Esther. You folks just butcher the calf and enjoy it." He turned and walked back to his horse. "I want to talk to you and your sister together," he said to Berryhill. "Can we go inside?"

Inside the hut, Zack seated himself on the block of wood he was offered and began to look around him. Though sparsely furnished, the hut was livable. A few pots and pans were clean and stacked neatly in one corner, while buffalo robes used for bedding were in another. Nails had been driven into some of the posts for hanging clothing. But even though the hut was dry and comfortable at the moment, Hunter knew that it would be woefully inadequate when the winter winds arrived from Canada. He could easily empathize with the plight of the Berryhills, and he wanted them off of this hillside before bad weather set in.

Continuing to sit on the wooden block, Zack offered the Berryhills a better way of life: he would build them a small house at the ranch that would be comfortable year-round. Wilf could help the farmers and work as a utility man, doing whatever needed doing at any given time. His sister could work as a domestic for the ranch's headquarters, looking after the boss's house and cooking a meal occasionally.

Wilford had already heard enough. "I c'n tell ya right now, Mister Hunter, that sounds like th' best deal we ever had." He turned to his sister. "Whatcha thank 'bout what he's a-sayin', Esther?"

"I thank th' same as you," she answered. "I've been worried ta death 'bout winter ketchin' us here." Then to Zack, she said, "I prob'ly ain't never eeb'm been in a house as nice as yore'n, but I'll shore try ta please ya."

"You'll do fine," Zack said. Twenty minutes later, he and Bob Human rode down the hill toward County Line Ranch. They had another cabin to build, for the Berryhills would be moving to the ranch in two weeks.

20

I t'll scare the hell out of most players in a big-money game, Zack," Rollins was saying as he pointed to the blank sheet of paper Zack had just signed, "and even get respect from a rich sonofabitch like Clyde Post." Turning the paper and picking up the pen, Rollins added his own signature. "Everybody in this country knows that you and I own County Line Ranch as partners. When the gamblers see that I can produce an IOU signed by both of us, they'll think two or three times before raising one of my bets. That's why I'm just gonna leave the upper part of this paper blank. I can write in whatever is necessary above our signatures."

Zack sipped at his coffee, then thumped the paper with a forefinger. "Don't know how well I'm gonna sleep at night, knowing you might be betting everything we own in a poker game. As far as I'm concerned, the ranch is big enough already. I just don't see any reason why we need more land."

"We need more land because we're gonna build us an empire, Zack. The H and R Cattle Company is gonna be the biggest outfit in Texas one of these days." Rollins walked to the kitchen, refilled his coffee cup and reseated himself on the bed. "Besides," he continued, "who says I'm gonna be betting everything we own? The IOU is just to put the fear of God in some of the bluffers." He blew air into his cup, then took a sip. "I'm not saying I wouldn't bet the ranch if the cards fell just right, but I'd damn sure have to be holding a lock. If somebody deals me a hand that can't lose, then wants to bet me a ranch or two, I'll sure as hell call his bet."

Zack got to his feet. "I'll be getting on back to the ranch, Bret. We're still putting up hay." He opened the door, turned and pointed to the paper. "Just be sure you've got a lock," he said. Then he began the short walk to town.

Zack had arrived in Lampasas late yesterday afternoon and spent the night at Bret's cottage. He had left the sorrel at the livery stable, requesting that Oscar Land trim the animal's hooves and nail on new shoes. Land had promised that he would be on the job at sunup, so Zack supposed that the horse was ready to travel by now.

After ten minutes of brisk walking, he realized that he was hungry and turned into the Hartley Hotel dining room for a late breakfast. Though he had never eaten a meal in the Hartley that he would recommend to others, breakfast was another matter entirely. There were not many ways to mess up an egg. Even Zack himself could fry one without breaking the yolk.

Half an hour later, he left the dining room, vowing to himself that he would never return. He had been served what was obviously yesterday's biscuits, a slab of fatty ham that was so salty he could not swallow it, and two eggs fried so hard that they were no longer even moist. Even the coffee was old and bitter, and barely lukewarm. He left the food and the coffee largely untouched and paid without complaining. Out on the boardwalk he set a fast pace for the livery stable. He would be home in a little over two hours, and Dixie Dalton would fix him a decent meal.

Twenty minutes later, Zack was on the road to the ranch, alternating his gait between a trot and a canter. He was thinking of his conversation with Rollins this morning and of Rollins' determination to build a cattle empire. And he was also thinking of the paper he had signed. Never before had he been asked to sign a blank sheet of paper, but Rollins' explanation that an IOU signed by both partners would give him a tool with which to manipulate the betting procedure in a high-stakes poker game made sense.

Zack himself had played enough poker to know that a player

who could put a little fear into an opponent gained an edge. In a no-limit game, where a player could bet any amount of money he wished, it was possible for one player to send another to the poorhouse on the turn of a single card. Consequently, any player who commanded such betting capabilities gained respect and could easily create shyness and timidity in his opponents. Bret Rollins was a master at such intimidations.

One reason Zack had put up no argument when asked to sign the paper was that he himself had no financial stake in County Line Ranch. Every acre and every cow had been bought with money that Rollins had accumulated through one scheme or another. Though Zack had invested his time and a certain amount of labor, he had lived well. The past three years had been the best he had ever experienced, and he had wanted for nothing. And he knew that he owed it all to his association with Rollins, without whom he might still be in Shelby County, Tennessee, harvesting crops from land that he did not and could never hope to own.

He stopped his horse and dismounted to relieve himself, then climbed back into the saddle. He resumed his pace and his thinking, smiling and nodding at his thoughts: nope, Bret would never lose the ranch in a card game, for just as the nickname Zack had given him implied, Bret was slick. The man knew the game so well that he always kept the odds in his favor, making it highly unlikely that he would lose money in the long run. Besides, no man ever lost a dime on a lock, and that's what Bret said he would be holding if he ever bet the ranch: a lock. Zack kicked his horse to a faster pace and nodded again. Bret just might pull it off, and Zack knew nothing whatsoever about bossing a cattle empire.

Several hundred second-generation calves and yearlings now roamed County Line Ranch. The purebred Hereford bulls had bred the half-Hereford cows, and the resulting young cattle revealed none but the characteristics of the Hereford strain. Shortly after the first of the year, John Peabody, owner of the Circle P across the river, had put in an order for thirty young bulls from this year's crop. The animals were now weaned, penned and ready for delivery. The price agreed upon before the bulls were even born was twenty-five dollars each. Today

Zack sent a rider to inform Peabody that he was ready to do business.

An hour after sunup the following morning, five Circle P riders appeared in Zack's yard. A tall, lanky redhead, who introduced himself as Willie Osborne, did the talking. "The boss sent the money for those young bulls," he said, "and we're here to pick 'em up."

When Zack stepped from the porch and into the yard, Osborne laid a roll of bills in his hand. "Seven-fifty," he said, a cigarette dangling from his lips. "If you'll give us a bill of sale and show us the bulls, we'll start trying to get 'em across the river. I'll bet a dollar that ain't gonna be no damn picnic."

"You're probably right." Zack had already written the bill of sale. He handed it to Osborne now, then pointed up the slope to the holding pen. "The bulls are young and scared," he said, "and about as wild as jackrabbits. You can probably get 'em across a lot easier if you drive some of the older stock ahead of 'em."

"I already thought of that," Osborne said, beginning to put another cigarette together. "Just didn't know how you'd feel about it."

Zack nodded and pointed to the pen again. "Just round up a few head of cows and drive them into the pen with the bulls. Let 'em mix for a few minutes and I believe you can drive 'em all across the river together. You might even be lucky enough to get one of the bulls's mammy in the bunch."

The riders, all of whom appeared to be less than twenty years old, turned their horses and headed up the slope at a trot. Zack walked toward the corral to saddle his own mount. The young men from the Circle P would probably need all the help they could get.

By the time he saddled the sorrel and rode up the slope, the men already had half a dozen cows in the pen with the bulls. Then, after allowing the animals a minimal period of time to sniff and investigate each other, Osborne opened the gate. With one man inside the pen yelling, the cattle rushed through the opening.

Zack sat his horse watching for the most part, only occasionally having to bluff a young bull back into line. The riders, excellent cowboys all, very quickly turned the small herd toward the river.

At the shallow crossing, where the river was less than two feet deep, the bulls balked at the water's edge. Not so with the cows. With only a little prodding, four of them took to the water and began to wade across. The young bulls, seeing that they did not have to swim, quickly followed. After only a few minutes, the entire herd was milling around on the west bank. Within half an hour, the riders had cut out the cows and driven them back across the river. Then, waving good-bye, they began to move the bulls west.

Zack released his horse in the corral and walked to the house. Esther Berryhill, accompanied by her young son, was standing on the porch. "I made a fresh pot o' coffee," she said, pointing toward the kitchen. "If ya don't need me fer nothin' else, I'd better git down there'n clean up my own place."

"No, no, Esther, you go right ahead." He tousled the youngster's hair, then added, "You keep things too clean around here anyway, lady. I'm not used to it." She smiled, then led the child toward her own cabin.

Zack filled a coffee cup and returned to the porch. All of the hands had ridden out to their respective jobs, and the cook was no doubt busy preparing dinner. He sat sipping the hot liquid and staring at the corral, reliving his most recent conversation with Rollins. Rollins had said that the big game might take place any time now, and that it might last as long as a week, with the participants spending as many as twelve hours a day at the table.

Though Zack had no doubt that Rollins had the stamina to wear down the much older Clyde Post, he also believed that Rollins might wait a year for the perfect poker hand and never get it. Situations where one player drew a lock without his opponent knowing it were rare. Incidents of a man drawing a lock without his opponent even suspecting it were rarer still. And Rollins himself had said that Post was a good poker player.

Zack dashed his coffee grounds into the yard and got to his feet. Rollins might have a long wait in front of him, he was thinking. Bret had beaten Post before, and it only made sense to expect the man to be more wary this time. Even as Rollins was setting him up for the big ambush, Post would no doubt be setting a few traps of his own.

Zack set his empty cup in the dishpan. Then, taking some cheese for bait, he walked to the shed for his fishing pole. Even as he dropped his line in the river several minutes later, he was still thinking of Rollins' ambition to build a cattle empire at Clyde Post's expense.

Zack himself needed no empire to be happy. County Line Ranch was larger than most, and more than a thousand head of Herefords roamed its acreage. Less than four years ago, neither of the partners had had a pot to piss in. Now they owned the H and R Cattle Company lock, stock and barrel, and owed money to no man.

While it was true that the partners had acquired their holdings through nothing more than Bret's conning and poker playing, Zack believed that County Line Ranch would provide a lifetime of financial security for both men, and he spent none of his time dreaming of an empire. He also believed that part of being a good poker player was knowing when to quit. He wished that Bret would do exactly that and move back to the ranch. If he could get truly interested in the outdoor things in life, maybe he would quit gambling altogether, or at least learn to be happy playing for smaller stakes.

After an hour, Zack grew tired of baiting an unproductive fishhook. He returned his pole to the shed, then caught and saddled the sorrel. Mounting the animal, he headed north. He would spend the rest of the day riding about the land that he had grown to love and waste no more time thinking about the big game. And a waste it was, because Bret Rollins was going to do exactly what he wanted, and no suggestion from anyone, including Zack, would make the slightest difference. Zack dismissed the whole idea from his mind. What would be, would be.

21

Rollins was sound asleep when the pounding on his front door began. He opened his eyes and lay still, listening. There it was again: five loud knocks. "Hold your horses!" he called loudly. "I'll be there in a minute." He struck a match to the lamp, then pulled on his pants. Never one to answer a knock at night without easy access to a weapon, he opened the door with his Colt in his hand. Shirley Doolen stood there.

She chuckled softly. "You don't need a gun to make me surrender," she said, then laughed again. "I just got lonesome after the restaurant closed and decided to come down and spend some time with you." She handed him an object wrapped in brown paper. "I brought you a pie."

Rollins accepted the pie, but continued to block the doorway. "I . . . it's . . . we just can't get together tonight, Shirley," he stammered. "It's just not a good time for me. I've been going nonstop for more than twenty-four hours, and I don't feel very good. I—"

"Nonsense," she interrupted. She ducked under his arm quickly and was suddenly inside the house. "I'll rub your back and make you feel better all over." She headed for his bedroom.

Rollins stood in his tracks for a moment, then shrugged and walked to the kitchen, where he placed the pie on the table. He returned to the bedroom and stood in the doorway.

Shirley stared at Rollins' bed and its rumpled covering. In the middle of the bed, holding a blanket to her chest to hide her nakedness, sat a young woman whose skin was as white as cotton. The women stared at each other, but for the moment, neither spoke.

Sensing Rollins standing behind her, Shirley spoke over her shoulder: "I can see why you might be tired, Bret. As you said, twenty-four hours nonstop should be about enough to do any man in." Rollins said nothing.

Shirley recognized the woman as the wife of Reverend Thomas Jones, pastor of the little brown church a quarter mile east of town. Shirley had heard the young pastor preach on two occasions, and had once sat through a Sunday-school class taught by none other than the woman who now sat in the middle of Bret's bed. Somehow she looked less saintly holding up a blanket to cover the tits that Rollins had probably been nibbling on all night.

Shirley seated herself on the side of the bed, clearly enjoying the other woman's discomfort. "How is the Reverend doing nowadays, Mrs. Jones?" When the lady offered no answer, Shirley continued: "Don't you know that sneaking out behind the good preacher's back with another man will send you to the bottomest pits of Hell? Do you think the Lord or your husband either one is going to forgive you for lying around down here with your legs wrapped around a no-good sinner like Bret Rollins?"

Shirley got to her feet as if to leave, then seemed to have second thoughts. Standing at the foot of the bed, she addressed the woman again: "Guess the preacher's out somewhere spreading the Word tonight, huh? Is he gone from home so much that he just doesn't have time to take care of you? Or maybe he just doesn't know how to please you. Is that it, Mrs. Jones?" The woman did not answer.

"Yeah, I guess that's it," Shirley said, answering her own question. "I'll say one thing for you, you chose the right man. Bret knows all about pleasing women. Of course, any man with as much experience as he's had would learn about all there is to know. You and I are just two of the hundreds of women he's talked into his bed, Mrs. Jones." She spoke to Rollins over her shoulder, "Or should I have said thousands?" Bret continued to look at the floor and said nothing.

Shirley squeezed past him and walked to the kitchen, where she repossessed her pie. Then she stormed through the front door, slamming it so hard the small building seemed to shake.

Rollins stood just inside the front door for quite some time.

The small scratching and bumping sounds that he could hear outside told him that Shirley Doolen was still on the premises. A smile appeared at one corner of his mouth as he considered what she might be doing.

Five minutes later, convinced that Shirley was gone for the night, Bret picked up the lamp and walked to the front porch. As he had expected, the pie was everywhere, and it appeared to have been made from blueberries. The door had been smeared as high as a short woman could reach, as had both front windows, part of the wall, and the posts that held up the roof over the porch. The remainder of the pie had been splattered in one large gob against the bottom of the door.

Smiling broadly, he returned to the bedroom, blew out the lamp and climbed into bed. He would have to get up again before daybreak to walk Mrs. Jones to her own home.

He saddled his roan at sunup, intending to visit County Line Ranch. After walking the lady home, he had cooked sausage and gravy for his breakfast, then sat around drinking coffee as he waited for his horse to eat a bucket of oats.

Mounting, he rode to the front of the house and sat looking at the mess Shirley Doolen had made. She had done him up good, all right, and he believed that the stains would be difficult to remove. Nevertheless, the job must be done. He would make it a point to get back from the ranch in time to take care of it. Lye soap and a pan of hot water should work nicely.

He rode through town and turned left on County Line Road. The roan was frisky in the cool morning air, and Bret gave the animal its head. A steady canter brought him to the ranch in less than two hours. He tied his horse to the hitching rail in the ranch-house yard, then began to look around. The only sign of life he saw was the gray smoke coming from the flue down at the cookshack. He headed in that direction. Stepping up onto the small porch, he knocked once, then entered the building. "Where is everybody?" he asked loudly.

Dixie Dalton was busy preparing something at the stove. "Hey, Mister Rollins," he said, reaching for a coffee cup. "Don't reckon there's nobody here but you and me right now. All the hands are out at work, and Mister Hunter and Jolly took a wagon and went up north to butcher that bull." He set the steaming cup in front of Rollins. "Damn bull broke its leg, and wouldn't you just know that it would be one of them expensive Herefords?

"Anyway, they went up to see how much of the meat they can save. They could leave it all for the coyotes as far as I'm concerned. You have to boil it all day before it gets tender enough for stew, and it damn sure ain't worth a shit for anything else."

The cook poured a cup of coffee for himself, then joined Rollins at the table. "I probably drink enough of this stuff to kill me," he said, pointing to his cup. "Bet I drink no less than thirty cups a day."

Rollins smiled, then shook his head. "I never heard of coffee killing anybody," he said with a chuckle, "but thirty cups a day sounds like an awful lot of coffee. Fact is, thirty cups a day is an awful lot of anything, Dixie."

When Zack and Ross returned from their butchering job, Zack jumped off the wagon at the cookshack, while Jolly hauled the meat on to the smokehouse.

"Whose good-looking roan is that tied in my yard?" Zack asked jokingly as he entered the cookshack.

Rollins chuckled. "I heard you needed somebody to tell you how to run a ranch," he said. "I got here as quick as I could."

Zack poured himself a cup of coffee and joined Bret at the table. "Guess Dixie told you about the bull."

"Uh-huh. He must have stepped in a hole, huh?"

"I don't know how he broke that leg, Bret. I shot him right where he was standing, then looked around the area for a hole. I sure didn't find one. There was a pile of logs close by that he might have gotten tangled up in. One thing is for sure: he didn't travel far after that leg popped,'cause he was just too heavy. One of the two biggest bulls on the premises."

"Was he one of the original Herefords?"

"Yep. Best-looking one of the bunch."

The partners walked to the house, where they seated themselves on the porch. They talked for more than an hour about one thing or another. Then Rollins told him about Shirley Doolen smearing his house with blueberry pie.

Zack slapped his leg and laughed loudly. "That's a good one, Bret, best one I've heard lately." He continued to chuckle, then added, "Shirley caught you right in the act, huh?"

"She found a naked woman in my bed."

Zack laughed again. "I wish I'd been there to listen to you explain the situation, old buddy. Do you remember what you said?"

"Sure do. I didn't say a damn thing. What can you say? Shirley's a lot sharper than some of the women. Anyway, a naked woman lying in your bed at midnight speaks for itself, and any denial I made would have just made her hate me more."

Zack's laughter trailed off. "Well, maybe she won't shoot you."

Zack had spent much time thinking about fencing the ranch with barbed wire, and had recently spent three days riding the boundaries and counting imaginary fence posts. Now he brought up the idea to Rollins again. "I've made up my mind to fence the ranch, Bret. I'm just waiting on you to give me the word."

"I've thought about it too, Zack, and I believe it's the right thing to do. Just give me a little time to sit down with Clyde Post once more, so we'll know how much wire to buy."

Hunter nodded. "The wire and staples are all we'll have to buy—we'll cut the posts right here on the ranch. That'll not only save us money, it'll be good for the grass. We've got too much shade, Bret. We're up to our asses in cedars."

Rollins sat biting his lower lip. "Cut 'em," he said.

"Even after I order the wire, it'll probably take me two or three months to get it, plenty of time for us to cut the posts and sink 'em into the ground. Then when the wire gets here, all we'll have to do is stretch it and build a bunch of gates."

"Have you got an estimate on how much money the fencing is gonna save us on the payroll?"

"Well, about all I can do is guess. But I believe that after we get some cross-fencing done, it'll save us a lot more money than it's gonna cost. Right now, four men are wearing out eight horses a day keeping the cows on the property. The fence'll put them out of work the very first day and at the same time, give us the means to eliminate overgrazing."

"I like the sound of it," Rollins said, getting to his feet.

"I'll let you know something as soon as I can."

Zack followed Rollins into the yard. Rollins led his roan to the watering trough and stood by while the animal drank its fill. "I'll be getting on back to town," he said, mounting. "Gotta go see if Shirley's burned my house down." He kicked the horse in the ribs and pointed it toward the road.

It was midafternoon when he reached town, and he was hungry. He tied his horse to the hitching rail at a little Mexican restaurant, well off the beaten path. The establishment was owned and operated by a middle-aged Mexican couple named Alvarez, and Bret had eaten there many times. He took a table by the window and ordered stuffed peppers and a bowl of Mexican beans.

He was enjoying his food and casually looking through the window when a man rode down the street on a prancing gray gelding. Occasionally the rider would jerk the nervous animal to a halt while he looked over the people on each side of the street. He gave Bret's roan the once-over, then moved on slowly. He was obviously looking for someone in particular.

Though Rollins did not think he had seen him before, the man nevertheless had a familiar look. Wearing tight-fitting range clothing, he had yellow hair that hung almost to his shoulders, topped by a black, flat-crowned Stetson. Appearing to be about six feet tall, he sat his saddle as straight as a fence post, and Rollins could easily see the Peacemaker tied to his right leg.

Rollins continued to watch until the rider disappeared down the street. He was not a local man, Bret was thinking, and he certainly did not look like a cowboy. Rollins gauged the man to be in his late twenties, and in excellent physical condition.

After a while, he dismissed the rider from his mind and began to flirt with a young waitress. After making a date with her for Sunday night, he sopped his plate clean with a tortilla, paid for his food, then left the building. Mounting the roan, he turned the animal toward home. He had a mess to clean up.

A few minutes later, he sat his saddle in front of his cottage, a broad smile on his face. The front of his house was clean, with no sign that the blueberry pie had ever existed. He chuckled softly. Shirley Doolen had been here again. He would thank her and buy her a nice trinket, but he would not invite her back to his house. Not for a while, anyway.

He curried and fed the roan, scooping an extra portion of oats into the trough. The animal had a hard day's work coming up, for Bret intended to ride to the town of Llano tomorrow. He would seek out Clyde Post and convince him that the time was right for the big game. He would also insist that the game be played at the White Horse Saloon, right here in Lampasas.

At the house, he shaved, bathed and laid out clean clothing for tomorrow. Then he lay down on his bed and began to read. He was about halfway through a book—about a half-breed Indian named Sequoyah—that was very interesting. The man had no doubt been exceptionally brilliant and had, among other things, invented the Cherokee alphabet, which eventuality led to more than half of his people being literate. He had died in 1843, after gaining profound respect from whites and Indians alike. The sequoia trees, the giant evergreens of California, were named in his honor.

Sometime before dark, the book fell to the floor. The next time Rollins opened his eyes, he struck a match and looked at his watch. He had slept the night away, and it would be daylight in less than an hour. Just before the match burned his fingers, he raked it across the wick of the lamp, then got to his feet.

He soon had a fire in the stove and the coffeepot on. He dressed himself, then set about stirring up some breakfast. He would eat his ham and eggs without bread because he did not feel up to making biscuits this early. Baking bread was mostly a waste anyway, for he seldom ate more than half a biscuit.

While his ham was cooking, he fed his horse by lantern light. The frisky roan trotted around and around while the oats were poured in the trough, no doubt sensing that he was going to get out of the corral this morning.

Rollins ate his breakfast and washed the dishes, then sat down for one last cup of coffee. On the chair next to him hung his fleece-lined coat with the fur collar. Though the weather was unseasonably pleasant at the moment, he would carry the coat anyway. The weather was highly unpredictable in this part of the country, particularly in the fall, and the temperature could plummet in a matter of minutes.

It was broad daylight when he left the house, his coat in one hand and his Winchester in the other. He carried no bedding or blankets, for he did not intend to spend the night on the trail. He saddled the roan, shoved the Winchester in the boot and mounted. Then, guiding the eager animal to the road, he kicked it to a canter and headed southwest. It would take most of the day to reach Llano.

Rollins returned to Lampasas one hour before sunset three days later. He had met with Clyde Post and found the man ready to play poker. The game would take place a week from next Saturday, nine days from now, and would be played at the White Horse Saloon.

He rode straight through town to the livery stable. He had no more than a quart of oats at home and was completely out of hay, so he would leave the roan with Oscar Land for a few days. Riding through the wide front door, he dismounted and handed the reins to Land.

The hostler quickly stripped the saddle and began to wipe the animal down. "Pretty horse you got here," he said. "I've always liked him. I remember that you don't have to hold his feet up when you shoe him. He'll hold his foot right up there for you himself, just as pretty as you please. It's like he knows you're doing something good for him, so he's helping you out."

Rollins nodded. "Yeah." Then he jerked his thumb toward the nearest stall. "I saw that high-stepping gray there on the street a few days ago. Who does it belong to?"

"It's been here about a week. Belongs to a man who's been staying at the Hartley Hotel."

Rollins was not satisfied with Land's answer. "That was not the question, Oscar. What the hell is the man's name?"

"Denning," Land said dejectedly. "Told me his name was Leo Denning."

Leo Denning! Rollins repeated to himself. He immediately thought of Al Denning, the man he had shot in the alley beside Shirley Doolen's house. He now understood why Leo Denning had looked so familiar riding down the street: he was a close relative, maybe even a brother, of Al Denning. Of course he was in Lampasas looking for a man, and that man's name was Bret Rollins.

Feeling a little uneasy now, Bret walked to the open door and looked down the street, seeing nothing that aroused his suspicion. He turned back to Land. "Did Denning say anything about what he's doing in Lampasas, Oscar?"

"Nope. He don't seem like much of a talkative fellow. Just told me what he wanted, and that was it."

"What was it, Oscar? What did he want?"

Land let out an audible sigh. "Hell, Bret, he just told me to take care of his horse. Said he didn't know how long he'd be in town. He comes after the horse every day and rides it an hour or two, then brings it back."

Rollins stood in thought for a few moments, then nodded. "Thank you, Oscar," he said. "I want you to do the exact same thing with my horse. Just take care of the roan till you hear from me again." He looked down the street once more, then began to walk toward his house, his coat and saddlebags over his shoulder and his Winchester cradled in the crook of one arm.

He continued walking through town at a fast clip and encountered only a few people, most of whom were acquaintances. The first thing he did after arriving home was to bring a bucket of water from the spring. Then, with his rifle leaning against the wall and a cup of cold water in his hand, he took a seat on the porch to enjoy one of his favorite pastimes: watching the sun disappear into the earth.

He sat on the porch till dark, his thoughts mostly on a man named Leo Denning. The man was obviously looking for somebody, but maybe it was somebody other than Bret Rollins. Rollins was thinking that if he himself was the reason for Denning's visit to Lampasas, the man would have found him long before now. Hell, Rollins was well known in the area, and almost any drinker in any saloon in town would be able to tell Denning exactly where he lived.

A hired killer might very well choose to attack a man while he was sleeping. A gunfighter, however, would be careful about choosing a neutral location for a showdown. A gunfighter would know that shooting a man in his own home could easily result in a date with the hangman. After thinking long and hard, Rollins came to believe that Denning was indeed a gunfighter and that he himself was the man's probable target. Never one to put off the inevitable, he decided to find out.

He bathed, shaved and changed into clean clothing, then walked to Toby's T-Bone for supper. A Mexican waiter took his order, and Rollins managed to eat his meal without catching Shirley Doolen's eye. As he paid for his food, he saw her watching him from across the room. He waved and she returned the gesture. She smiled and mouthed something, but Rollins could not read her lips.

Then he was on the street, determined to make himself easy to find. He walked up one side of Main Street and down the other. He made a left turn at the livery stable and wandered up and down some of the streets on the north side of town, eventually ending up at the Twin Oaks Saloon.

"Haven't seen you in a while, Rollins," Jake Smith said, walking down the bar with a beer in his hand. He placed the foamy mug in front of Rollins. "You been doing all right?"

"Doing fine, Jake. Been out of town for a few days." He looked around the room for a moment, then smiled. He was the only customer in the building. "Is business always this good?" he asked jokingly.

Smith nodded and chuckled softly. "Business has been terrible all this year, Bret. Then about two weeks ago, it got worse. Hardly ever a day that I take in more than twenty dollars."

Rollins shook his head sympathetically, then reached for his beer. He had the mug almost to his lips when he heard the front door slam. Out of the corner of his eye he could see a man standing just inside the door. He set his beer down slowly, then turned on his stool to get a better look at the newcomer: Leo Denning!

Denning looked just as he had the first time Rollins saw him, and in fact, seemed to have on the same clothing. His yellow hair hung out on all sides of the flat-crowned Stetson, but seemed to be cut short enough in front to keep it out of his eyes. What Rollins noticed most, however, was the Colt on his hip. The Peacemaker rode in a cutaway holster that had no thong and was tied to his right leg with rawhide.

Denning stood in his tracks for quite some time, staring straight ahead. Then he took a few steps forward. He pointed to Rollins and spoke with a snarl: "You've just been walkin' around darin' me, ain't you? Struttin' all over town!"

Bret was on his feet now and had moved away from his stool. He was watching Denning like a hawk. "I've always considered myself too smart to dare anybody, fellow. I don't even know you, but if you're who I think you are, it's pretty easy to figure out what's on your mind."

"Guess by God it oughtta be easy. I'm Leo Denning, younger brother of the man you waylaid in the alley and shot down in cold blood. I'm takin' up his fight, fellow. By God—"

The man was dead before he hit the floor. Even as Denning was talking, Rollins, always one to seize the upper hand, had shot out his right eye. Denning never moved after falling.

Jake Smith stood behind the bar with his mouth open. "I tell you right now, Bret, that man was fast."

"I know," Rollins said, holstering his weapon. The man had been fast indeed, for even though Rollins had moved first, Denning had almost matched his draw. He had gotten his gun out of its holster, but had died before he could raise his shooting arm.

Rollins reseated himself on the barstool. "Give me a drink of that good whiskey, Jake."

The bartender complied, then set the bottle on the bar. "I guess somebody from the sheriff's office might have heard the shot," he said. "If not, I'll send the first customer who comes along out to fetch Sheriff Pope."

Sheriff Pope and Deputy Hillman were on the scene within the hour. Pope picked up Denning's Colt and sniffed the barrel, then spoke to Smith: "Did you see the whole thing, Jake?"

"Yep."

"Did you hear everything that was said?"

"Every word."

"Would you mind letting me hear those words?"

"Hell, Pete, there wasn't all that much said." He pointed to the body. "That fellow there just as much as told Bret that he'd come to kill him. Said he was a brother to that Denning fellow Bret shot a while back and that he was here to take up his brother's fight. Simple case of self-defense, Sheriff, cut and dried.''

Pope bit his lip and sniffed the Peacemaker again. ''I guess so,'' he said. He ordered Deputy Hillman to recruit some help and remove the body from the premises. Then, on his way out of the building, the sheriff spoke to Rollins: ''Seems like every time I see you lately, there's a dead man close by.''

Rollins looked the lawman squarely in the eye. ''I don't plan it that way, Sheriff.''

Pope spun on his heel and was quickly out the door. A few minutes later, Rollins also left the building. With the knowledge that nobody was stalking him, he would sleep well tonight.

22

Hunter made it a point to be in Lampasas during the weekend of the big game. Late Friday afternoon he sat at the bar in the Twin Oaks Saloon sipping a beer and talking with Jake Smith. At the moment, Smith was discussing Rollins' most recent gunfight. ''I tell you, Zack, if Rollins hadn't moved first, I don't believe he'd still be with us. That Denning fellow was quicker'n a damn cat. He got a late start on his draw, but he damn near beat Rollins anyway.''

''That's what I've heard,'' Zack said, pushing his mug forward for a refill. ''Bret says the same thing. He knows how close he came to losing.''

Smith served the beer, then poured himself a stiff drink of whiskey. He seated himself on his own stool and changed the subject. ''I'm sure you know about the high-stakes poker game that's starting tomorrow up at the White Horse,'' he said.

"Gonna be some heavy betting in that game, Zack. Can't no poor folks even get a seat at the table. I hear tell it's a ten-thousand-dollar buy-in."

Zack nodded. "I believe that's the way they set it up."

Smith reached for a pitcher, added a little water to his whiskey and took another sip. "Good poker players," he said, "every single one of 'em. And they've all got plenty of money to play with. Don't guess Clyde Post even knows what he's worth, but Pascal Peters and Hiram Wooten ain't far behind. It's gonna be a four-handed game, and that's the three men Rollins is gonna be up against." He touched his drink to his lips. Then, apparently deciding that he had added too much water to the glass, he poured in a little more whiskey. "I tell you right now, if I was a betting man, I'd bet my money on Rollins. He don't always win a whole lot, but he just damn nearly don't ever lose. He's real bad about letting somebody else win the little pots and then dragging all the big ones himself."

Zack chuckled. "Bret says that's the way the game is supposed to be played."

"No doubt." Smith scratched at the label on the whiskey bottle with a thumbnail, apparently in deep thought. "It sure would have helped my business if the game had been played here at the Twin Oaks," he said finally. He sat shaking his head for a moment. "I've known Clyde Post for more than twenty years, Zack, and the man has never paid me the courtesy of having a drink in my saloon. I don't reckon he dislikes me or anything like that, he just by God don't come around."

"Maybe it's only because your place is off the beaten path, Jake."

Smith shook his head. "Nope. I used to think so, but not anymore. Post owns at least a thousand saddle horses, so he could certainly come by here without walking. Besides, coming into town from the southwest like he usually does, my place is just as close as the White Horse. No, sir, Clyde Post has got a reason for staying clear of this saloon, and for the life of me, I can't figure out what it is." He got to his feet and dropped his empty glass into a pan of water. "One thing is for sure," he added, "I'll certainly never ask Mister Post to explain it."

Zack left the Twin Oaks a few minutes before dark and walked to Toby's T-Bone for supper. The restaurant was filled to capacity, and he stood leaning against the wall, waiting. When a small table became available a short time later, he was motioned forward by the Mexican waiter.

He ordered roast pork and applesauce, then leaned back in his chair. Though every seat in the building was occupied, he could see very few people that he recognized. A few men were treating their ladies to supper and were dressed in their Sunday best, but the crowd for the most part was made up of working men who wore overalls or, like himself, jeans and flannel shirt.

Zack continued to look around the room. Even the few faces that he recognized, he could not put a name to. Putting names to faces had certainly never been a problem for Rollins, he was thinking. Zack would not have been surprised if Rollins could call the name of every person in the restaurant, including the businessmen and their wives. Especially the wives. Zack smiled at the thought.

When he had eaten and paid for his meal, he headed for the front door, returning Shirley Doolen's greeting as she smiled and waved flirtatiously from across the room. He was still smiling when he reached the street, thinking of the girl's blueberry pie and wondering if she had gotten back into Bret's good graces yet.

Zack had arrived in town at noon today and immediately ridden to Rollins' cottage. His knock at the door had gone unanswered. The fact that Rollins' roan was in the corral, however, meant that he was somewhere around town. Zack had ridden around for the next two hours peeking through the doors and windows of one business establishment after another, but had seen no sign of his partner. Then, intending to spend the night in town anyway, he had ridden to the livery stable and turned his horse over to Oscar Land.

Now, standing outside Toby's T-Bone just before sunset, he decided to check Bret's house again. Walking at a fast clip, he had traveled only a short way when he met Bret walking toward town. "I checked all of your hangouts that I know about," Zack said, grasping Bret's hand, "so I figured you'd be back home by now."

"I had a jillion things to do, Zack. Been going all day. I

finally walked back to the house and slept about an hour. I feel pretty good now, so good that I'll buy you a drink at the White Horse.''

"I'll take you up on that," Zack said. "Seems like I need one to hold my supper down."

They were soon seated at a small table near the back wall of the saloon, well away from the gaming tables. Looking around the room, Zack decided that the crowd was much smaller than normal for this place. Even so, there were more men here than he had ever seen in the Twin Oaks. Once again, he wondered how Jake Smith managed to survive.

Rollins had brought a bottle and two glasses from the bar and was now busy pouring drinks. He set the bottle down and nodded toward a group of men in the center of the room. "I see Mister Post is already celebrating the things he's gonna do to me in the poker game tomorrow."

Zack turned his head for a better look. A group of eight men had pushed two tables together and were seated around several bottles of whiskey. Somebody had obviously just told a funny joke, for the boisterous laughter of the group seemed to shake the room. An old man sitting at the end of the table, whom Rollins identified as Clyde Post, laughed loudest of all.

Zack watched the men for a while, then decided that it had been Post himself who had told the joke. The laughter subsided several times but erupted again each time Post decided to chuckle. It was the same old story, Zack was thinking: the worker was compelled to laugh at the boss's jokes, and if a rich man thought something was a bit humorous, it was hilarious to everybody else.

Rollins topped off their whiskey glasses and set the bottle down again. "Peters and Wooten are over there, too," he said. "That's Wooten at the opposite end of the table, and the bald-headed younger man seated on Wooten's right is Pascal Peters. I've heard that Peters was a cattle rustler in the old days, but now they say he's got money to burn. I guess that's true,'cause he sure throws it around like he's got plenty more in his sock. He'll bet you two or three hundred dollars on a damned pair of deuces.

"Now Wooten I don't know much about, except that he was born rich. Everybody says that his folks were originally from Chicago and that they brought a bundle with them when they moved to Texas. Wooten owns several ranches, and I heard that he sent half a dozen herds north to the rails last year. By God, I'm talking about money now, Zack.''

Zack took a sip of whiskey, then cleared his throat. ''I believe you, Slick,'' he said, taking another look across the room at Wooten. He had long thought that people with money had a certain look, and he could easily see that Wooten had it. Appearing to be about sixty years old, he was clean-shaven, with thinning brown hair and a look of confidence that said the world could kiss his ass, that he would make it just fine even if syrup went to a thousand dollars a sop. He was also the man who had laughed the least at Post's jokes.

Zack had been told so much about Clyde Post that he spent little time looking him over. He was more interested in Wooten and Peters. Pascal Peters appeared to be no more than thirty-five years old, and though his head was poked partway into a Stetson, it was easy to see that he was prematurely bald. A beefy man who probably stood at least six feet tall, his pinkish complexion suggested that he had once been a blond or a redhead. ''Where does Peters live?'' Zack asked.

''His main spread is a few miles west of Llano. I believe he also owns at least one saloon in Austin. This is not the first time I've seen him with Wooten. I think he follows the old man around and kisses his ass every chance he gets. Wooten is probably the man who taught him how to get rich.''

When the men at the long table recognized Rollins, each of them waved and called out a greeting. Rollins nodded, smiled and waved his arm back at them, then ignored the table. Anything else he had to say to the men would be said over a poker hand less than twenty-four hours from now.

Hunter slept the night away in Bret's extra bed and was up at the first hint of daybreak. He built a fire in the stove and put on the coffeepot, then walked to the corral to feed Bret's roan. As the animal ate its oats, Zack chuckled and began to speak to it. ''How do you like living in Texas, old buddy?'' he asked, scratching the horse's ears. ''You don't have the slightest idea that you used to belong to a rich doctor in Shelby

County, Tennessee, do you?'' He gave the animal's neck a final pat, then returned to the house.

Rollins was sitting at the kitchen table in his underwear, opening flat tins of fish and dumping them onto plates. ''I don't remember us ever having fish and crackers for breakfast before, but there ain't a hell of a lot else around here to eat. I've been eating all my meals in town lately and just haven't bought anything for the house.''

Zack pulled up a chair and reached for one of the plates. ''Don't worry about it,'' he said. ''I've been fish-hungry for quite a while and this might be the only chance I get to eat some. I sure as hell haven't been able to catch any from the Colorado River.''

Rollins filled two cups from the coffeepot. ''The fish are in there, Zack. You just don't know how to catch them.''

Zack blew into his steaming cup. ''I suppose you do know how, huh?''

''Nope. But I do know that Toby's T-Bone serves somewhere between a dozen and forty fish plates a day and every damn one of those fish comes right out of that river. Some people fish for a living, Zack. If you could watch a few of them and see how they do it, I think your own stringers would be a little heavier.''

''Professor Rollins,'' Zack said sarcastically and began to wash down the fish and crackers with hot coffee.

Zack could not think of many things more boring than watching a poker game and said so. He informed Rollins shortly after breakfast that he intended to be somewhere else when the game got underway. He left the cottage at midmorning.

Rollins stood on the porch as Zack was leaving. ''Spend the rest of the weekend in town, Zack,'' he said. ''Rent a room at the Hartley and have some fun. Get yourself a woman, let her take some of that swelling out of your neck.''

Zack turned up his lip and shook his head, then walked to town and did exactly as he had been instructed by Rollins.

Hunter left the Hartley early Sunday morning. He had been at the hotel for almost twenty-four hours and had left his room only once. His supper in the dining room last night had been the only good meal he had ever eaten at the Hartley and he decided to quit while he was ahead. This morning he would eat breakfast at home. Dixie had smoked ham and sausage, fresh eggs, maple syrup, and from somewhere he had gotten hold of some special pancake flour. Zack licked his lips and headed for the livery stable to get the sorrel.

The morning was cool and he gave the frisky horse its head. Two hours later, he released the animal in the corral and walked to the cookshack. Poking his head inside the door, he spoke to the cook: "Give me about four eggs, sir, and everything else you can think of."

"Good morning, boss," Dixie said, pulling the coffeepot to the front of the stove. "Got ham and eggs and some warmed-over coffee and biscuits."

Zack seated himself at the table. "Sounds better than anything I could have bought in town, but I'd really like a stack of those light pancakes you've been making lately."

The cook shook his head. "Can't make 'em, Zack. I'm all out of that kinda flour, and so is the store in Lampasas. I told Lacy to hold me back two hundred pounds the next time he gets some in, but there's no telling when that'll be. That special flour is pretty hard to come by, Zack. It's an extra fine grind that's put out by a company in Dallas, and it's called Bulah's Best. I guess the reason it's so hard to find is 'cause the company can sell a hell of a lot more than it can make."

Zack smiled. "Makes sense," he said. "Just fix me whatever's easiest." A short while later, he was served a breakfast that no restaurant in town could match.

He was sitting on the porch mending a bridle when Jolly Ross returned from town Monday afternoon. Zack watched as the foreman unloaded supplies at the cookshack, parked the wagon and loosed the team in the corral. Then Ross walked up the hill to the house, taking a seat on the doorstep. He sat staring across the river for a while, then spoke softly: "I've got bad news, Zack."

Zack laid the bridle aside. "I've heard bad news before," he said. "Keep talking."

Ross began to fidget, kicking at a small stone. "Well, some folks might say it's none of my business, but it seems to me that it concerns us all. The big poker game in Lampasas broke up yesterday afternoon. The talk around town is that Rollins lost big, lost everything he owned. The bartender at the White Horse says he even lost this ranch, and everything on it. Hayes says Bret turned the deed over to Clyde Post this morning, along with every dollar the ranch had in the bank.''

Zack's expression turned to granite. He stared at the floor for a long time as a feeling of numbness crept into his very soul. "Thank . . . thank you, Jolly,'' he finally said in a low, indistinct tone. He got to his feet and turned toward the house. "I'd . . . like to be alone now,'' he said.

Zack sat at the kitchen table in a daze, sipping lukewarm coffee. There was little possibility that Ross was mistaken, he was thinking. Jolly was a very intelligent man and would surely have checked with more than one source before repeating the story. He nodded at his thoughts. The story was true, and he must accept the fact that he was once again homeless and owned nothing except the horse he would ride away from here. Well, two horses; he would ride the sorrel and use the bay for a pack animal.

He swallowed the last of his coffee and banged the empty cup against the table. Why had Rollins not been satified? With more than a thousand head of full-grown Herefords running about, the twenty-thousand-acre ranch was just now getting into a position to pay off handsomely. Why had Rollins spent every waking hour trying to figure a way to get more? County Line Ranch had been all the partners really needed. Indeed, it would have provided them with financial security for life.

Just before sunset, Zack was back on the porch. He sat looking down the hill to the river, knowing full well that this might be his last day on the ranch that he had built from scratch. He was not angry with Rollins, for it was just about impossible to stay mad at the man. Rollins was Rollins, and he could no more stop gambling than he could stop breathing. In Rollins' mind, he had done the right thing. He wanted a cattle empire and firmly believed that he was entitled to it, no matter that he might acquire it at somebody else's expense.

Nope, whatever happened to Zack in the future, he would never be angry at Rollins. He had, however, made a decision during the past two hours: it was time for the partners to part. The two men should go in opposite directions, each seeking his fortune in his own way. Rollins would probably be along tonight or tomorrow and then the two would say good-bye.

Rollins rode into the yard at ten the following morning, a bedroll and a bundle of clothing tied behind his saddle. He tied the roan to the hitching rail as Zack walked down the steps to meet him. Rollins found something interesting to look at on the ground for a while, then raised his eyes. The perpetual smile was missing this morning. "I guess you've heard the news by now," he said softly.

Zack nodded.

"I lost it all, Zack, lost everything we owned." Neither man said anything for a while, then Rollins added, "I played just as carefully as I ever do and thought I had a lock. I misread one of the cards." He took a seat on the bottom step and told Zack about the game.

The cards had run in his favor most of the day on Saturday and he had won two thousand dollars. Then on Sunday afternoon, Rollins himself had dealt the hand that broke up the game: the hand was five-card stud, and both Wooten and Peters folded when the fourth card fell, leaving Rollins and Post to contest each other for the pot. Rollins had two sixes and a nine faceup, and another nine in the hole. Post had three hearts showing: the ten, queen and king. With the only pair showing, Rollins was high man and it was his turn to bet.

"Possible straight flush," he said, tapping the table to indicate that he was checking his hand to Post. "I'll put it on your back, Clyde. I'm not about to bet into something that looks that mean."

Post said nothing, just made a sizable bet, which Rollins called.

When Rollins dealt the final round, he dealt Post the ace of hearts and himself a third six. He now had a full house. He set the deck down very slowly, his eyes on his opponent. Post leaned back in his chair, showing no signs of weakness. Even though he was looking at Rollins' three sixes, the old man was still very much in the pot.

Rollins decided quickly that he had a lock. The only card the old man could have in the hole that would win the pot was the jack of hearts. The jack of hearts was already among the discards, for Wooten had turned it when he folded his hand. Any old heart in the hole would give Post a flush, however, and Rollins was hoping the old man had it. Knowing that his own full house would beat the flush, Rollins slid fifteen thousand dollars into the pot.

The old man matched the bet, almost beating Rollins into the pot. "You didn't bet near enough!" he said loudly. "I intend to raise that bet considerably."

Rollins smiled. "How much?"

Post chuckled. "Everything you own. We can do it this way: you put up County Line Ranch and everything on it, along with whatever amount of money you've got in the bank. Put it all in the pot. If you win, we'll get an unbiased appraisal of everything you've got. Whatever value the appraiser puts on it, I'll pay you that amount in cash."

Rollins spoke quickly: "You'll put that in writing? Get some of these witnesses to sign it?"

Post spoke to Peters: "See if the bartender has a pencil and something to write on, Pascal."

When the old man had written and signed the agreement, he passed it across the table for Rollins' approval. Then, when Peters and Wooten had each signed as witnesses, Post dropped the paper in the center of the table. Rollins' bet was already in the pot. It was showdown time.

"All right, Mister Post," Rollins said, "I've called your bet. Let's see that hole card."

Rollins' smile faded, then disappeared, as the old man turned over the jack of hearts. A royal flush!

Rollins read the cards instantly, then reached across the table for the hand Wooten had discarded, still lying facedown. He turned the cards faceup: a ten, a five, a four, and the jack of diamonds. The jack of diamonds! Rollins stared at the card for a long time, wondering how he could have mistaken it for the jack of hearts. He had long prided himself on his ability to read and remember cards at a glance, and though the cards in question were very similar in appearance, that was no excuse for a man with his experience.

Finally, Rollins dropped his cards on the table and pushed back his chair. "Guess today was just your day, Mister Post. If you'll meet me at the bank tomorrow at nine, I'll give you the money. I guess you can take charge of the ranch about the middle of the week.'' He started to leave, then stopped and turned to face the old man again. ''I know you'll do whatever you want to, but I'd sure like to ask a favor.''

''Ask away,'' Post said.

''Well, we've got some mighty good people on the payroll, and I was hoping you might keep them on.''

''Everybody working there's got a job,'' the old man said, nodding several times. ''Same job they've got right now.''

Rollins bought a quart of whiskey on credit and headed home. He was very soon drunk and slept till Monday morning.

Now he got up from the doorstep and walked around behind the house to relieve himself, then returned to the yard. ''Nothing left for us around here, Zack. I think we should go out to El Paso for the winter, then make it up to one of the gold camps next spring. I hear that the miners throw money around like there's no tomorrow.''

Hearing Rollins talk about somebody else throwing money around was humorous to Zack, but he did not laugh. Instead, he walked back and forth and began to speak softly: ''I'm not going to El Paso, Bret, or anywhere else you might be going. You and me are as different as daylight and dark, and it's time we went our separate ways. We've had some good times and a few things we've done have turned out pretty nice, but I just can't live my life worrying about what the next turn of a card will do to me.''

Rollins shifted his weight from one foot to another nervously, a look of dejection on his face. ''I guess you've made your decision, Zack, but it sure is a hard one. I've never had another friend like you.'' He reached into his back pocket and pulled out a small roll of bills. ''Yesterday I sold those two lots I owned in town, got seven hundred dollars for 'em. I want to give you half of it so you'll have some money to get started somewhere else.''

''No, no, Bret. I've still got that seven-fifty Peabody gave me for the young bulls, so we're in about the same shape.''

Rollins motioned down the hill to the road. ''El Paso's a long ride,'' he said, ''and I can't get there till after I start.''

When Zack pushed his right hand forward for a parting handshake, Rollins ignored the hand and grabbed him in a bear hug. Moments later, when Rollins had mounted, Zack spoke again: "No matter where you end up going, Bret, I'd change my name if I were you." He pointed to the Peacemaker on Bret's hip. "Word of that thing has already spread far and wide."

"I know, and I'll change my name when I leave this yard. From now on, my name is Bill Brown. If you ever decide you want to see me again, start asking after me by that name: Bill Brown." Then he turned his horse toward the road.

"I'll be thinking about you!" Zack called after him. "You take care of yourself!" Then he took a seat on the porch and with a lump in his throat, watched his friend ford the river and disappear toward the western horizon.

Zack spent the remainder of the day going over some of the things he had accumulated over the past three years, sorting out the smaller stuff that he would carry on his own journey. He had no idea where he would be going yet, but just as Rollins had said, there was nothing left for him here.

He dug out the packsaddle and the tent, then laid aside cooking utensils and heavy blankets, determined that when he left this place tomorrow, everything he needed to spend the winter outdoors would be riding on the packhorse. Finally, he took a seat on the doorstep and studied his Texas map for a long time.

Zack had asked Jolly Ross to assemble the crew in the cookshack after supper, saying that he wanted to personally thank the men for their outstanding service and loyalty and to bid each man good-bye. Shortly after dark, he could see that more than one lamp was burning in the cookshack, and he was down the slope quickly.

As he entered the building, every man got to his feet and began to applaud. Zack shook his head and waved his arm to discourage the adulation. He walked to the stove and filled a cup from the coffeepot, then turned to face the crew. "I suppose you all know by now that the H and R Cattle Company is no more!" he began. There was a nodding of heads and some soft mumbling.

"The new owner's name is Clyde Post, and he'll be taking charge of the ranch any day now. Mister Post has assured us that he will keep every man who wants to continue working here. Every man on the same job at the same pay. When the first of the month comes, he'll pick up the payroll right where I left off.'' He caught Wilf Berryhill's eye. "I also believe he will continue to employ your sister Esther, Mister Berryhill.''

Zack set his cup on the table, then continued: "I never made a speech in my life, men, and I don't intend to start now. I just came down here to say good-bye to everybody and to thank you for . . . for just being who you are.''

"Where you gonna go, Zack?" one of the hands shouted.

"I haven't decided for sure yet," Zack answered. "I'll probably head east, maybe go down around Houston or Beaumont.'' He shook hands with every member of the crew, then took a seat at the table and ate his supper. An hour later, he was in bed, where he tossed and turned for the entire night.

He ate breakfast in the cookshack the following morning, long after the hands had eaten and gone to their jobs. Dixie Dalton had prepared enough trail food to last Zack several days, and had also raided the storeroom. The supplies now lay in a neat pile at the end of the table. "You take care of yourself, Zack,'' the cook was saying, "and you oughtta do right well in Houston. Lots of money around that town, and it's growing fast.''

An hour later, Zack mounted the sorrel, then led his loaded packhorse to the cookshack. When he had added his provisions to the bay's pack, he remounted and spoke to the cook, who was standing in the doorway. "So long, Dixie. It's been a pleasure knowing you.'' The cook nodded and waved good-bye.

Hunter rode down the hill. When he reached the road, he stopped and sat his saddle for a long time, looking first in one direction, then in the other. "Aw, hell!" he said finally, almost shouting. He turned the sorrel west and kicked the animal to a fast trot. If he traveled steadily and did a little night riding, he could easily overtake Bill Brown before he reached El Paso.

Westerns available from

TOR
FORGE

TRAPPER'S MOON • Jory Sherman
"Jory Sherman takes us on an exhilarating journey of discovery with a colorful group of trappers and Indians. It is quite a ride."—Elmer Kelton

THE PUMPKIN ROLLERS • Elmer Kelton
When Trey McLean leaves his family's cotton farm and sets off on his own, he's about as green as they come. But Trey learns fast—about deceit and love when he meets the woman he's destined to marry.

CASHBOX • Richard S. Wheeler
"A vivid portrait of the life and death of a frontier town."—*Kirkus Reviews*

SHORTGRASS SONG • Mike Blakely
"*Shortgrass Song* leaves me a bit stunned by its epic scope and the power of the writing. Excellent!"—Elmer Kelton

CITY OF WIDOWS • Loren Estleman
"Prose as picturesque as the painted desert..."—*The New York Times*

BIG HORN LEGACY • W. Michael Gear
Abriel Catton receives the last will and testament of his father, Web, and must reassemble his family to search for his father's legacy, all the while pursued by the murdering Braxton Bragg and desire for revenge and gold.